# BANISHED

## Street Rats of Aramoor
### - The Beginning -

written by

# MICHAEL
# WISEHART

# Copyright

# STREET RATS OF ARAMOOR: BOOK 1
# BANISHED

# To View Map in More Detail

« www.michaelwisehart.com/map-of-aldor »

# To View Map in More Detail

« www.michaelwisehart.com/map-of-aldor »

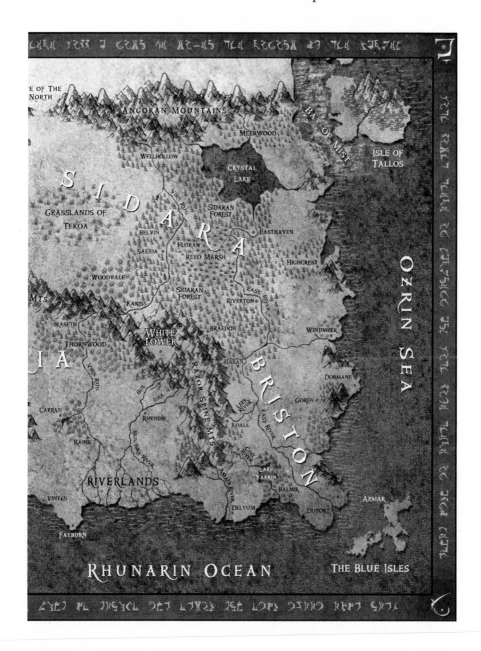

# Foreword

BANISHED IS THE first book in the Street Rats of Aramoor series. It takes you deep underground within the ruins of the Lost City and gives you a glimpse into the life of an Upakan warrior.

This series ties directly into the Aldoran Chronicles saga, twenty years prior to the first book: *The White Tower*. Both series are completely stand-alone.

As with my other books, there is a Character Glossary at the back if you need it.

# Books

## THE ALDORAN CHRONICLES

Book 1 | *The White Tower*

Book 2 | *Plague of Shadows*

## STREET RATS OF ARAMOOR

Book 1 | *Banished*

Book 2 | *Hurricane*

Chapter 1

"MOVE IT, AYRION! You stop, you die." My words echoed off the mountainside as I fought to make it up the steep granite wall in front of me. The shelf I needed to reach was close. I was nearly there. The excitement of finishing before the others had me climbing even faster. My right hand slipped, and for a moment, the only things that stood between me and the deadly rocks below were my left hand and a few hundred feet of nothing.

*This is what I get for yelling at myself.*

A freezing gust of wind lashed against me, whipping me around. Even in the middle of the night, I could see the ruins of the Lost City in the distance. My home had never looked so small. Dragon Fang was the tallest of the peaks in the Northern Heights, and it was the final stage of the Tri'Nephrin. We weren't expected to climb all the way to the summit, only to the top of Howling

Gorge.

I kicked my legs and twisted around to find another hold. The wind shrilled as it pushed through the gaps in the deep ravine, coming in heavy gusts.

The rock face was sharp in some places, smooth in others. From one swing to the next, you never knew what you were going to get. Deep crevices and cracks made for strong grips if you could find them, as long as you stayed away from the ones with webbing. One bite from the wrong spider and it would be a quick trip down.

I found another handhold a few feet to my right. I had to hurry; my fingers weren't going to hold much longer. I waited for the next gust to pass and then kicked out and swung for it. My fingers latched on to the textured part of the rock, and I let go with my left hand to reach for the next one up. Just as I did, the rock gave way and time seemed to stop. I felt what it was like to fly, suspended in the air, as free as a bird.

The moment didn't last.

Before my mind had even registered what had happened, I was falling. I tried to scream, but the wind ripped the air from my lungs. I looked down and watched as the ground grew closer. This was it. My short life was over, all thirteen years of it. I'd spent my entire life training to become an Upakan warrior, the youngest to ever claim the title, and here I was, about to die before completing my first real advancement. Worse yet was the thought that after working so hard to get a full day's lead ahead of Flon and the other trainees, they were going to find my bloody remains, laugh, and go on without me.

It's amazing what runs through your mind before you die. I closed my eyes and waited for the impact.

My head cleared, and I realized I was still hanging by my left hand, my body swaying against the side of the mountain. My stomach heaved from the sensation of having fallen to my death. I swallowed, forcing myself to take a breath as I tried to slow the beating in my chest. Even knowing how my magic worked, I still had a hard time getting used to it.

The visions were so real.

My knuckles were white as I held on to the small crack in the rock with everything I had. I couldn't feel my fingers. Any moment, they were going to give way. Frantically, I searched for another hold. Thanks to my vision, I knew where *not* to grab, so I swung for a small outcropping just above it.

It held.

I pulled myself up and reached for another just under the shelf I was trying to reach. The ledge over my head extended too far out for me to climb. I considered my options. It seemed my only choice was a bad one. Almost as bad as having decided to undergo the Tri'Nephrin in the first place. No one had ever attempted to complete the advancement course at my age. It was unheard of. The course was made for trainees at least three or four years my senior.

On my left, about six or seven feet below me, was a small section of rock jutting out from a wall adjacent to the one I was clinging to. It was just enough to stand on, but not much more. The only way I could see to reach it was by jumping.

Now would have been a good time to have anchored a rope to

the wall, but since I had left my pack below in order to increase the speed of my climb, not to mention the bragging rights, I had to make do without it. Instead, I opted to use one of my picks. Letting go with my right hand, I grabbed it from its holder at my waist.

Not wanting to give myself time to reconsider, I planted both feet and aimed myself at the shelf. "Here goes nothing." I released my grip and kicked off the wall.

The wind pounded in my ears as I flew across the gorge. My eyes never left the small outcropping on the other side. My feet landed first, and then the rest of me hit the side of the mountain. A sharp pain tore through my legs and chest where they struck the hard granite, letting me know I was still alive.

I slammed my pick into a small crevice and yanked myself back against the wall. I released a heartfelt sigh of relief as my face pressed against the cold stone. This was as good a time as any to take a breather. My hands were shaking as they clung to the pick's handle. My legs weren't doing much better.

I glanced over my right shoulder at the shelf above me. It was so close and yet just out of reach. As desperate as I was to finish, I needed to slow down and think. The other trainees hadn't made it this far. They were probably still in the caverns below the city, trying to get through the previous three obstacles. Not a single trainee had volunteered to team with me, so I had gone on alone. I wasn't too worried. I worked better alone.

My fingers prickled as the blood and feeling returned. I gave them a few more minutes to rest before moving on. Carefully, I tapped the end of the pick to release it from the rock, then slipped it back into its hoop at my waist and started climbing.

The problem now was that to reach the final shelf, I was going to need to jump back across the gorge. Unfortunately, the two walls separated farther up, making a jump all but impossible.

"Why is it never easy?" I moaned. Talking to myself helped. I was an excellent conversationalist. I very rarely argued, but if I did, it was for a good cause.

My anticipation grew as I climbed high enough to see over the top of the shelf and spot the five flags bracketed to the walls on the other side, one for each of the trainees. Mine was second from the left—a black background with a white rune at the center. The rune was from the old tongue and supposedly stood for my name, *Ayrion*. There were few who could still read the ancient language, so I had to take their word for it.

At the back of the rise was a door with torches on either side. Behind the door was a set of tunnels leading down to the bottom of the gorge. In the old days, they had used rises like this as look-outs for oncoming armies. No guards were in sight, which wasn't too surprising, considering they wouldn't have expected the train-ees to make it this far for at least another day.

A little farther up, I found a small outcropping for my feet, which took some of the weight off my arms. I rested as I studied the gulf between me and the ledge where I needed to be. It was too far to jump. I didn't need a vision to tell me how stupid I'd be to try it. Yet that was exactly what I needed to do.

I studied the wall above me and then looked back at the shelf. What was I going to do? The only way to make it that far would be to jump from higher up to add distance. Even then, I wasn't sure it would be enough. And if it was, it would be a very hard landing.

I took an extra few seconds to let the blood flow back into my arms while I looked for the next set of holds I'd need to reach to get high enough to attempt something this ridiculous. Two deep breaths, and I reached for the first of what looked like eight pulls.

The first wasn't a problem; it was close enough to reach without having to stretch. But the next two were a different matter. There were no toeholds for my boots, which meant I had to heft my entire weight with my arms. The fourth and fifth had small ledges beneath, large enough to place the tip of one boot. I used them to ease some of the weight on my arms as I readied myself for the final three pulls up to where I estimated I needed to be to make the jump across.

By the time I'd reached the top of the narrow ledge on my side of the gorge and stood looking across to where I needed to jump, I had all but talked myself out of it. If it weren't for the fact that I had nowhere else to go, I would have been tempted to give up and climb back down. But I'd rather fall to my death than let Flon and the others see me quit. So, I pushed all doubt and fear aside and focused on the task. Even from this height, I could see I wasn't going to be able to jump far enough to land on the shelf, which meant I needed to try something else.

I could have kicked myself for not taking the full pack of supplies offered before the climb. I figured the lighter load would cut my climbing time down and allow me to gain even more distance from my fellow trainees. That had been a mistake. That grapple would have come in rather handy right about now. In fact, if I had carried it along, I probably wouldn't have been forced to resort to such a foolish stunt.

Without the grapple and rope, my only options were my picks. I removed both from their holders and held them in front of me, testing their balance. Each had a small leather loop at the end of the handle for me to stick my wrist through in case my hand slipped.

I took a moment to glance over the side one last time. It was a long way down. At least it would be a quick death if I missed.

Tightening my grip, I concentrated on what I was about to do, picturing it in my mind—the jump, the swing of the picks, the jerk as they struck the ledge. Each time, the image ended with me falling to my death. So far, I hadn't received another vision, so maybe I would make it. Then again, my visions only gave me a few seconds' warning. With my luck, the vision would come halfway across the gorge and make me miss the strike.

I walked back from the ledge until I reached the face of the mountain behind me. I needed as much room to run as I could manage.

My breath coursed through my lungs—in and out. In and out. I started counting down.

*Three.* I locked my fingers around my picks.

*Two.* My legs tightened, and I bent to run.

*One.* I screamed, hit three steps, and pushed off the ledge as hard as I could.

There was no question. I wasn't going to make it.

I raised my picks and swung at the top of the ledge.

They missed.

My picks sparked as they scraped down the side of the shelf, one of them snagging on a boulder protruding from the bottom. The force of the catch nearly pulled my arm from its socket. I screamed in pain. My fingers came loose, and for a moment, I was hanging from the side of the mountain with nothing but a leather strap holding me up.

I looked down and wished I hadn't. The fear of heights had been trained out of me years before, but something about hanging there by my pick's strap had me on the verge of losing my stomach. I closed my eyes and fought through the pain, praying to anyone who'd listen that my strap wouldn't break.

Opening my eyes, I raised my other pick and swung. It stuck.

"Come on, Ayrion! Pull!" I bit down and hauled myself up with one arm, far enough to pry loose the first pick and reach for something higher. I swung, but the rock I hit gave way, raining pieces down on my face. I shook my head and tried again. The pick held. I tested its weight before releasing the other.

Arm over arm, I swung and pulled, swung and pulled, until I reached the top of the shelf and crawled over the edge. I rolled onto my back, panting harder than I ever had before.

I couldn't move.

My entire body was shaking. I couldn't believe I'd made it. That was by far the stupidest thing I'd ever done, and yet the most thrilling. I wished the other trainees had been there to see it. I shook my head. No. If they had been, that would mean they had made it up the mountain in front of me, and I wasn't about to wish for that.

The wind howled above me as I lay there gasping for breath, and the moon flooded the top of the rise with pale light. With what strength I had left, I rolled onto my side and tried to stand, but sitting with my back against one of the smaller boulders on the side of the rise was as far as I got. I looked out over the edge of the cliff into the depths of the gorge below, and I wondered if all of this was really worth it. Did I really want to become a warrior after all?

I got my answer when my legs pushed the rest of me up to a standing position. From there, I hobbled over to where the flags waved in their brackets and lifted the black one with the white rune. I tucked it under my arm, hobbled over to the door, and knocked. While waiting for someone to open, I raised my hands to the torches to warm them.

It was a while before someone lifted the latch on the other side of the door and the hinges groaned. I stepped back to keep from getting hit.

A short man with a round face stuck his head out, took one look at me, and then went back inside. "Hey, Jesup. You were right. It was a knock."

"Here, let me see." A taller man with a rather bulbous nose stuck his head out, then finally opened the door the rest of the way. "I don't believe it. How'd you get up here?"

"I climbed."

The man stepped around me and scanned the top of the shelf.

He turned back around. "Where's your pack?"

"I didn't carry one."

"What do you mean, you didn't carry one? How'd you climb up here without a pack?"

"I used my hands and my picks." I patted the picks where they hung at my sides.

The two men stared at me like they'd seen a specter.

"Well, I never," the second guard said as he scratched the top of his head and glanced at the first. "Mark this down, Argust. Could be for the records."

I smiled. I couldn't wait to see the others' faces when I walked in carrying my flag a full day in front of the others. They couldn't deny me my right to be there anymore.

Chapter 2

**H**E'S A CHEAT!" Brim said as he leaned his intimidating torso forward in his seat. Brim was the head of our clan and the overly proud father of a not-so-distinguished son named Flon. The same Flon who had taken it upon himself to be my personal tormentor.

"Ayrion is no cheat," my father said, quick to come to my defense.

I stood quietly beside my father at the center of the stone chamber that was used by the members of the Peltok to administer clan justice. Other than the platform holding the council's seats at the center of the room, the chamber itself was rather bare. Torches lined the walls, illuminating their sad state of disrepair. There was a pile of stone blocks stacked near the back of the room, where a section of the wall had fallen and had yet to be replaced.

The room was as dark and cold as the mercy I was sure *not* to receive. Like the crumbling walls of this once-great city, our way of life was slowly unraveling.

"Then he's a liar," Brim said with a sneer. "No one finishes the Tri'Nephrin in a single day. It can't be done."

I scanned the faces of the two other council members. Neither showed signs of being influenced by my father's words. Mostly, they looked frightened. Of course, if I had been known for strangling my own father with my bare hands just to take his place as head of the clan, I'm sure they'd have been afraid of sitting beside me as well.

It was no secret that once Brim had taken over as Primary, he had seeded the Peltok with people he knew he could control, those who wouldn't question his decisions. He was as cunning as he was ruthless.

To the right of Brim was Talarin, a member of Brim's extended family. Not too close, but enough that Brim didn't need to worry about the man challenging his authority. On Brim's left was Ness, no relation. She hated conflict, and the easiest way to avoid it was simply to agree with whatever the Primary said. Real backbone, that one.

"Obviously, it can be done," my father said. "Because Ayrion did it."

Brim pounded the arms of his chair. He looked like he was ready to jump off the platform and challenge my father to combat right there on the spot. "Are you saying *my* son couldn't have?"

"Of course not, Primary." My father's voice was tempered, but

I knew him well enough to hear the soft hint of anger. Brim, who rarely controlled his own emotions, didn't catch it, and glowered at my father's apparent calm. "I'm simply stating a fact. Ayrion made it through the Tri'Nephrin in a single day."

"And that's why I say he's a cheat!" Brim roared, his eyes bloodshot as he attempted to stare my father down. Brim seemed to think that if he glared long and hard enough, my father would see the error of his ways and recant.

He didn't.

Talarin glowered in my direction, as if expecting me to fall on my knees and confess that the entire thing had been a lie and beg for mercy, but I kept my face emotionless, just as my father had instructed. I wasn't about to give them the satisfaction of seeing me look weak, especially considering that the outcome of this inquiry was all but inevitable. Who was I kidding? As many times as I'd been called to stand in front of the Peltok, I'd never once had it go in my favor. Not when the Primary's son was the one constantly ratting on me. Flon was a poor loser.

Brim wouldn't allow his son to come in second place, and certainly not to someone who was four years Flon's junior. In Brim's mind, no thirteen-year-old should have been able to even finish the Tri'Nephrin's course, let alone in front of the older trainees.

In Upakan society, your skill as a fighter was your most valuable asset. Those at the top, like Brim, were able to claim the most lucrative jobs for themselves, raising their family's standing within the clan. However, those like my father, who didn't care for the ruthlessness it took to reach the top, had to be content with the leftover contracts. The ones that didn't pay as well or were too risky to take on. My victories during training helped bolster our standing.

Ness leaned forward in her seat and broke the tense silence. "Narris, can you please explain to us how Ayrion managed to complete the course in such a record time without help? It seems unlikely that Ayrion could have come out that far ahead of the others without cheating." She glanced at Brim to ensure he approved of her question.

The Primary waited for my father's answer.

My father broke his gaze with Brim to answer Ness. "He trains longer and harder than any of the other contenders. Is it that difficult to assume he'd come out on top?"

"No one's that good," Brim said with a smirk that left me twisting inside. "Not even Ayrion, which means he's either a liar or a cheat." Brim drummed his fingers on the arms of his chair. "And both are subject to punishment."

"Punishment?" My father's hands tightened into fists.

Talarin and Ness looked surprised as well, as if they hadn't expected Brim to go that far. I wasn't sure why. Punishing me was one of Brim's favorite pastimes.

"How in the flaming Pits of Aran'gal can you punish him for completing part of his training?" my father asked, face reddening.

My heart was racing. I took a step closer to my father, afraid he was going to lose his composure altogether and do something foolish, like challenge Brim. The head of the last person to challenge the Primary decorated the entrance to the Justice Hall for a full half-year. Watching the man's face desiccate day after day had been a great deterrent.

"You cannot punish someone for doing their best," my father stated plainly.

Brim's eyes narrowed. "We can if we believe there is just cause."

I cringed. The last punishment I'd received had been to spend a full day without food or water in one of the lower caverns where the molten rock flowed. I'd been so weak after that my father had been forced to carry me all the way home. It had taken another three days before I could manage to get out of bed.

Brim leaned forward in his seat. "Ten lashes of Dorin's whip for the cheating, and ten more for the lying. That way, we can make sure he gets punished for the right thing."

My legs nearly gave out.

"Twenty lashes?" My father's eyes were the size of ripe figs, and his mouth was open wide enough to have poured an entire bushel in.

Talarin remained silent. The grin on his face said it all.

Ness, on the other hand, fidgeted in her seat. "Primary, sentencing something we cannot prove may raise questions."

Brim's glare in her direction made me glad I wasn't the one sitting next to him. "Are you questioning my judgment?" His tone made it clear that her answer would determine whether or not she joined me at the post.

"I . . ." She turned and looked at me. I already knew her answer. She lowered her head. "No, Primary."

"Twenty lashes?" My father shook with rage. "Twenty lashes

for making your son look like the fool he is? Why not fifty? *Nu'Tarin Fu'Tok*! Why not just take him out and execute him while you're at it?"

I nearly choked as the air wheezed from my chest. Only twice had I ever heard my father curse, and never in the old tongue. I had to do something. If I didn't stop him, Brim might actually try having me executed out of spite. The Primary hated our family. Always had, not just because my father wasn't afraid of Brim, but because he couldn't explain why I kept coming out on top. This would be the perfect excuse to be rid of one of us.

I took a slight step forward. "I accept." I heard the words, but I couldn't believe I had said them. I must not have spoken them loudly enough, because my father was now telling Brim what he thought about his son, his wife, his house. I think I even heard him say something about his manhood.

This time, I took a deeper breath and shouted, "I accept!"

My father's tirade faded as he—and every other member of the Peltok—turned to look at me. "What?"

"I said . . . I accept."

"You most certainly will not! No son of mine is going to be punished for doing what is required of him."

"Done!" Brim said, pounding his fist like a mallet on the arm of his chair. "Guards, take Ayrion to the post."

My father started to argue, but I shook my head, and he bit his tongue.

As the guards led me out, I found myself wondering once again how I had managed to end up in yet another mess.

Chapter 3

I FOLLOWED THE TWO guards down the long corridor leading back to the foyer of the Justice Hall. The name seemed ironic. There was about as much justice in this place as there were adornments on the walls, and they were as empty as Bulrin's tankard on a slow night after work.

My father and the Peltok followed a short distance behind. I was amazed Brim hadn't ordered my father tied to the post along with me after the vitriol he had just spewed.

No one spoke. The crackle of the torches and the echoes of boots on broken tile were the only sounds to be heard. It did little to quench the fear bubbling in my gut. I'd been forced to endure Dorin's whip before, but never with so many lashes.

Dorin was one of five instructors in our clan, but he considered himself responsible for single-handedly maintaining our clan's high passing rate. His influence had nothing to do with his ability to teach and everything to do with his use of the whip on students he believed weren't measuring up. No one slept through his classes.

We reached the second floor of the foyer and started down the center of three staircases. The other two curved outward to connect to adjoining corridors on the sides. All three staircases merged about halfway up to form a single set of stairs wide enough to fit all five members of my family standing side by side with arms outstretched.

Although little more than ruins, the buildings of the once-great capital city of Keldor were impressive in size. After the eruption of Mount Ash centuries earlier, it was said that the entire city had been lost in a single day, that the ground had shaken with such violence that it had opened its mouth and swallowed the city whole. Pretty disgusting image, if you ask me. It was no wonder they called it the Lost City.

I looked up. The floors above were shrouded in darkness. With the majority of the city resting underground, the sunlight from above rarely found its way in. For most people, this would have been a problem, but not for the Upaka. Our eyes allowed us to see in lower light. My father said it had something to do with our people having spent so much time underground. The few times we did go above required the use of shaders. Without them, the light was too bright for us to see.

The guards raised their torches to light the way across the broken tile of the main floor as we headed toward the entrance. I let my imagination wander. I tried thinking about exploring the deeper tunnels under the city, or bathing in one of the underground falls, but every time I attempted to think of something other than what awaited me outside, my mind kept returning to Dorin's whip.

There was always a good turnout for public punishment. We Upakans enjoyed our entertainment. Personally, I didn't find it all that agreeable. I took after my mother in that regard, especially considering I was the one, more often than not, receiving the punishment.

It was nearly as dark outside as it was inside. There were streetlamps lining the square in front of the building as well as down the street. Along with the lamps, the underground caverns themselves held a unique form of crystalline structures that produced a greenish-blue phosphoric glow, perfect for our overly sensitive eyes.

As predicted, there was already a growing crowd standing around the seven-foot-tall stone pillar at the bottom of the stairs. It seemed they had already known what the verdict would be before the session had even taken place. But considering who was on trial, I guessed it was to be expected. In a close-knit community such as ours, standing out wasn't always a good thing.

Upakans weren't exactly known for being softhearted. We were mercenaries, after all. Our stock-in-trade was our ability to fight. It was also the reason why we were shunned by all normal society. But it never stopped the *good* citizens of Aldor from using our services when it suited them. There was always someone who needed killing.

My hands shook as we started down the steps. The thought of

those lashes and the damage they would cause had me walking as slowly as the guards would permit. I certainly wasn't in a rush to get there. I hadn't made it halfway down when my father and the members of the council exited the building. Brim seemed to be waiting for me to reach the bottom before he made his grand procession down the stairs. My father had no such notion and was halfway down before my foot reached the final step.

The crowd parted, leaving just enough room for me and my armed escort to pass.

The guards slowed their pace. Part of the ritual was to force the criminal, or in my case *victim*, to endure the scrutinizing glares of their clan before receiving punishment. They wanted the experience to be as shameful as possible. The goal was to make an example of the wrongdoer in the hope that the people would learn from the experience and change their ways. I held my head high. They weren't going to see me break. I'd done nothing wrong and had no reason to be ashamed.

"Cheater."

I didn't need to look to know who'd said it. *Flon.*

The Primary's son was four years older than I was, which made his bullying of me seem even more petty, not that anyone would ever tell him that. At seventeen, he was nearly as tall as his father and certainly as nasty. It would be just like him to show up and taunt me throughout the entire ordeal. I ignored him and kept walking.

As I marched through the crowd, I could hear snippets of whispered conversations. Some were wondering with a great deal of concern what else the Primary would be willing to start dishing out punishments for if he was going to go this far. Others wondered if I wasn't getting off too easy. Those closest to the front clicked their tongues and shook their heads in disgust. Most had no real idea what was going on.

The guards came to a halt in front of the blood-spattered pillar. Four rings, each with a set of shackles, had been mounted to the top of the post, one per side.

My legs wanted to run, but I was determined not to bring shame to my family.

Dorin stood off to the side, uncoiling his whip. The leather strands had been tightly woven into a cord that stretched a good twelve feet. Dorin prided himself on his ability to break skin with every swing.

"Take it off," one of the guards said as he propped his spear against the post.

I removed my top, and the guard proceeded to shackle my wrists. The iron was cold to the touch. My hands wouldn't quit shaking. I didn't want them to see how frightened I was.

Behind me, Brim's voice silenced the crowd. "The council's decision was unanimous." I turned to see what was happening. The three members of the Peltok were making their way down the stairs, Brim one step ahead of the others. "Ayrion has been convicted of cheating during the Tri'Nephrin and lying about it after the fact."

The crowd parted to let them through.

"The punishment has been set at ten lashes for cheating and

another ten for the lying."

There were a few gasps. Hushed whispers sifted their way through the crowd. I got the feeling that those watching felt the punishment rather severe, but none would ever voice that opinion, at least not loudly enough for the Primary to hear.

My father pushed his way to the front. My older sister, Rianna, was there beside him, as well as my younger brother, Jorn. There was rage in my father's eyes. I shook my head to let him know not to interfere.

My sister had tears running down both cheeks. Like our mother, she had a tender heart. She had spent two days weeping in her room after Father had killed one of the cave lizards she had rescued when it had run across the dinner table and tried helping itself to a piece of meat from his plate. It had taken weeks for Rianna to finally forgive him.

Jorn, on the other hand, had no tears to shed for his older brother, only contempt. He had always been jealous of my abilities, and it only seemed to get worse the older he got. The growing divide between us was definitely one of the worst downsides to having magic. Unfortunately for me, magic wasn't going to get me out of this mess. In fact, it was the reason I was in it in the first place.

A loud *crack* caught my attention. Dorin had finished his stretching and was now testing his whip. He swung the long cord over his head and then brought it back around with a snap of his wrist. The sound echoed off the surrounding buildings like a clap of thunder.

The people standing closest moved back, nearly tripping over themselves as they attempted to get clear of Dorin's aim. No one wanted to be standing anywhere near the open end of the lash.

"That looks like it's going to hurt," a familiar voice said off to the right, causing my jaw to tighten even further. This time, I couldn't ignore Flon. He had pushed his way to the front, opposite my family, only a few paces from where Dorin stood. I was hoping a stray lash would catch him in the mouth, or maybe one of his eyes.

Dorin took great pride in the dispensing of punishments. He seemed to take a fair amount of pleasure in it as well. The enthusiasm on his face made me sick. The lanky instructor finished the last of his practice swings before moving in behind me. I was so busy focusing on keeping my legs from shaking that when he spoke, I almost yelped.

"The more you jump, the worse it'll be." Dorin always said that to his victims before he began. It was just another part of his ritual.

My entire body was trembling. I took a step closer to the post and grabbed the extra slack in the chain with each hand and held tight. I made sure to keep my tongue from between my teeth. There had been stories of others who'd bitten clear through theirs from the pain.

"Dorin, you may begin when ready," Brim said.

I turned my head just in time to see Dorin fling the whip back over his head. I closed my eyes and tightened every muscle in my body. The whip struck. I felt it sear across my back, burning like a hot iron. I wanted to scream, but I held it in.

"One!" Dorin called out loudly enough for everyone to hear.

Again, the whip found its mark, and I clung to the chains to keep my legs from giving way.

"Two!"

I could hear my sister whimpering off to my left. I was thankful my mother wasn't there.

"Three!"

The pain ripped through my body, and I found myself pressed against the post. The cold stone on my chest was no small relief. I gasped for breath. Each new lash ripped the air from my lungs.

"Four!"

"Five!"

"Six!"

Dorin continued to swing, showing no mercy. My knuckles were white, and my teeth ground together under the strain of holding my mouth shut. I could feel warm blood running down my back. Small sprays had joined countless others in the mural at my feet.

"Eight!"

"Nine!"

"Ten!"

I tried desperately to focus my mind, to concentrate on a single moment, or object, something emotionally strong enough to allow me to block out the pain. It was a tactic we had been taught during training to keep from breaking under torture.

It didn't work.

There was a brief pause from the lashing. I tried to turn my head to see why, but my neck wouldn't move. Tears burned the corners of my eyes as I fought to hold them in.

I could hear some whispers in the crowd. I wondered if the Peltok had decided to show lenience, but then Brim's voice boomed above the crowd. "That was ten for cheating. Ten more to go."

My heart sank. It would have been easier had they never stopped. By now, I could have been halfway through the final ten instead of just getting ready to start. The familiar clap of thunder resounded and my back spasmed.

"One!"

*One? Why couldn't he have kept on at eleven? Now it feels like they're starting all over again.*

"Two!"

The pain was overwhelming. I couldn't take it any longer. I wanted to give in. I wanted to beg for mercy. I might have recanted right there and told them whatever they wanted to hear if they'd been willing to stop.

"Three!"

My legs gave way. My hands slipped and I landed on my knees. My father started forward, but others in the crowd grabbed him and held him back. My sister had covered her face with her hands, while my brother simply stared at the cobbles around his feet.

"Four!"

A yelp fought to break free, but I snatched it back before it could get away.

"Five!"

Another crack of the whip and my mind began to slip. I was growing dizzy. I could feel something cool against my face. I peeked through my lids and dimly realized I was pressed against the post. The rough stone rubbed my cheek.

"Six!"

I groaned. At least I thought it was a groan. I wasn't even sure I was the one who'd done it. I tried imagining it was Flon. That somehow Dorin had swung wide and the tip had caught him in the face.

"Seven!"

Dorin's counting faded into the distance. I could no longer feel the pain. In fact, I couldn't feel anything. It was a strange euphoric sensation, like when leaving one of the tunnels from the city to walk in the light above. Except it was the opposite. I could see the light, but it was growing more distant. I was being pulled further and further into darkness. Pretty soon, it had completely enveloped me.

I had no idea if Dorin ever finished his counting. The last thing I remembered was my mother's gentle voice telling me to sleep.

Chapter 4

SOMETHING PULLED ME from the darkness. As my mind cleared, I wondered why I had even bothered to wake up. Gut-wrenching pain enveloped me like liquid fire bubbling up from the deepest of the wind tunnel caverns. I closed my eyes and tried to find my way back to the darkness. It was peaceful there. No Peltok sentencing me to an undeserved punishment, no Dorin practicing his skills on my hide, no Flon mocking me as my skin was peeled from my back. I wanted to stay in the darkness and never return.

"Ayrion? Are you awake?" My mother's voice pulled me back from the precipice. "He's waking up, Narris."

"Good. I was starting to worry. He's been out for hours."

"He needs the rest."

"Yes, but if he hadn't awoken by this evening, I was going to pay Dorin a little visit tonight."

I didn't need to ask what my father had meant by that.

"Hush, Narris. The children could hear you."

My father grumbled something under his breath, but it was too soft for me to hear. It was clear I wasn't going to be able to find my way back to the dusk of sleep, so I decided to step into the light. At least, as much light as one can find living underground.

The amber glow of the lamp burning on my bedside table cast deep shadows across the faces of my parents, which were already haggard from worry. Like the rest of the Upaka, my parents had the same fair skin and dark hair. My father kept his hair cut short. He didn't want to give an opponent something to grab hold of during a fight. My mother would have probably preferred to do the same, but she knew how much my father liked her longer curls.

My father was shorter than most Upakan men, something he said was a benefit when having to sneak in and out of places while fulfilling his contracts. My mother, on the other hand, was taller than average. She stood eye to eye with my father, which she said made kissing him much easier.

"There he is," my father said, laying an encouraging hand on my shoulder. "There's my little warrior."

I wanted to smile, but it came out more of a wince than anything.

"No one has ever stood before Dorin's whip like that before. I've seen grown men weep under the lash. But not my son. No, they couldn't break my Ayrion." My father leaned in a little closer. "You should have seen the look on Brim's face. I've never seen him look so disappointed." He rubbed the top of my head. "I couldn't be prouder of you, son."

"Proud or not," my mother said, "this wouldn't have happened if you hadn't been using your gifts during training." Her words were harsh, but the look on her face let me know they were given out of sincere concern. "Using magic only draws attention."

I took a breath, but the pain from the wounds in my back nearly snatched it away. "I have these gifts for a reason," I said, my voice weaker than I had anticipated. "I shouldn't have to hide them."

"Perhaps not. But what should be and what is are two very different things."

"Your mother's right. You've got to be more careful. If Brim was to ever discover that your advancement was due to magic and not cheating, he'd take you to the White Tower and drop you off at the front door himself."

I shivered at the thought. Those taken to the Tower were never heard from again. "I suppressed my magic during the whipping."

My mother sighed. "I wondered as much."

"Wondered what?"

"Your grandfather used to speak of how the magic affected him. He said he was able to turn it on and off at will."

"The last thing I wanted was to see the lashes coming and not be able to stop them. It was easier not knowing."

My grandfather had had the gift of pre-sight. But unlike me, he only had the one gift. The magic had skipped a generation. However, none of my siblings had it, at least not yet. My mother said that magic sometimes took longer to manifest in some than others.

Normally, being able to see things before they happened was a good thing, except of course when you're tied to a stake and publicly beaten. I wasn't an actual seer like my grandfather, though. I couldn't predict future events or anything. My visions only gave me that few seconds of warning when something was going to affect me in a physical way. It came in handy whenever I faced Flon in the ring.

My second gift was just as useful. My mother said I was a repeater. The name sounded silly to me. It was a type of muscle memory. It allowed my body to learn things much faster than anyone else. For most trainees, it took years of work and repetition to master the elements of Upakan fighting, but with my gift, it only required me to perform something once, and my body could repeat it immediately.

My parents had warned me not to use my gifts. They told me to let the other trainees win occasionally so I didn't stick out so much. I didn't see the point. I was already disliked by the other kids, so I wasn't about to give them the satisfaction of beating me. If I was going to be shunned, then it might as well be for good reason. After today, I was starting to think that maybe they had been right after all.

My mother gently rubbed my cheek. "Get some rest, Ayrion. You need to heal. I'll check in on you later."

My parents stood and walked to the door. I closed my eyes and listened to the latch fall back into place behind them. It didn't take

long for the darkness to find me as I floated away into peaceful silence once more.

The days and nights tended to blur together as I started my long journey of recovery back to health. Rianna spent a great deal of time reading to me as I dozed off and on. I wasn't sure if Jorn made an appearance. If he had, it must have been while I was dozing.

My mother washed my wounds every day, and Father coated my back with a special herbal salve, a secret recipe passed down through his family that was said to speed healing. It seemed to be working. By the end of the first week, I was out of bed and moving around the house. By the end of the next, I was walking down through the tunnels to my favorite spot at the bottom of Triple Falls.

The pain was still there, but not with the same intensity. The wounds had all but sealed, and the itchy scabs were driving me crazy. Pretty soon, even they would be a distant memory, a stern reminder to keep away from magic, at least in public.

I exited the tunnel to the thunderous sound of water pouring down off a hundred-foot ledge of granite, forming pools at the bottom. The larger pools at the base spilled over into smaller ones, forming a honeycomb of water holes.

I doused my torch. Anywhere else within the wind tunnels, I would have been left in darkness, but the pools were home to a type of algae that produced a soft bluish glow. The water was so clear that the bottom looked as if it were just below the surface, close enough to touch. In reality, it would have taken a deep breath and a strong pair of arms and legs to make it down and back.

The water was warm, perfect for swimming. I stripped down to my underpants and carefully slid off the shelf and into one of the smaller pools farther from the falls. Normally, I would have climbed higher and dived in, but I would have probably ripped my back open if I had, and then Mother would have given me a harsh scolding when I got home.

The water felt wonderful. It soothed the tension in my back. The buoyancy allowed me to float without strain. I paddled around for a while before finally turning over on my back to float.

"There you are!"

I opened my eyes and lifted my head. My sister was walking across the rock shelf in my direction. She opened the front of her lantern and blew out the wick.

"I thought I'd find you here."

I relaxed and lowered my head back into the water, continuing to float. "It's quiet down here."

Rianna turned to look at the falls. "*Quiet* isn't exactly the word I'd use for it."

"You know what I mean."

She sat on the edge of the pool and rolled her trousers up past the knee, letting her legs dangle in the water.

My sister was sixteen, three years older than I was. She was pretty for a girl, but so far, she hadn't been chosen by any of the boys for Mal'jinto.

"How's the back?"

"Healing." I watched her paddle her feet for a moment. I could tell she wanted to say something but was having a hard time getting it out. "What is it?"

Rianna was unusually quiet. "That was one of the hardest things I've ever had to watch," she said finally.

I smiled. "If it makes you feel any better, it was even harder for me."

She splashed me with her foot. "Hey, I'm being serious."

"Me too." I floated for a while without saying anything. I couldn't stop thinking about all the trouble I'd been in over the last couple of years, and wondered if Brim was right, that the problem was me. "Sometimes, I wonder if it wouldn't be better if I just left." Rianna looked at me funny. "No, really. I can't very well stop being who I am."

"No one's asking you to."

"Everyone is. Even Mother wants me to stop using magic so I'll fit in." I hit the top of the water with my palm and watched the ripples spread outward. "I'd like to say that I wish I'd never been born with magic, but I can't. It's a part of me. I can't just ignore it and hope it goes away."

Rianna sighed. "I know it's hard. But you must realize you're not the only one affected by it. We all are. Most of the other ladies won't talk to Mother anymore. And Father's contracts, if you haven't noticed, are getting smaller every year. And Jorn . . . well, he's ten. He just wants attention—"

"And most of it seems to be heaped on me, I know."

Rianna nodded. There was another moment of silence as we listened to the droning sound of the water beating against the granite floor of the enormous cavern.

Even though she never said it, I had a feeling I was partially to blame for my sister's lack of suitors. Very few people wanted to be associated with our family.

"Anyway, I just thought you should know."

She was right. Would it really hurt me to try being a little more careful? "I'll see what I can do."

Rianna smiled. "Good. Can't ask for more than that."

"Hey! Why didn't you tell me you were coming down here? I wanted to come." Jorn stood just inside the mouth of the tunnel on the left, his torch revealing the deep-seated scowl on his face.

"Come on in," I said, waving him over. "The water's warm."

"I can't. Father told me to come get you. He has news."

"What kind of news?" Rianna asked.

Jorn shrugged. "How should I know?" With that, he ran back up the tunnel.

"Guess we'd better go," Rianna said as she stood. "Give me your hand." With her help, I was able to get out of the pool without reinjuring my back. "I hope it's good news."

I grabbed my clothes and put them on over my wet underpants. "Don't know. With my luck, the Primary wants to give me another ten lashes for having the nerve not to cry during the last twenty."

My sister frowned. "That's not funny."

She was right. It wasn't.

Chapter 5

"HE'S TOO young, Narris."

"Nonsense. I was his age when my father took me on my first contract." Father rubbed the top of my head and smiled. "Besides, Ayrion is twice as capable as any of the other trainees. He'll be fine."

"He's hardly healed," Mother insisted. "Just look at him. He can't even put his clothes on straight." I looked down. In the rush to get out of the pools, I'd somehow managed to put my top on backward. Mother gave me a sharp look. "I don't like it. He's not ready."

Father huffed. "Lea, he'll be fine."

As much as I didn't like watching my parents argue, it was nice to see that look of pride in my father's eyes.

"The contract doesn't come due for another month," Father

said. "That's plenty of time for him to get his strength back."

"It's already coming back, Father," I said, so eager to join him on one of his jobs that I would have done or said anything. "See." I swung my arms in a slow circle, not letting the sharp pain in my back show on my face. "No pain. In a month, I'll be stronger than ever."

"That's the spirit," my father said with a wink. "After everything that's happened, I think some time away from here will do you good."

"Will he be in any danger?"

"No. It's a single contract with a good payout. Fanon said it came in a week ago. He's been holding it for me. He knew we needed the coin."

Mother sighed. "That was kind of him. Make sure to thank him for me when you get the chance." She looked at me and crossed her arms but didn't say anything more.

The days seemed to drag on forever. Sitting around waiting for something to happen was harder than I'd thought it would be. It reminded me of the time I'd ventured above ground and watched the sun move from one side of the sky to the other. It had seemed it would never make it.

I tried to stay busy. Most of my time was spent down at the pools. If I wasn't swimming, I was running through my exercise routines. The slick granite was a fantastic place to work on balance. If I slipped, I had warm water waiting to catch me.

When the day finally came for our departure, my father awoke to find me packed and waiting by the door.

"Someone's anxious to be underway," Father said with a chuckle. "You remind me of one of Master Selfer's wolf pups waiting for a piece of meat." He pointed at me with his long-stemmed pipe. "You start howling and I'm leaving you here."

I smiled. He was right. I stopped pacing and started double-checking my supplies. I had crammed everything I thought I would need into my travel pack the day Father had first told me I was to join him. Since then, the sack hadn't left my side, in anticipation of the event.

It wasn't just that I was being awarded the opportunity to go on my very own contract; it was also that I would be able to see my father in action. My father had quite the reputation among our clan. He was known as the Cleaner. When he finished a contract, there was nothing left. It was like the person had never existed. It had earned him a fair amount of respect among the other warriors. And up until now, it had been a dream of mine to watch him work and learn his secrets.

"You have your sword?" my mother asked as she started through the long checklist of items she always read off before my father left for a contract.

I tapped the hilt at my waist. "Got it."

"Throwing knives?"

"Yep." I ran my fingers across my leather jerkin. Mother had sewn pouches on the inside for them.

"Longbow?"

"Right here." I motioned to the unstrung bow and quiver of arrows sitting next to me.

My mother never looked up from her list.

"Have you restocked your fire pouch?"

"Of course," I said, listing off the items in the small red sack. "Flintstone, hemp fibers, resinous wood—"

"Birch bark?"

I rolled my eyes and huffed in frustration. "Yes, Mother, I have it."

We continued through the list, Mother checking off the items as she went. It was exciting. It made me feel older. I was running through the same routine I'd watched my father perform on countless occasions. This time, it was my turn. I was going on my first contract.

By the time we made it through, finished saying our good-byes, and started up the south tunnel that led to the surface, I was nearly ready to crawl out of my skin with excitement. I kept trying to walk faster, but Father just smiled and said, "No need to rush. We'll get there when we get there."

Half the tunnel we were walking through consisted of lined cobble from one of the old city's main streets. It had folded in on itself during the collapse, twisting its way up the wall before meandering back under our feet again.

The higher we climbed, the colder it got. One of the great things about living underground was that we rarely had to deal with the extremes of weather. The heat from the magma flows in the lower wind tunnels helped regulate the temperature. I took a deep breath and exhaled. I couldn't yet see my breath, but the nip in the air let me know that fall had arrived.

The tunnel ended inside the atrium of a large building. I had no idea what it had been used for back before the great quake, but from its size, I was sure it had been important. The back half had collapsed, leaving only the entrance and part of the west wing mostly intact and above the surface. Bright light shone through the broken windows at the front and sides, and I had to squint to see where I was going.

Father doused his torch, and we started across the once-elegant tiles now chipped and faded with age. The sound of our boots echoed off the walls. Two guards, standing on the other side by the entrance, motioned for us to stop as we approached. They wore the crests of their respective clans.

"It's a bright one," the guard from Clan Kovaa said as he walked over to a small desk. *Kovaa* meant *hidden* or *unseen* in the old tongue.

Father smiled. "It usually is."

The guard picked up a quill and dipped it in the ink jar. "Where're you headed?"

"Oswell."

The guard scribbled something in his ledger. "Contract?"

"Yes."

"Will you be taking the southern route around the mountains,

or will you be going west through the Squeeze and on past Norshag?" The guard stopped writing to look our way. "Norshag will
cut a good four or five days off your journey, but . . ." He looked
at me. "It's a sight more dangerous."

"We'll take the—"

"Squeeze," I blurted out. I wasn't about to look like I needed
coddling.

My father looked like he was about to say something but only
nodded. The guard went back to his writing. "And when will you
be expecting to return?"

"Put us down for three weeks. A full moon at most."

The guard nodded and added it to the ledger, then rejoined the
guard from Clan Raju to open the doors. *Raju* meant *swift*. Although, the way this particular guard moved, he gave no indication
of it. He lowered his shaders slowly into place and walked over to
the door on the left. He didn't seem all that eager to let in the light.

Of the three clans making up Upakan society, my family was
part of the third. Orpa. The name meant *strength*. There were times
I thought we had ended up in the wrong clan. Kovaa would have
been a better fit. Maybe then I could have remained unseen.

"Get your shaders," Father said.

I followed his lead and pulled the leather strap from my bag. I
didn't like wearing them all that much. They tended to give me a
headache.

Shaders were hard to come by, which meant they were rather
costly. Most families were lucky to have one pair. We had two.

My father had managed to land a contract in Aramoor before I was born. Because the capital city of Elondria was on the other side of Aldor, it meant contracts from there were few and far between. Also, a city as big as Aramoor already had plenty of options to choose from when it came to hiring killers. While my father was there, he'd found a blower who had specialized in unique glass and had him make some tinted glass for two pairs of shaders, and then he'd hired a girdler to sew the glass into leather bands. It had been much cheaper to purchase the items separately than to acquire a premade pair.

I cinched the straps at the back of my head, but not too tightly. The last time, I'd spent two days with a severe migraine. The soft leather on the inside band kept my skin from chafing, but they were still annoying to use. They narrowed my range of sight to what was directly in front of me, so I spent a lot of time shifting back and forth to watch my flank. I felt like a horse with blinders.

Once our shaders were secure, the guards opened the doors and we stepped outside. I lifted my hand over my eyes. Even with the tinted glass, the light was blinding.

"Good hunting," the guard from Raju said as they shut the doors behind us.

It had been a few months since I had been topside. I'd forgotten how different it was. The sun felt warm on my hands and face. Smells were unnaturally sharp without the familiar dampness of our underground home to mute them. The wind whipped across my face, sending tiny bumps skittering across my arms. Even the sound of my own breathing was unnerving without its normal hollow echo off the stone below. It wasn't bad, just different.

All around us lay the ruins of the former capital city of Keldor. The tops of some of the taller buildings burst through the ground as if trying to claw their way back up. The rest were either scattered debris or buried below the surface. Behind the city, the white-capped peaks of the Northern Heights stood as a protective barrier, a beautiful offset to the carnage of what now lay spread across its foothills.

"Let's get our horses and be on our way," Father said as he started down the steps. "I want to reach the Squeeze before night-fall."

I hefted my sack and followed him down to the worn path that led in the direction of the stables. The path wound its way through the ruins, making sure to avoid any of the red markers. The ground was unstable to walk across in some areas. Most of the holes the markers warned against had been discovered by people falling through—often to their death.

The stables were nothing more than half a building too stubborn to collapse. The front wall was missing, which was perfect for setting up a handful of stalls. I'd been given training in horsemanship, but it had been quite a while since I'd ridden one. The thought of doing so again brought a spring to my step.

Father rented us a pair—a medium-sized mare for me with a white stripe down her light brown face, and a stallion for him with a dark coat and an even darker mane. We tied on our gear, mounted, and slowly made our way back out into the light.

My father turned in his saddle. "Make sure not to let your horse wander off the path. You hit one of those sinkholes and Brim will get his wish."

I nodded and gripped the reins as tightly as I could. That would be my luck. My chance to finally go on my first great adventure, and I'd manage to plummet to my death before I even left the city.

I shivered at the thought.

Chapter 6

$\mathfrak{I}$T TOOK US THE rest of the morning to navigate through the city's remains. Once safely on the other side, we skirted the area designated for farmland. Those not training to be warriors, because of an infirmity, a lack of ability, or an absence of desire, were recruited to help grow the crops necessary to feed those living underneath. The land surrounding our home was rocky and difficult to grow in, but we Upaka never backed away from a challenge. What we didn't manage to grow ourselves, we purchased from the regular supply wagons that sold to us from Chorazin and Pinnella.

Off to the west, the smoke from Mount Ash rose into the sky, a clear reminder of the power it held over this part of Keldor. It burned night and day, feeding the lava flows deep beneath the city. Some said if it ever erupted again, it would finish the job it had started centuries before. I tried not to think about it.

We made good time in reaching the pass. The sun was still hanging above the ridgeline behind us when we stopped at a small grove of trees nestled against the sheer rock, the last oasis before entering the barren passageway through the Northern Heights.

Within the confines of the trees, the sun's last rays had little effect. I was thankful for the chance to finally remove my shaders and let my eyes readjust to the relative dimness, even if it meant losing the warmth of the sun. I rubbed the back of my head where the leather strap had flattened my hair.

Father dismounted and went about setting up camp in a small clearing off the main path leading into the pass. We could see the entrance to the Squeeze from where we were.

I slid off my horse with a rather sore backside and a stiff, bowlegged limp. After tying off the animals, I dug a small pit for the fire and gathered enough wood to last till morning. It didn't take the kindling long to light. There was a nip in the air, and I scooted closer to the flames as I watched Father slowly stew some cabbage, leeks, and a few pieces of meat in our small kettle.

In the distance, a pack of wolves joined their voices in song. It was a lonely sound, haunting and beautiful. We were happy to listen so long as they stayed at a distance.

Father finished his stirring, and I held out my bowl to be filled. He dipped a good portion and then froze, the ladle halfway to my bowl, dripping its contents on the needles below.

I looked around. "What is it?"

He held his finger to his lips. Another round of howling drifted in, but it didn't sound like the pack had gotten any closer. I opened my mouth to ask him what he'd heard when a twig snapped.

Father spun in the direction of the pass. The ladle hit the ground, and two knives appeared in his hands. I grabbed my dagger from my waist since my sword and bow were with my bedding on the other side of the fire. We both stood staring off to the left.

There was another snap, this time much closer. Father grabbed my arm, and we raced to the far-right side of the camp, away from the main road leading into the Squeeze. I grabbed my bow and quiver on the way by, and he snatched my sword, which was closer than his.

We melted into the trees and waited. A voice called out on the opposite side of the clearing.

"A warrior in life."

Father's shoulders relaxed slightly. "A warrior in death," he answered.

I followed him back to camp. Two men dressed in the familiar leathers of Upakan warriors appeared out of the shadows, leading their horses.

"Would you have any more of whatever that wonderful smell is?" one of the men asked. "Our journey took longer than expected. I'm sick of hearing Heflin's stomach growl." He elbowed his companion. "Not much in the way of game in there unless you count rock grubs and stripers. Another day without food and I might have resorted to either."

"Aye," my father said, gesturing for the two men to take a seat. "There's enough to go around. We can always restock in Norshag if we need to."

"Norshag?" The taller man, wearing a neat jawline beard, glanced my way but tried not to make a show of it. "That's a rough place to be taking someone so . . ." He cleared his throat. "I'd stay clear if you can manage it. The place grows worse every year; you know how the mountain folk feel about our kind."

"It's been a couple of seasons since I've been," Father said with a pensive look. "I thank you for your advice, uh . . ."

"Sorry about that," the taller man said. "I'm Nykl, and this is Heflin." He made a quick gesture to his comrade. Heflin, who was shorter than his companion and somewhat stocky, seemed more interested in what was in our cooking pot than whether or not we went to Norshag. Both men wore rings on their right hands like my father's, each with the mark of their clan. I studied them, eager for my own naming day when I would be given mine and recognized as a full-fledged Upakan warrior.

"Pleased to meet you both," Father said. "Let's get you something to eat."

"Much appreciated," Nykl said. The two men made no attempt to hide their haste as they tied off their horses, grabbed a couple of wooden bowls and spoons from their satchels, and plopped down beside the fire.

"How far have you traveled?"

Heflin leaned forward to get a good whiff of the pottage. "Syrel."

"That's quite the journey," my father said, adding another few cuts of meat to the pot and what was left of the onions.

"I couldn't agree more," Nykl said. "I'm looking forward to

getting back to the wife and kids. This contract took us longer than we would have liked. I'm sure Maritsa has been worried sick."

Heflin huffed. "If my woman were half the looker yours is, I'd be anxious too."

Nykl smiled at the compliment. "Your Lorna might not be the most handsome woman, but she can cook a circle around anyone in our clan, not to mention shoot the tick off a boar's backside."

Heflin grinned and patted his stomach. "Aye. Why do you think I chose her for bonding?"

Nykl snorted. "You chose her 'cause she didn't give you any other choice. Tell Lorna no and she'd mount your head in her bedroom and use your skin for a blanket."

"Aye," Heflin groaned.

"Not to mention her brothers catching the two of you down in the pools."

My eyes widened. This was getting interesting.

"That again? I tell you, nothing happened."

"Clearly, they didn't believe you."

My father cleared his throat and nodded in my direction.

Heflin looked at me and changed the subject. "Yes, well, regardless, my Lorna can make a mean pot of stew."

The two men ate their fill and were mighty grateful for it, not turning down the offer of seconds. Heflin even licked his bowl before laying it aside. "Best I've tasted in some time," he said with an honest smile.

The two men stretched out in front of the fire while I helped Father finish cleaning. I spent the rest of the evening enthralled as

I listened intently to the three of them swap stories of their adventures: battles fought, men they'd killed, interesting places they had seen. Being a warrior sounded like the most exciting thing in the world. I couldn't imagine living my life as anything else.

Morning broke early, and I awoke to the sound of my father's voice and the feel of his hand on my shoulder as he shook me awake. "It's time to get up. We've a long day ahead of us."

My teeth chattered as I yawned and stretched. The fire had died during the night, but the coals were still glowing faintly. "Are you sure?" I asked. "It's still dark."

My father smiled and started to pack his gear. Nykl and Heflin were already up and packed and ready to leave by the time I managed to drag myself from the warmth of my bedding.

"We wish you safe travels," Heflin said as they mounted. "Many thanks for sharing your fire with us."

"Our pleasure," Father said with a warm smile.

Nykl leaned forward in his saddle. "Do consider my warning, and stay clear of Norshag."

"We will. Thank you."

"Oh, and watch out for stripers in the pass. They aren't all in hibernation yet." With that, the two men waved, turned their horses, and headed west.

I looked at Father. "Stripers?"

"We'll keep our eyes out."

I groaned. I hated snakes.

After a quick meal of cheese and some dried apple slices, I refilled the bladders from a small stream near the camp. We let the horses drink their fill. Normally, Father would have been cautious not to let them drink too deeply and upset their stomachs, but our journey through the pass would be a slow one, with no chance for them to reach a full gallop. We saddled the horses, tied on our gear, and buried the remains of the fire with a blanket of fresh dirt.

Before the first hint of morning light had penetrated the canopy, we were mounted and riding toward the pass. I'd never been to the Squeeze, so I was excited to see it for myself, as long as there were no stripers there to greet us.

I was bubbling with anticipation. New adventures around every corner. Even the possibility of danger waiting for us at Norshag was thrilling. I knew Father would never allow us to go, especially after Nykl's warning, but one could always hope.

Chapter 7

IT WAS EASY TO SEE why the pass was called the Squeeze. It was barely wide enough for two horses to walk side by side. In some places, it was too narrow for even that. The sun wasn't yet high enough to illuminate our path between the rising walls of stone, so Father used a torch to guide the horses.

My shaders hung loose around my neck as I diligently scanned the path ahead for stripers. I clicked my tongue, and my horse slowly moved back in step with Father's. The rhythmic clopping of their hooves on the granite made it hard to stay awake.

My lids had drifted closed for the third time when Father shouted. I nearly fell out of my saddle as I grabbed for the reins. "What's going on? What happened?" I was awake now, the drowsiness frightened out of me.

Father roared with laughter. "You should have seen the look on your face."

I didn't find it all that funny at first, but soon enough, I was laughing right along.

Father shouted once more and then cocked his head to the side. "Just listen to that echo." His voice reverberated off the surrounding rock, slowly fading into the distance. "Give it a try."

I wasn't sure if he was being serious.

"Well, go on. What are you waiting for?"

I shrugged and shouted, "Hello!" There was a faint echo in the distance.

"You call that a yell? I barely counted three repeats. Your sister could have done better than that."

I straightened my shoulders. No girl was going to shout louder than I, not even Rianna. Taking a deep breath, I sucked in every last bit of air my lungs could hold and released it. "Ahhhh!" By the time I finished, my face had turned red and my head felt woozy from the rush of blood.

The echoes bounced back in all directions. This time, I joined Father in counting the number of repeats. "Eight," I said with a proud smile.

"Aye, now, that's more like it." He slapped me on the back with a firm whack. My eyes bulged as I coughed from where his hand had hit my lashes. Even though mostly healed, they were still tender. From then on, I made sure not to doze off.

By midafternoon, the sun had risen to its peak, cutting through the shadows ahead and lighting our path. There wasn't much to see but more rock. The pass was deep enough that we were able to travel most of it without our shaders. Every now and then, it would widen long enough to allow in chunks of sunlight, but I was finding that I needed the tinted glass less and less.

The stone corridor tunneled through the mountains like a snake. What lay beyond each new bend was a mystery, one I was anxious to explore—at least for the first couple of hours. After two or three dozen twists and turns with nothing to show for it but more twists and turns, I grew annoyed.

"How much farther?"

My father laughed. "It's a two-day trip through the Squeeze. Better get comfortable."

I groaned and tried to find a more relaxed position in the saddle. You would think that doing nothing more than sitting all day would be easy, but it wasn't. I'd forgotten how sore horseback riding could make your backside.

The rest of the day went about the same—jostling along in the saddle while watching for stripers. The only good thing about the endless miles of granite was that it reminded me of home.

Father wanted to reach our next campsite before dark, so we ate while riding, stopping only long enough to give the horses a rest, which wasn't really a stop. It just meant we led the horses on foot for a while.

The last of the light was slowly ebbing from the pass when we rounded yet another bend to find an opening large enough to make camp.

"Ah, good, we're here," Father said, hopping down from his

horse and stretching. "I was getting worried I'd misjudged the distance."

I slid from my mount and did the same, followed by a few well-deserved moans as I massaged my hindquarters.

There wasn't anything available to burn, so we had a cold meal of dried meat and cheese stuffed between a couple of slices of Mother's delicious rye bread.

The horses were unsaddled and fed. Father tethered them to a boulder in case they got the notion to wander on without us in the middle of the night.

Without the warmth of the fire, I made sure to lay my bedding right beside my father's.

"Make sure to tuck your blanket up under you," father said. "Don't want a striper finding its way in while you're asleep. They're attracted to heat, you know." He turned over. "Well, good night." I couldn't tell, but I thought I heard a slight chuckle.

After tucking every loose inch of blanket up under me, I lay there shivering, staring at the rock overhead. How was I going to go to sleep now, knowing I could awaken with a snake in my bed?

As worried as I was, exhaustion finally got the better of me. By the next morning, my teeth were chattering and my hands were shaking. Even under my winter blanket, it was unpleasantly cold. Father eventually turned over and crawled out of his bedding. It was hard to do the same knowing there were no warm embers waiting for me.

I slowly removed my blanket, careful to make sure there were no unwanted guests underneath. Once I realized I was the only one in my blanket, I stood.

We ate a quick breakfast, saddled the horses, packed what gear we had used—which wasn't much more than our blankets—and were heading back inside the narrow corridor before the stars had winked from view. I volunteered to be the one to hold the torch this time, hoping it would thaw my fingers.

I was more than grateful for the sun's eventual company once the pass widened enough for it to make its presence known. The warmth on my face and hands more than made up for the fact that I had to keep squinting. Father said the sooner we got used to the light, the better off we'd be, so I went most of the day without my shaders.

With the towering rock on either side of us, it was hard to judge how much time had passed. To me, it seemed to have been days, weeks, months. My backside was growing numb from the endless up and down in the saddle. I was starting to wonder whether the Squeeze actually led anywhere, or if it was taking us in a giant circle.

"We're getting close," Father said, no doubt sensing my impatience.

My fingers tightened anxiously on the reins as we rounded the last bend. The endless walls of granite were finally lowering, and I could see trees in the distance. I couldn't help but smile as I exhaled a huge sigh of relief at the sight of open skies, which was an odd thing, considering I had spent my entire life underground.

Father was smiling as well.

I urged my horse to move a little faster. The excitement of

reaching the end of the long, narrow corridor had my heart racing. "Come on," I said, glancing over my shoulder at Father as he trotted along behind me. "What are you waiting for?" I was about to spur my horse once again when something off to the side hissed.

My magic tore through me like a bolt of lightning, and I was suddenly ripped forward in time. I watched the long black-and-yellow snake uncoil as it dove out of a crevice in the left wall and struck my horse's leg. The mare bucked, and I grabbed for the reins. My grip wasn't strong enough, and I flew backward out of the saddle. My head hit the side of the wall on the way down and everything spun. The pain was excruciating. I opened my mouth, but before I could get anything out, I was suddenly yanked backward in time. The vision vanished, and I found myself once again in my saddle.

Quickly, I jerked the reins to the right, nearly colliding with my father as the enormous striper I had seen leaped out of its hiding place, just missing my horse's leg. The mare whinnied and reared, and just like in my vision, I lost my grip and tumbled out of the saddle. However, my head didn't hit the wall this time, since I had managed to get my horse far enough away.

Time seemed to slow as I waited for impact. My back hit first, and the pain sent my head to spinning. I gasped for air. I looked up in time to see my horse heading for the trees ahead at a full gallop. Stupid animal. I had just saved her life; the least she could have done was wait for me.

I barely had time to gather my thoughts before another vision whisked me away. Using it, I rolled to the right, and the viper missed my left arm. Frantically, I grabbed for my sword, but it wasn't there. It was still attached to my spineless horse, which was now probably halfway to Norshag.

I flipped over and drew my dagger instead. The snake lunged again. This time, I had the advantage of knowing when and where. With a single swing, I cut the snake nearly in two, throwing it to the side as I scrambled backward as fast as I could.

The snake coiled, not yet realizing it was dead.

"Are you injured?" Father asked, trying to keep his own horse in check. "Were you bitten?"

I shook my head. "No. I'm fine," I said, putting on a brave face. In reality, I was as frightened as my worthless horse. At least she had possessed enough common sense to get out of there. I scooted up against the right wall and scanned my body. Other than a sore back and injured pride, I didn't have any lasting damage.

"Good. I'm going after your horse! We can't afford to lose the gear." He slapped his reins and took off for the trees.

I scrambled to my feet. The snake was still flopping as I edged away. I didn't wait to see if it would ever realize it was dead before chasing after my father.

Finally breaking free of the mountainside, I plopped down on a fallen log and attempted to catch my breath. I didn't dare venture into the woods on foot without knowing where I was going, so I waited for Father to return with my horse.

I shook my head. This was my luck. We'd traveled the entire length of the Squeeze without seeing a single striper, and one had waited till the very last few feet to make an appearance. Worse still,

I'd lost my horse in the process. Not the best way to prove my worth on this contract.

After an hour had passed, I began to worry. The dumb animal couldn't have run that far. Then again, these woods were dense; no telling how hard it would be to track the crazy thing if she ever got out of sight.

Another hour passed, and I was more than a little anxious, when I finally heard someone coming. I hid behind a large boulder up near the rock face—checking for stripers first. It was Father. However, my excitement at seeing him disappeared when I saw only the one horse.

"I couldn't find that rotten animal anywhere," Father said as he came to a stop. "Who knows how far she went before slowing. Dumb thing probably ran herself to death."

Now I really felt bad. "I'm sorry," I said, worried Father would call the whole thing off and go back home.

"Sorry for what? It's not your fault that flaming snake was there." Father climbed off his horse and looked me over. "Are you sure you're not injured?"

"I'm sure." I was too embarrassed at having lost my horse and our supplies to worry about anything else. That snake could have bitten me a hundred times and I wouldn't have admitted it. "What are we going to do?"

Father sighed and ran a gloved hand down his face. "Something I don't want to." He turned and looked to the south. "We can't go on with only one horse and half our supplies, not to mention the loss of your weapons."

I grimaced. "I still have my dagger." I held it up, only to realize I hadn't cleaned all the blood off yet.

"It looks like we don't have much of a choice. We'll have to resupply at Norshag."

"But Nykl said—"

"Doesn't much matter what he said. We can't go on with one horse and only half our supplies."

I shrugged. "I guess not."

Father walked over to his horse and mounted. "Here, give me your hand. We'll have to ride double for now."

With his help, I swung up behind him.

"When we get there, you do exactly what I say. You hear me?"

"Yes, sir."

"Just keep your eyes open and remember your training. You'll be fine."

I found his words less than comforting.

## Chapter 8

$\mathcal{O}$HE LAST SWATCH of color in the sky was fading from view by the time we reached our destination. Father brought the horse to a stop on the outskirts of town.

"Remember what I said. Keep your eyes open, but don't say anything. People 'round these parts don't care much for the Upaka."

"Why?"

There was a slight pause. "Because of who we are."

I didn't say anything more. Instead, I spent the time studying the small village. There wasn't much to see. Norshag seemed to grow right out of the surrounding forest. It certainly wasn't one of those exotic locations that Father had described from his travels. The buildings were older and poorly crafted. They looked to have been built from the trees cut to make room for the withering community.

Father started us forward, slowly. I scanned the faces of those we passed. The people on the street, as well as those mingling around the buildings, stopped to stare. Most were dressed in rough leather and thick furs, and everyone was armed, from the youngest to the oldest. There were swords, daggers, bows, bludgeons, and even hatchets, but it wasn't their dress or even their weapons that held my attention.

"Look at their eyes," I leaned forward and whispered in Father's ear.

"Yes, I know." There was a slight edge to his voice.

These were the first outsiders I'd ever seen. I was never around when the supply wagons came through from Chorazin and Pinnella. I'd never seen anyone with colored eyes before. They looked frightening, as though they could see right through me.

"Why are they so different?"

"They aren't. Ours are. Now keep quiet and put your hood up."

A few of the people we passed shook their heads, some spit, but most just stood there watching. Whispers of conversation floated from one person to the next as we rode by. Even the scraggly mutt we passed bared its teeth.

I followed my father's lead and lifted the hood of my cloak over my head.

The road leading through town was a muddy rut. The sludge sucked down the horse's hooves with each step. There were a few rundown shops scattered to either side, with a smattering of single-story homes filling in the rest. A large building at the center of town seemed to be the main attraction. It was also the only building—apart from a barn farther down—to have two floors. The sign swinging at the front declared it THE BLOSSOM. Seemed appropriate, considering the amount of brightly colored paint on the outside.

Shouts drifted through the open doors at the front while rough screams and uncomfortable moans floated down from the windows above. Women with painted faces lined the front porch. They seemed to have more clothes off than on.

"Don't look," Father said as we got a little closer.

I turned my head, but a loud crash from one of the second-floor windows had me spinning back around. A man, wearing nothing more than his underpants, had been thrown from one of the top windows. He rolled down the porch roof and landed in the dirt below. Another half-dressed man climbed out of the window after him.

"Stop, Fulton!" one of the painted women said from the window as she tried reaching for the second man. "You're gonna kill 'im."

"That's the idea." The second man jumped off the roof and just missed landing on the first. The two started throwing wild punches as they rolled in the dirt. The building's remaining occupants turned out to watch the entertainment. People were shouting, laying wagers, urging the two men to do their worst.

Father stopped the horse before we reached them.

The half-naked women on the front porch were waving their arms and shouting, their shrill voices overpowering the men's.

The second man made it to his feet and pulled the other one up far enough to punch him in the face, knocking him down again. He repeated this action a couple more times before a hefty man in a full apron pushed his way through the crowd and pulled them apart.

"I told you, you could both have her. You just have to wait your turn."

The two brawlers dusted the dirt from their clothes as they stood. The crowd grumbled at the fight having ended and stomped back inside THE BLOSSOM. The man who'd clearly won grabbed the half-naked woman who'd been standing at the window and shuffled her inside. The loser wiped the blood from his mouth and stumbled toward the front porch. Two of the more heavily painted women took pity on him and helped him in. The bright smile on his face as they wrapped their arms around him was a strange contrast to his bloody nose and swollen eyes.

Once the people had dispersed, my father urged us on. He directed the horse toward the barn on the south side of town. There was a corral built on to the side with several horses mingling about.

"Father." I tapped him on the shoulder. "That's our—"

"I know. I see it."

My horse was one of those prancing around the small fenced-in area. The saddle was still on her back, but my travel packs were gone, including the one with all my weapons.

A couple of gruff-looking men stood at the gate. They turned when they saw us coming.

"They don't look too friendly," I whispered. In fact, they looked like wild animals, with their fur coats and untamed beards.

"What's your business here?" a large bear of a man asked as he stepped out of the barn and started our way. His shirt was only half-buttoned, revealing he had more in common with a bear than just his size.

I slid off the back of the horse so Father could get down.

"Stay here," Father said as he handed me the reins, "but be ready just in case." He spared a passing glance at his sword but left it tied to the horse as he walked over to meet the man.

*Be ready for what?* I wondered.

The two men leaning against the railing kept a close eye on my father. One of them stopped digging into the top of the fencepost with his knife and looked at me. He spent a good deal of time eyeing our horse or, more accurately, the bags tied to it.

"I see you found our mare." My father's tone was polite, almost cheerful. He even wore a friendly smile, probably a good tactic. These weren't the kind of people you wanted to anger. He made his way over to the corral's gate, and the grizzly-man joined him.

Father pointed to our horse. "That one there with the saddle. She got spooked by a striper back at the pass and took off. Spent a couple of hours looking for her this afternoon. I guess she made her way down here. I appreciate you taking care of her. Here," he said as he pulled a small coin pouch from around his neck. "How much do I owe you for stabling her?"

My father was clearly trying to direct the conversation.

The big man leaned one arm on the top rail and placed one foot on the bottom. "Nothing."

"Nothing? No. I won't hear of it." My father loosened the drawstrings on the purse. "Come now, at least I can pay you for the time and feed."

The big man eyed the coin pouch. I couldn't exactly tell because of the thickness of his beard, but he appeared to be smiling. "No need. The horse isn't yours."

Father raised his head. "Of course she is. See there. That's our saddle. And if I'm not mistaken," he said, pointing in the direction of the barn where my travel bag was hanging from a peg, "that's one of our satchels."

The big man didn't move. There was no need for him to turn and look. He knew what my father was referring to. The other two men started creeping around the side of the pen.

While the two men were preoccupied with the conversation taking place at the front of the corral, I loosened the strap holding my father's sword. I slid it partway out of its sheath. I didn't like the way those men were sneaking up behind my father. I could have grabbed his bow, but if things turned ugly, I wouldn't have time to string it, so I kept my hands close to the sword.

"You're mistaken. That's Haran's horse." The big man looked past my father to the two men working their way around the front of the pen. "Ain't that right, Haran? That's your horse there with the white nose, isn't it?" It sounded more like the big man was telling him rather than asking.

"Aye," the man on the left said, stopping to look at the animal in the pen. "That's mine for sure. Bought her off a peddler two seasons back. Cost me . . . uh, three gold pieces."

So, that was what they wanted. Ransom. We couldn't afford to pay that for the horse. Then again, if we returned without her, we'd be liable for her worth.

"If you bought her off a peddler," my father said, "then you bought stolen property. You can see by the brand there on the back she's clearly an Upakan horse."

Father didn't say anything else, but his smile disappeared. He looked at the big man in front of him for a moment, then turned and looked at me. Was he trying to tell me something? I took a step closer to the horse and reached for the sword, but Father simply shook his head and turned back around.

A few more people stepped out of the stables and started toward my father, two men and a woman. The woman was just as big as the men. All three were heavily armed.

My father glanced at the newcomers and then over his shoulder at the two men moving up from behind. "Fine. How much do you want for her? It seems I don't have much choice but to buy her back from you."

"She's not for sale," the grizzly-man said. This time, I could see his smile. He was clearly enjoying himself. The three from the barn moved alongside him, obviously eager to get in on whatever was happening. None of them looked my way, and even if they had, Father's horse blocked their view. I took the opportunity to draw his sword from its sheath, slowly so it didn't make any noise. I stuck it tip-down in the dirt, then untied and strung the bow. It seemed I was given the opportunity after all. I nocked a single shaft and waited to see what would happen.

"We don't want any trouble. We just want to get our horse and be on our way."

I found myself nodding in agreement, not that anyone could see me.

"Upakans bring trouble wherever they go," the man said before spitting on my father's boot. "The last time one of your kind showed his face in Norshag, a cousin of mine wound up with his throat slit. Ear to ear." The man rested one hand on a long knife tucked in his belt. "So, you see, you've come to the wrong place if you ain't looking for trouble."

Father removed his hood. There was only one reason to do that. "Fine," he said, tucking his purse inside his shirt before raising his hands to show submission. "We'll just leave." He took a step back.

"Where do you think you're going?"

Father stopped, and I raised the bow and drew partway.

The men had him nearly surrounded. I couldn't believe this was happening. I'd always wondered what it would be like to be in a real fight. Never had I imagined being this nervous. My mouth was as dry as one of my father's jokes. I'd been in hundreds of fights, but none where I was expected to actually do real harm, maybe even kill.

"Please, my son is with me. You don't want to do this." The distress in my father's voice surprised me. He wasn't one to plead. He never backed down from anyone, not even Brim.

"Oh, but I think I do. Why take a couple of gold coins in ex-change for the horse when I can just take your gold and the horse, and do the world a favor by ridding it of two more filthy Upakans?"

My father raised his hand. "I'm warning you. This will not end well for you."

The big man smiled. At least I thought it was a smile; it might have been a snarl. "I tell you what. I'll let you and your runt go if you . . . if you clean my boots." He winked at the others.

My father stared at the man for a moment and then dropped to his knees.

My mouth hung open. My father was an Upakan warrior, and here he was kneeling in the mud, groveling for our lives. What turned my stomach even more was the fact that I knew he was only doing it because of me.

The others were openly laughing as my father leaned forward to wipe the man's boots with his sleeve.

"With your tongue." The grizzly-man's voice dripped with contempt.

I raised my father's bow the rest of the way and drew to my chin. My arms were trembling. The anger boiled inside me, vying to break free. I wanted to kill them all. I'd never felt hatred like that before. It frightened me.

Father had stopped halfway to the man's filthy boots.

"You heard me, dog! Lick them clean!"

Those gathered around laughed and jeered, drawing others from across the street.

"You tell him, Orvil."

"Teach that filthy Upakan where his place is."

"Mercenary scum."

My father bent over once more, but this time, I caught a flash of something in his hands. It was one of the two blades he kept tucked in his sleeves. With a single swift movement, he buried one in each of the grizzly-man's feet. He yanked them back out as the man reared back and howled, his arms swing outward as he fell, knocking a couple of the others off their feet in the process.

I stepped out from behind the horse, aimed, and released the bowstring. Haran, the man claiming to own my horse, screamed as my arrow decorated his backside. I shrugged. I'd have to work my way up to the killing part. For now, I'd settle with just incapacitation.

My father was on his feet before I had a chance to grab another arrow. He moved with the grace of a mountain cat. Three of those standing closest were dead before they knew what hit them. Just a single pass with his two blades left necks open, chests pierced, and guts spread wide. It was horrifying and beautiful at the same time.

I nocked another arrow, and everything around me disappeared as my magic yanked me forward once more into another vision. Two men from across the street rushed me at once. I ducked underneath the first man's cudgel only to have the second man's rusty blade pierce my gut. Before the blade made it all the way through, I was yanked back. That was one of the downsides to the visions. I was forced to endure whatever warning of danger they were sent to give.

Quickly, I turned with just enough time to draw halfway and

release. One of the men caught the arrow in the right shoulder and spun around.

I dropped the bow and grabbed my father's sword, managing to get it up in time to parry the second man's swing. Before he could bring his sword back around, I stabbed him in the thigh. I was surprised how easy the blade slid in. The man howled and dropped his weapon. He attempted to help me pull the blade out, nearly cutting his fingers off in the process.

I yanked the blade free and spun around on the heels of a new vision. I let my magic take over as three men rushed me at once. Each vision showed me what was coming, giving me time to counter.

My magic seemed to have a mind of its own as it acted and reacted to each attack. My gift as a repeater moved my body with precision. I blocked left. Spun and countered right. I cut the legs out from under the first man, then stopped the second by removing his sword hand from his arm. I swallowed hard at the blood, a wave of nausea threatening to overpower me.

The third man was more cautious after witnessing how quickly his comrades had been dispatched. I blocked his first swing and parried the second, driving back each attack, then countering with my own. It didn't take long to find an opening. Ducking under his swing, I spun around behind him and cut through both calves. The man dropped.

I retreated toward the corral's gate, where my father was holding off five or six men of his own. He had acquired a sword, blocking with it in one hand while delivering swift, fatal strikes with the dagger in the other. He was amazing. I'd never seen him fight like this before.

Another vision struck, and I spun, bringing my sword around and barely dodging three swift blows from a pair of hatchets. The man wielding them was short but stout, with more hair on his face than on the top of his head. He snarled and swung every which way, trying to cleave me in two.

I pivoted to the left, and a hatchet sailed past. The throw was deadly accurate—but not for the intended target. It struck one of my father's attackers in the back, and he fell without a sound.

My assailant was so stunned at having killed the wrong person that he swung wide and I knocked the remaining hatchet from his hand. With a swift backswing, I slammed the pommel of my sword into the side of his head, and he crumpled.

The townsfolk—those still standing—determined we were far more hassle than we were worth and retreated. I stood back to back with my father as we waited to see what they intended to do. My father didn't appear to even be winded. I, on the other hand, was having a hard time keeping my hands from shaking.

I snuck a glance at the pile of bodies strewn across the lawn in front of the corral. Some were still writhing, but most would never move again.

"Get your horse and satchel," my father hissed.

I crawled through the fence and grabbed my horse, pulling her by the reins toward the gate. Father retrieved his, which surprisingly hadn't run off in the middle of the battle, and opened the gate for me.

He held my horse while I ran to get my pack from the peg at the front of the barn. The other two bags, along with my sword and bow, were piled just inside the door.

"Everything there?" Father asked.

I took a quick look inside the packs. "Looks like it."

"Good. Let's go."

By the time we had tied everything off, those who had retreated had rallied help. It looked like half the town was heading our way. By their unsteady steps, most appeared to have come directly from the tavern. Even the half-naked women were rushing down the street to see what all the fuss was about.

I mounted, slapped the reins, and took off after Father. We headed out of town as fast as we dared in the dark, not slowing until we were sure no one was following. Some miles down the road, Father slowed, and I brought my mare up alongside. We kept our pace to a brisk trot from there.

"Are you injured?"

In all the excitement, I hadn't thought to look. I gave myself a quick inspection, then shook my head. "No. You?"

"Not that I can tell."

Neither of us spoke for some time. I didn't know what to say, but the silence was even more disconcerting. Just when I thought I couldn't take it any longer, my father finally turned in his saddle.

"Best we don't tell your mother about this."

I shivered at the thought. "Agreed."

## Chapter 9

WE TRAVELED THE REST of the night without stopping. We were worried that the good townsfolk of Norshag would throw a hunting party together and come after us while we slept.

By the time the sun had risen high enough to break through the trees, Father had directed us off the main path and into a dense grove of underbrush. We quickly covered the horses' passage with fallen branches and loose leaves.

"You need some rest," he said. "And frankly, so do I."

He wasn't going to get an argument from me. I hadn't been able to quit yawning for the last four hours.

We stopped next to a small stream, not bothering to unsaddle the horses in case we needed to make a run for it. After refilling our waterskins, we fed and watered the horses before bedding down. I was too exhausted to eat.

Father took first watch. I turned over and pulled my blanket up over my face to hide the light. As tired as I was, sleep was slow in coming. The events of last night kept playing over and over in my mind. My first real battle wasn't what I had imagined. Sure, we won, but I didn't have that excited energy I'd seen so many of the other warriors return with after a good fight. I felt numb. Guilty. As if I had something to be ashamed about.

I lowered my blanket. "Is everyone out here like that?"

Father was sitting against a large oak, keeping an eye on the surrounding wood. "Like what?"

"Like those people back there."

"What . . . crazy?" he asked with a slight chuckle. "No. They aren't all like that." He shifted position to see me better. "But we aren't the most welcomed people in Aldor either, given what we do."

"You mean killing people?"

Father nodded.

I thought about it a moment. "Then why do we do it?"

"Because . . ." He seemed to be searching the surrounding foliage for an appropriate answer. "It's just the way it's always been."

Not exactly the response my curious mind had hoped for. "But why?"

He shrugged. "I guess out of necessity. It allows us to live our own lives away from the burdens of their society. And," he said with a slight pause, "we're good at it." He leaned his head back against the rough bark. "When you find something you're good at, something others are willing to pay for, you stick with it."

"Why are we so different?"

"I don't know. Some say we weren't born this way but made. Others say we are faerie-cursed." He shrugged. "Doesn't much seem to matter one way or the other. Can't change who you are."

I lay there for a little while, listening to the birds. "So, what makes us such great fighters?"

Father rolled his eyes with a frustrated grunt. "Ayrion, if you aren't going to go to sleep, then how about sitting up so I can?"

I quickly rolled over, pulled my blanket over my head, and closed my eyes.

Something grabbed my shoulder. I threw back the covers and shot up, ready to fight.

"Calm yourself. It's just me."

I shook my head to clear it. When my eyes focused enough to recognize my father's face, I let my fists drop. I had to squint just to see him. "Is it my turn already?"

"No, I let you sleep. We'll eat and be on our way."

"Why didn't you wake me?" My words were distorted by a deep yawn.

"That's why."

I stretched my limbs and rubbed my eyes. "What time is it? How long did I sleep?" It felt like I had just managed to doze off when Father had awoken me.

"Midafternoon, judging by the sun. Now get a move on. We have quite a bit of road to cover today."

I stood slowly and repacked my bedding. My movements felt groggy, like after a long night of hard drinking. Not that I had ever done such a thing; I just knew that whenever Dorin stayed out longer than he should, we suffered in class the next day. It was always best to remain silent when he came in smelling of ale.

We spent the next couple of days traveling through the wooded regions south of the Northern Heights. I'd never seen so many trees. I was beginning to wonder if they'd ever end when the forest eventually started to thin. Pretty soon, there was nothing but open countryside in all directions.

It didn't take long before I found myself missing the trees or, more importantly, the shade they provided, as the direct sunlight covered us with its warm and blinding rays. I tried resorting to my shaders, but Father said we couldn't keep relying on them. "Being solely dependent on something is dangerous," he said. "It's a weakness that could be exploited."

We traveled another day or so without seeing another living soul. By the third day, the air in that part of the region had changed. There was a stale taste to it that clung to the nose and mouth like the leftover bits of a dead scalenbat in full rot, the parts that even the cave lizards didn't want.

"What's that smell?" I finally asked, pinching my nose.

"That's the Slags."

"The what?"

"The Slags. It's a marsh just north of here," he said, pointing off to the left. "It runs between Norshag and Oswell."

"That's the city where the contract is, right?"

"Yes. The marsh runs for days in both directions. It feeds off the Shemoa River."

"Why does it stink like that?"

"It's filled with bog holes that emit gases from under the soil."

"Why?"

Father groaned. "I don't know, but you never want to get close enough to find out. A lot of dangerous predators live in there, including razorbacks."

I'd read about razorbacks. They were monstrous, lizard-like creatures that devoured anything stupid enough to wander into their territories. We had cave lizards back home, I'd even kept a few as pets, but they weren't much longer than my forearm. It was hard to believe that these razorbacks could grow as large as twenty feet.

Father smiled at my pinched nose. "The winds are coming from the north. That's why the strong smell. Once they shift, you'll never know the Slags are there."

Somehow, I doubted that. The next few nights, I found myself sleeping with one eye open, jumping at every unexpected sound and wondering if it was a razorback coming to eat us.

A full week had passed since our narrow escape from the mountain people of Norshag. Of that, five days had been spent traveling parallel to the marsh, and five days we'd been forced to bear the stench of its bog holes. If it smelled this bad from here, I couldn't imagine what it must be like up close.

Two days later, the smell finally lifted. I almost didn't notice. I'd grown so accustomed to the lingering stench that it took my father calling my attention to it for it to register.

"We should reach the Shemoa River by tomorrow," he said.

It was a good thing, too. We'd used the last of the waterskins on the horses and had only a single spare between the two of us. It had been days since we'd come across anything drinkable. The water holes we'd found smelled as bad as the marsh. We didn't dare fill our skins from them. If the foul water didn't kill us outright, it would have turned us into bog toads or worse. At least, that was what I imagined would happen if I was ever desperate enough to drink the dark liquid.

We made camp in a small clearing surrounded by high grass, which helped block some of the cold winds gusting across the open plain. Father had me dig the pit much wider than usual. The last thing we wanted was to accidentally ignite the dry brush.

I looked up at the stars as I ate.

"Beautiful, aren't they?" Father said when he noticed me staring.

"Yes." The thick, billowing clouds that had followed us for the last few days had moved on, revealing a sky so wondrous, it could steal your breath. More stars than I could count in a lifetime lit the heavens like a traveler's map pointing our way. Not even the cavern crystals back home could compare. I took a deep breath and slowly released it, the mist fanning out in front of my face.

"Best we turn in," Father said as he cleared the meal. "Got another long day tomorrow." He yawned. "I'll take first watch."

I nodded and crawled the rest of the way under my blanket. It didn't take long for sleep to arrive. Sitting all day in a saddle tended to be more tiring than a hard day's march.

I'd barely nodded off when something jostled me awake. I tried to say something, but a firm hand was clamped over my mouth. It was Father. He had a finger pressed to his lips. My first thought was that those people from Norshag had caught up with us.

Father waited until I nodded before releasing my mouth. Neither of us moved. All I could hear was the wind whipping through the grass. I concentrated. A nervous tension began crawling down my back, threatening to overpower me. What had he heard? I listened harder. There was nothing there. Wait. I thought I heard . . . It was faint, like nothing I'd heard before. It was something between a hiss and a deep-throated grunt. I heard it again, this time closer, more distinct.

Father leaned in and whispered, "Razorbacks."

Now I knew why my hands were shaking. My body had sensed the danger before I had. I leaped from my bed, dragging it behind me as I rushed for my horse. Most of our gear was already packed. I stuffed my blanket into the saddlebag as fast as I could. A loud hiss sounded behind us and I spun around. I could hear the grass swishing around the creature as it moved.

My horse was already prancing about, trying to break free of my grip. I swung into the saddle and yanked her around.

Father was already mounted and halfway across the small clearing when another barking croak broke through the tall grass in front of us. We were surrounded. I still couldn't see them. I'd grown so accustomed to the light that I was finding it difficult to pierce the darkness as I once had. My head swung back and forth as I waited to catch my first glimpse.

Another barking cry rose out of the grass.

How many of them were there?

Father grabbed his bow and nocked an arrow before I had time to even consider my options.

The horses backed away from the edge and closer to the fire. I grabbed my bow as well, my eyes darting from one side of the clearing to the other for something to shoot at. I nocked an arrow and waited. That was when I saw it.

The first creature pushed its way out of the dense weeds. It was even bigger than I had imagined. For once, the stories were true. It stood at least eight or nine feet tall, and its back was armored with thick scales. There were flat spikes running the length of its spine, no doubt the reason for its name. I wondered how something that size had managed to get so close without being seen.

I turned my horse at the sound of the second creature. It was almost as big as the first, maybe seven feet tall. It pushed its way out of the grass behind us and released a screeching hiss so loud that I accidentally released my bowstring. My arrow flew across the camp and bounced off the creature's protected hide. It opened its jaws, giving me reason to truly fear. Two rows of razor-sharp teeth smiled back at me.

"The arrows won't penetrate!" I shouted as I fumbled for another shaft. My horse whinnied as she spun around with nowhere to go. It was taking all my effort just to hold her in place. The razorbacks circled but from a distance. They stayed on the outer edge of the grass. "Why aren't they attacking?"

"I don't know," Father said. "Aim for the eyes." I heard the *twang* of his bow behind me, and the first creature shook its head violently with a disturbing screech. I glanced over my shoulder to see my father's arrow protruding from its left eye.

That was when it charged.

My father whipped his mount out of the way just in time, but the creature spun and hit mine with its long tail, knocking her to the side. She managed to stay upright, but her cry let me know she'd been hurt. My heart was about to beat out of my chest. I hadn't known a person could be this scared.

I drew my arrow, aimed, and fired, but the creature managed to turn its head at the last moment, and my shaft ricocheted into the night.

The creature charged, but like the first, it stopped just shy of the fire and tried using its tail as a bludgeon. This time, I was able to maneuver my horse to the right, and the spikes hit the ground beside us. Both times, the creatures had purposely kept away from the center of the camp.

It had to be the fire.

Without thinking, I jumped off my horse, holding on to her reins in case she tried to leave me behind.

"What do you think you're doing?" Father released another arrow, but I heard it bounce off the razorback's scales.

"I think they're scared of the fire." I grabbed a stick of wood from the pit and waved it like a torch in front of the second razor-back's face, hollering as loudly as I could. The creature recoiled, hissing at me as it did. I pushed forward, dragging my horse behind me. The creature withdrew even more. It backed all the way around to where the first razorback stood, shaking its head to try to dislodge my father's arrow.

One small torch wasn't going to be enough. The flame was sure to burn out, and then it would be over.

The second creature spun, but warned by another vision, I leaped over top of the spikes as its tail flew under me.

In a move of desperation, I leaned over and lit the fallen grass at my feet. The dry weeds ignited, and my horse yanked me away from the flames. The fire spread like it was alive, creating a wall between us and the creatures. I threw my torch at them and jumped onto my horse. One look at the flames and the two razor-backs turned and retreated the way they had come. They cut a trail straight for the Slags.

"Pray the wind doesn't shift!" Father said, giving me a harsh look as he turned his horse east and snapped the reins. I did the same and we let them run. Galloping blindly or not, we couldn't afford to get caught in the middle of the grasslands with a fire on our heels.

Behind us, the sky burned a deep orange. I shook my head. I hadn't been away from home two weeks, and I'd already burned down part of Keldor. Not exactly the most promising start as an Upakan warrior. I was beginning to question my reasons for com-ing. It seemed like things were going from bad to worse. I

wondered if this was how every mission went, or did it have something to do with me?

Chapter 10

I YAWNED. My back was stiff and my bottom sore. We had ridden through the night and only stopped twice during the next day. The first to stretch our legs and eat some dried meat and cheese; the second was to let a herd of zyntar pass. It was the first time I'd seen one. They were even taller than the razorbacks but quite a bit slower. They had six legs and long snouts that hung all the way to the ground. Some of the bigger ones had tusks that curved upward from their mouths. I wondered how they ate with something like that getting in the way.

By the end of the day, we had reached the edge of the Shemoa River. All hint of the fire had disappeared. Even the smoke we had seen rising into the sky earlier that morning was no longer visible. I hoped it had hit the Slags and burned itself out.

Father directed us north along the river's bank. I'd never seen so much water. It made the underground river back home seem like a mere trickle in comparison. I tried throwing a stone across, but it barely made it halfway.

We continued north until we reached a small outpost that looked to have been built by the same people responsible for designing Norshag. The quality was no better.

There were a couple of rundown buildings that looked to serve as a way station for travelers, and a long set of stairs leading down to a dock with a large, flat boat.

"What's that?"

Father turned to look. "That's a ferry. It's going to take us across the river." On closer inspection, I saw that the boat was connected to a thick cord spanning the entire width of the river.

"The horses, too?"

"That's right."

I twisted the reins with excitement.

"I guess we made it just in time," Father said as he turned in the saddle to get a look at the sun's position. The sky had already begun to color, signaling the close of another day. "We'll bed down here for the night and cross in the morning." He guided his horse down the path to the front of the first building. It was the only one with smoke rising from its chimney.

We hadn't made it past the gate when the front door opened and a rugged-looking man stepped out. He was about my father's height but a good bit rounder in the chest. His hair was thinning on top, and his arms—where the sleeves had been rolled up—were dark from too much time in the sun. He held a rather large cross-bow, casually stroking the trigger with one hand.

"You're the first to travel through this way in nearly a moon. Where you headed?"

"Oswell," Father said, coming to a stop at the foot of some steps, which led to a full wraparound porch.

"Oswell?" The man leaned against the doorframe and spat off to the side, wiping his mouth with the top half of his sleeve. "No need to tell me where you're traveling from. I can see by your eyes you're from the Lost City." He stood there for a moment without saying anything, continuing to stroke the bow's release. He appeared to be weighing his options. "You ain't here for me, are you?"

Father chuckled. "You wouldn't be standing there if we were."

The man grunted. "Good point. I take it you'll be looking for a ride across, then."

"We will, plus some shelter for the night if you have the room."

"Aye, plenty of room. I'm the only ferryman around these parts. Few people travel east from here. They prefer the longer route farther south, keeping as far from the Slags as they can." The man chuckled. "Personally, I don't know what they're all so afraid of. I've lived here close to twenty years, and the most dangerous thing I've seen were some of those folks coming out of Norshag."

I smiled. After our run-in with the razorbacks, the man was either very brave or an idiot, but I liked the friendly sort of way he babbled on. I wondered if he lived there alone.

The man lowered his bow and started down the steps. "I've got some bunks out back; five coppers for the room, three more for grub." He glanced at the horses. "I'll even throw in some hay at no additional charge."

"Much appreciated," my father said with a slight bow of his head.

"The name's Hobb." The man paused at the bottom of the steps and looked at us.

"I'm Narris. And this is my son, Ayrion."

Hobb nodded. "Welcome to Hobb's Crossing. If you follow me, we'll get you tucked in for the night."

*Hobb's Crossing?* Not exactly original, but I liked it.

Hobb took us around back past the long flight of stairs leading down to the dock. There was a small stable between the two buildings, no more than a couple of stalls, but dry enough to give the horses a place out of the weather. We tied them off and then joined our host as he worked to turn the apparently stubborn lock on the building where we were going to stay.

"No telling what shape she's in. Like I said, I haven't seen another soul in quite some time, and they didn't stay the night."

"As long as there's a roof and a mattress, you won't get any complaints from us."

"Well, you'll certainly find those. And I can vouch for the stew." His mouth curled into a wicked grin. "Caught some fresh coneys this morning. Pesky things won't stay out of my cabbage."

My mouth watered at the thought of a hot meal—anything besides salted pork.

The lock finally snapped, and Hobb pushed the door open. The hinge whined the entire way, stopping only when the door hit something on the other side.

"Here, just a moment." Hobb laid the bow down on one of the bunks and grabbed a small tinderbox from the mantel over the hearth to start a fire. "There you go. She'll be warm in a jiff." He grabbed his bow. "By the time you finish unpacking, I should have supper ready. Come on up to the house, and I'll set you each a bowl."

The ferryman opened his hand and waited.

Father lifted his coin purse from under his shirt and counted out eight coppers.

The ferryman jostled them in his palm. "Right, then. I'll be seeing to your meal, gentlemen." With that, he turned and walked out the door, shutting it behind him.

"He seems nice enough," I said, dropping my pack on the cot closest to the fire. I sneezed at the dust I'd disturbed on top. "Nothing like those people in Norshag."

"Not everyone is going to be as hostile as they were, but it doesn't mean you can blindly trust people, either. Best to always err on the side of caution."

We finished unpacking, then unsaddled the horses and made sure they had plenty of water before heading up to the main house.

"Come in. Come in," Hobb said when Father knocked.

Father opened the door, and I followed him inside. Hobb's home was cluttered with all sorts of knickknacks, tools, and lumber. It had all the makings of a fine workshop.

"Have a seat. Food will be ready shortly."

Hobb stirred a large kettle hanging over the fire. It smelled wonderful. He dished up three wooden bowls and placed them in front of us. Steam curled around my face, and I took a deep whiff, savoring the moment. He poured us each a glass of something from a pitcher he had sitting in the middle of the table and then sat down.

"Eat. Eat."

Eat we did. In fact, we didn't stop eating until we'd emptied every last scoop from the pot. You'd think we hadn't eaten in days, the way we stuffed it in. The pitcher turned out to be watered-down ale. Even that tasted good to me tonight as I shoveled down Hobb's excellent rabbit stew.

"That's quite the healthy appetite you have there," the ferry-man commented as I licked the droppings from my fourth and final bowl. He lit his pipe and took a seat by the fire. "So, tell me of your travels. I don't get out much myself, and when I do, it's only to Oswell for supplies. It's always nice to hear what's going on in the world." He puffed out a couple of smoke rings, which circled his face before rising into the rafters.

I didn't say much, this being my first time out in the *world,* as he'd put it, but Father spent some time regaling him with a few of his expeditions. Hobb paid attention, but I think he was more interested in the company than the stories.

Once Father finished with his adventures, he asked Hobb about Oswell.

"The city seems to be doing better ever since Magistrate Egleman was ousted and this new fella, Sirias, took his place. Things are beginning to quiet down. I've even heard talk of expansion."

Father slowly directed the conversation. The questions were subtle, innocent enough, but I recognized the information he was trying to gather—Oswell's politics, leaders, militia—information he would probably need to fulfill his contract.

From the information Hobb gave us, it sounded like Oswell was like most of the other communities in Keldor that I'd read about. They had an elected magistrate that acted as the city's head. There was a council that saw to the day-to-day decision-making as well as keeping up the town's militia, most of whom were volunteers. Oswell was protected by a wall that had been built decades before. It was manned by a rotation of guards posted at various stations around its perimeter. Apparently, the new magistrate was encouraging new growth, and there had been talk of rebuilding the wall.

We absorbed every detail. With all the excitement of being able to accompany Father on this mission, I'd forgotten to ask him the particulars. Who were we supposed to kill?

After a few more well-placed questions, my father finally stood. "We better be turning in if we plan on getting an early start."

"I'll have breakfast ready before you go," Hobb said as he stood and walked us to the door. He'd barely gotten it open when a loud crack of thunder shook the house. We stepped outside and followed him to the edge of the porch. "Looks like a bad one." He rubbed the top of his head, where his hair was thinning, and stared out across the water on our left. "It's gonna flood the banks for sure. Passage tomorrow will be difficult at best."

We said our good-byes and thanked him once again for the

food and the company, stopping only long enough to make sure the horses were secure in their stalls before heading for our bunks.

"Will they be okay?" I asked when a flash of lightning streaked across the sky, followed by a deafening roll of thunder.

"They'll be fine," Father said, but his face held a hint of concern as the first drops hit the tops of our heads. I was feeling very thankful for the shelter. I would have hated to have been caught outside on a night like this.

I plopped onto my cot as my father stoked the fire. I was too tired to do much more than remove my boots. By the time my head hit the feather pillow, all thoughts of finding out more about the contract had been forgotten. Rain drummed on the roof, and the soft sound lulled me into sleep.

Chapter 11

MORNING BROKE and so did the storm.

I awoke to a strange animal making all kinds of ruckus outside our window. "What in the name of Aldor is that?" I tried blocking out the noise with my pillow, but it did little good.

"It's a rooster."

"Well, kill it. It sounds like it's dying anyway."

My father laughed as he got out of bed and walked over to the window to take a look. "Storm's passed. Looks like it's going to be a beautiful day."

I yawned. Getting out of bed was even harder when the place you were staying was dry and warm. Unlike most mornings when I awoke to the sound of my own teeth chattering and a face covered in dew, I had no desire or need to go stand by the fire. I was already in a state of complete relaxation. Eventually, Father managed to coax me up.

Actually, it only took two words.

"Get up."

We packed our bags, made our beds, and tidied up the bunk-house before heading to breakfast. We stopped at the river and rinsed off as best we could. The water was freezing, but it felt good to be able to wash off some of the smell.

"I know a place in Oswell where we can stay that has a tub on every floor," my father said as he pulled his shirt back over his head. "We'll be able to get a thorough cleaning there."

"Good," I said, trying to hold a serious expression. "'Cause you stink." It faltered when my father lifted his arm and took a deep whiff.

"I don't know what you're talking about." With a smile, he turned and walked out to the end of the dock.

I decided while I was there to go ahead and dunk my entire head in the water. It felt like a thousand small needles all poking me at once. I was certainly awake now. After shaking the droplets from my hair, I joined my father at the dock's edge and stared out at the river.

"That water's moving awfully fast," Father said. He looked concerned as he watched the ferry bump against the dock's braces.

"Aye," a voice called out behind us. The dock shook slightly as the ferryman joined us. "Her banks are higher than I expected." Hobb rubbed his chin as he took a moment to study the current. "I don't care for the look of it. Best we wait a couple of days for her to get it out of her system. Rains came from the north, which means more flooding. Yep, I'd say two, maybe three days." With that, he turned and left. "You coming? Food won't stay hot forever."

We left the river to its meanderings and followed Hobb up to the house.

The next couple of days were a relaxing break from the dreariness of more riding. Father spent most of his time up at the house talking with Hobb. I, on the other hand, spent as much time away from it as I could. There was nothing more exhilarating than exploring new places.

The days came and went at an alarmingly slow pace. By the end of the third day, my father looked ready to swim the river himself just to get underway. It wasn't that he didn't enjoy the ferryman's company or minded sharing his table; he just wasn't one for sitting around. My father needed something to do.

We awoke on the fourth day to a knock at the door. Father was the first up. He crossed the room and opened the door to find Hobb standing there with a wide grin on his face and an unlit pipe in his mouth. "I believe she's down far enough to give her a try, if you're up to it."

My father didn't have to be told twice. We were up, dressed, and heading out the door for breakfast before Hobb even had a chance to set the table. After a hot meal of oats with a dab of honey, Father and I rounded up the horses and followed Hobb down to the ferry.

The water was as murky as dirt soup but had dropped considerably since the morning after the storm, and the boat no longer thumped against the dock.

"Careful with the rope," Hobb said, already standing on the ferry. "You don't want to snag their heads."

I lifted the heavy cord while Father coaxed the two horses on board. The flat-bottom boat rocked back and forth in the current, making me grateful for the railing around the outside to keep us from falling off the edge.

"She still has some life in her," Hobb said, looking out over the water as he waited for us to get our gear stowed.

"Is it safe enough to cross?" Father glanced over the side. "The boat's already rocking."

Hobb waved his hand. "No worries. I've crossed in worse, trust me. I'll have you on the other side in no time." He released the last of the lines, and the boat started to move. The current tried its best to pull us downstream. If not for the rope, which spanned the river, it would have. "All hands to the line," Hobb called over his shoulder as he grabbed the rope and yanked.

I joined them and started to pull. We walked the rope back five paces to the far end of the boat, then walked five paces to the front and did it all over again. A few minutes of heaving and I could see why Hobb's arms were so big. My shoulders and back were on fire, and we'd barely left the dock. My fingers were a little stiff from the cold morning air, but the rush of blood from heaving the rope quickly warmed them.

The horses didn't seem too bothered by the movement. It probably had something to do with the hay Hobb had piled for them in the middle of the raft. The man certainly knew what he was doing.

"The current's stronger than I thought," Hobb said, straining under the weight of the rope. All around us, debris floated by. The tone of his voice didn't sound very encouraging, but his face was calm despite the effort it was taking to keep the ferry on course. The water was now lapping over the sides of the boat and onto the deck.

"How do you plan to get back across?" Father asked. "The current's too strong for one person to manage."

Father grabbed the rope and started to walk it backward, but his foot slipped on the wet planks and he lost his grip. He reached for the rope, trying to hold on with one hand, but his other arm swung wide, and he fell backward into me.

A quick warning from my magic and I scrambled to get out of the way, but not before hitting a patch of slick board myself. My feet flew out from under me, and I hit the small railing at the back and started to fall over, but Father somehow managed to catch his fall and grab the front of my trousers before I tumbled headfirst into the icy water.

He yanked me back on board, and I stumbled to my knees beside the pile of hay. My heart was racing. I tried to catch my breath as the thought of what had nearly happened hit me. As fast as these waters were moving and with the strong undercurrent, I'd have been pulled downstream before they could have done anything about it.

I glanced at my horse, and she glanced at me. A shake of her head and a quick nicker let me know I wasn't the only one who thought I looked foolish.

"What do you two think you're doing back there? This ain't no time to go swimming. Get back on the line before I lose her."

I stood and brushed the muck off my pants from where I had slid across the ferry.

"Blazes! I spoke too soon." There was something in Hobb's voice that had Father and I scrambling for the rope. The ferryman pointed upriver. "Look!"

I gasped. Something enormous was sticking out of the water and heading in our direction. It was one of the largest trees I'd ever seen, at least as wide as the ferry. The roots looked like hundreds of brown stripers all writing together as they headed straight for us.

Father grabbed the rope. "What do we do? Should we try going back?"

"Won't help!" Hobb said. "We're already halfway across. Now pull!"

I grabbed the line and heaved with all my might. It felt like I'd lassoed a mountain. No matter how hard we pulled, we didn't seem to be going anywhere. I'd seen rock slugs travel faster. I glanced at the approaching tree and wished I hadn't. We were still in its path, and it was coming fast. There was no way we were going to get clear in time.

"Pull! Pull!" Hobb kept shouting the same order as though it would produce a better result. The horses had stopped eating. Their ears were perked as they sensed the danger.

I dropped the rope and grabbed the railing. There wasn't anything we could have done anyway. The tree was close enough to spit on. I ducked in time to miss catching one of the roots in the face.

"Brace yourselves!" Hobb shouted.

The tree hit the left side of the ferry, throwing Father and me into the horses. The horses screamed as they fought to keep their footing.

"Help!" came a panicked cry.

I turned to see Hobb hanging off the front of the ferry, clinging to the rope for dear life.

"Pull me in! Pull me in!"

I scrambled after Father to help, but the line behind us snapped with a loud *crack*.

Hobb plunged into the icy waters of the Shemoa.

"Hold on!" Father shouted.

"Tie it off! Tie it off!" Hobb bellowed as he fought to keep his head above water.

I turned around. *Tie what off?*

Father flew past me and wrapped what was left of the rope around the closest corner post. The slack in the rope snapped taut, and the boat started swinging back toward the far shore like a pendulum.

"Ahhh!" Hobb cried as the sudden tension in the line jerked him clear out of the water. He lost his grip and landed a few feet from the boat. He went under before we could get to him, only to reappear on the opposite side, arms flailing.

"We need to help him!" I shouted as Hobb went under again.

"There's nothing we can do for him now. Keep those horses calm."

I reached for the reins, and then it hit me. "The horses." I looked at the mare, then back at Hobb, who was bobbing like a cork in the current. "That's it." I swung up into the saddle.

"What do you think you're doing?"

"Going after him."

"The blazes you are! Get off that horse!"

I didn't bother looking. I could already guess the expression on my father's face as I dug in my boots. My horse crashed through the railing and over the side.

"Ayrion!"

We hit the water, and its icy tendrils stole my breath. I clung to the saddle as the mare fought to keep our heads above the surface. She swam straight for shore, forcing me to yank her in the opposite direction. The current was powerful. On our right, the last of the great pine's branches were passing. I kept us back far enough to keep from getting caught in them.

"Hold on! I'm coming!" I glanced over my shoulder. The ferry had reached the shoreline, and Father was grabbing up lengths of rope as he pulled his horse off the boat and onto the far bank.

I turned back around. Hobb had heard me shout and was trying to fight the current to reach us, but with little success. We were being pulled toward the middle of the river at an alarming rate. Soon, we were going to be too far out for the horse to make it back to shore. She was already panting from the strain, and her movements were getting sluggish.

"Swim!" I shouted. "I can't get to you. You need to swim!"

Hobb swung his arms with everything he had, but the current was too strong. He was within twenty feet, but it just wasn't enough.

I wrapped the reins around my left hand and leaped into the water, swimming out as far as the leather straps would allow.

"Grab my legs." I stretched them as far as they would go, and Hobb grabbed my ankle. I pulled with all my might. I wasn't sure if I was moving us toward the horse or the horse to us. Either way, we both managed to grab ahold of the saddle. "Don't get on her," I said, spitting water with every word, "or she'll never make it." At this point, I didn't think she'd make it either way.

"Hold on! I'm coming!" Father shouted, galloping down the bank with a coil of rope over his shoulder.

He stopped farther down the bank, waiting for us to catch up. "Catch!"

He threw the rope, and it struck the water right in front of me. I let go of the horse and grabbed hold. My entire body was numb. I could barely feel my fingers, so I wrapped the rope around the horn of the saddle instead of trying to tie it. As soon as I waved, my father slapped his horse and started towing us in.

In a matter of moments, I was sprawled out next to Hobb in the mud, neither of us able to move much beyond offering a satisfied smile at having survived what should have been a watery grave.

"That's quite the boy you have there," Hobb said, his teeth

chattering against the cold.

"Yes, he can be quite stupid sometimes." My father shook his head, but there was a proud smile on his face.

"Where's my ferry?" Hobb asked, trying to lift his head high enough to get a look.

"She's safe. I managed to tie off the line like you said and ride her to shore."

Hobb released a sigh of relief. "I owe you my life."

"No. You owe that to Ayrion. You owe me another ride back across on our return."

The ferryman smiled and reached over to pat my arm. "You'll have a free place to stay anytime you need it. And that's a fact. There will always be an extra seat at my table for you."

I wished I had one of his steaming bowls of delicious coney stew right then. The thought of it almost made me forget the chill in my bones. Almost.

"We just might take you up on that," my father said as he stood to his feet. "But for now, I think we need to get a fire started before the two of you freeze to death."

It didn't take him long to gather some semi-dry wood from a nearby thicket. Pretty soon, the two of us were sitting naked by the fire while our clothes dried on a line.

As we continued to thaw, Father went through what was left of the supplies. "Most of the food is ruined. The pork and cheese will be fine, but the rest is like soup. We should have enough to get us to Oswell if you don't decide to take another swim."

I smirked.

My father turned to Hobb. "What will you do about the ferry?"

Hobb looked at his boat. The force of the current had buried the right side deep into the bank. "Nothing for now. At least not until the river lowers, which will probably take a few days." He stretched his hands toward the fire. "If you gentlemen don't mind, I'll ride along with you into Oswell. I've got friends there I can stay with. I'll borrow a horse from them and ride back. If the current's still too strong, there's a crossing about a day's ride south of here."

"No objection here," Father said.

"Don't worry about the food," Hobb said with a wave of his hand. "When it comes to rustling up some game in these parts, there's no one better."

Father nodded. "We'll have to take turns walking. I don't want to wear the horses out by riding double while carrying supplies."

"Won't get any complaints from me," Hobb said with a smile. "I can walk for miles. That is, after I get some feeling back in my toes." With that, he lifted both legs and waved the bottoms of his feet at the open flames.

I started to laugh. It was hard not to, looking at the naked man with his feet in the air.

The other two joined in.

Chapter 12

HOBB WAS TRUE to his word.

He didn't complain once about the rotation for walking, and each night, there was fresh game he'd managed to hunt during our time on the road. He seemed to have the eyes of a hawk when it came to spotting coneys. I wasn't sure what he had against the fluffy things, but I didn't care as long as his disdain resulted in a hot meal.

For the next few days as we continued crossing the plains between the Shemoa River and Oswell, I followed Hobb around while he taught me the art of tracking. He showed me how to hunt off the land: how to spot rabbit holes, pigeon cubbies, even wild boar wallows. He explained the difference in tracks, rubs, and rooting. I wasn't sure how useful it would be to see caked mud on the bottom of a tree and know a hog had been that way, especially when the only time we saw a pig in the Lost City was when the market carts rolled in from Chorazin and Pinnella to sell their goods, but I soaked up the knowledge anyway.

The journey took longer than we had planned, but that was expected, considering we were short one horse. Father didn't seem to mind, and I was having too much fun learning how to hunt to worry about how it might affect our contract.

By the fourth day, we found ourselves standing outside the gates of Oswell. A large stone wall surrounded the city. According to Hobb, it had been built to keep out some of the more dangerous creatures living in the Slags. He said the marsh was close enough that it wasn't unheard of to have the occasional razorback venture out in search of food.

At the gate, Father and I kept our hoods up and let Hobb do the talking. He seemed to know one of the guards. During their rather lengthy conversation, the guard kept looking in our direction. I could tell that my father was getting anxious. His hand slid toward his sword. A few more exchanges and Hobb finally walked back over, and the watchman waved us through.

"That was Treppin," Hobb said as he led us through the gates, "my late wife's younger brother. I told him my predicament, and he agreed to let me borrow a horse to take back in a day or two. Unfortunately, I might have overestimated his willingness to offer me a room, so I guess I'll be joining you in looking for a place to stay."

"What did you tell him about us?" Father asked, his brows lowered slightly.

"The truth. I told him you were a couple of travelers that fished me out of the river and saved my life. Don't worry; your identities are safe."

Hobb turned and we started up one of the streets on the right. "This will take us into town. I know a couple of good inns, if you're looking for a hot meal and a bath. The price is fair and the food fresh. I've stayed at both. Although," he said with a slight grin, "I'd suggest the Golden Tassel. Best pie in town and the service is excellent. Milly will do us right." The way he said her name indicated there was more to his choice than the food.

Finding the two inns didn't prove difficult. They were hard to miss. The Golden Tassel sat on one side of the road and the Cockatrice on the other. Both establishments appeared well kept. Their signs were newly painted, their porches swept and lined with occupied chairs. They even had curtains in the windows. The upper rooms had vases of wildflowers on the sills.

Both establishments seemed inviting. If it hadn't been for Hobb, it would have proved a difficult choice. The only noticeable difference, apart from the names on the signs, was the curtains. Those hanging in the Golden Tassel were a deep yellow, no doubt due to its name, while those at the Cockatrice were soft purple.

"Just get a whiff of that, would you," Hobb said as he directed us behind the inn toward the stable. "Smells like Milly's already in the kitchen."

I followed his advice and took a deep breath. Something did smell good.

"Greetings, and welcome to the Golden Tassel," a boy said,

standing just outside the open doors leading into the stable. He was about my age and overly dressed for someone who worked outside. His vest and tunic were clean, and he wore a yellow sash from his neck down to his waist. It matched his cap. "Will you be staying long?"

"One night," my father said as he dismounted. "Two at most."

The boy's smile was as bright as his vest. "Very good, sir," he said with a tip of his cap. "Shall I take your horses? They'll be watered and fed with the finest oats in Oswell." I wanted to like the stable hand, but he seemed a little too friendly. I'd never met anyone, other than my sister, who was that cheerful without an ulterior motive. His wide smile and eager disposition faltered momentarily when he walked over to take the reins from my father and got his first good look at our eyes. To his credit, he didn't gasp.

Before I had time to swing off my horse, his smile was back in place. He even whistled as he guided the horses inside. There were two open stalls near the back, away from the others. "Will these do, gentlemen?"

My father studied the two stalls and pursed his lips as if having a hard time deciding. "I suppose they'll do," he said before tossing the boy a couple of coppers. "There'll be double that in it for you if you keep a close eye on our gear."

The boy's eyes widened, and for the first time, the expression on his face seemed genuine. He pulled the cap off his head and placed it over his chest, offering a deep bow. "Yes, sir. I'll make sure no one comes near it. You have my oath."

My father grabbed his weapons along with one of the smaller

carry bags, and I did the same. "We'll be back for the rest later."

The stable boy bowed again and then proceeded to scoop some oats from a large grain sack in the corner. We left him to his work and headed back outside.

Hobb looked impatient. "Good. Now let's get a room so we can eat."

My stomach growled at the thought of food.

"I think the folks inside might appreciate it more if we had a dunk in the tub before we did," Father said, pointedly staring at Hobb's mud-spattered clothing.

Hobb looked down. "You might be right." He pulled back the top of his tunic and sniffed. "No, you're definitely right. Milly gets one whiff of this and she'll try to drown me herself." A mischievous grin spread across his face. "I think we'll go this way." He nodded toward the back of the building.

Father hefted his sack and bow. "Lead the way."

There were two sheds behind the inn with an extensive clothesline running between them. A large woodpile leaned against the smaller of the two buildings, and a well sat just off to the side.

We followed Hobb past the first door leading into the inn and stopped at the second. There was a nervous twitch in his eye as he grabbed the handle and turned. Instead of opening it fully, he peeked inside. There was a curious grin on his face. He turned and put his finger to his lips before opening the door the rest of the way.

We followed him in.

I pushed my way past Father to get a better look. Father closed the door quietly behind us, and we watched as Hobb tiptoed across the kitchen. On the other side of the room, a woman hummed as she stirred a large mixing bowl, completely unaware of our entering.

I realized I was holding my breath. A couple of the attendants saw Hobb and smiled, but no one said anything. Like us, they stopped what they were doing to watch.

Hobb made it all the way up behind the lady without her noticing. She was still humming when he reached out and grabbed her by the waist with a heavy growl.

The woman screamed. Her bowl flew into the air, its contents spilling over the counter and floor.

She spun around. As soon as her eyes lighted on Hobb, she slapped him across the face; and if that weren't enough, she proceeded to beat him on the arm with her stirring spoon for good measure. "How dare you scare me like that, you sorry excuse for a man!"

The workers smiled, some openly laughing, but a single look from the innkeeper sent them rushing back to their duties. I happened to be one of those who had been laughing; my father elbowed me to be quiet.

"You told me I'd better stop by the next time I was in town. So . . ." Hobb spread his arms wide as if expecting a warm embrace. "Here I am."

"I have half a mind to throw you in the oven for scaring me like that." The innkeeper waved her spoon in Hobb's face threateningly.

Hobb's lower lip dropped. "Milly, sweetie. How long's it been?"

"Don't you *sweetie* me, you old bear." She turned up her nose. "What's that smell?"

Hobb smiled. "Natural attraction. It's the smell of a man who's traveled a great distance to see you."

"It's the smell of a hog's wallow." She pointed her spoon at him again. "If you think you're coming within ten feet of me looking and smelling like that, think again." She noticed Father and I standing at the back door and lowered her spoon. "Who's this you got with you?"

"Ah. Allow me to introduce my rescuers."

"Rescuers?"

"Aye. The river flooded a few days back. I nearly lost my boat and my life. If it weren't for these two gentlemen jumping in to pull me from those icy waters, I wouldn't be here today."

She struck him once more on the arm, but not quite so hard as before. "I told you that you were going to get yourself killed one of these days living out there all by your lonesome." Hobb led her back across the kitchen to greet us. She held out her hand, but when she saw our eyes, she recoiled. She grabbed Hobb by the arm and pulled him to the side. "They're Upakans."

"Good to see your eyes still work."

"We can leave if it's going to be a problem," Father said kindly.

"No problem at all," Hobb said with a bright smile as he looked at Milly for a response. "Right?"

Milly didn't look as convinced, but she nodded. "Right. No

problem. The Golden Tassel prides itself on its hospitality. What kind of host would I be to turn away a couple of rescuers?" She looked at our gear. "You'll be wanting a room?"

"If you have one to spare."

"Better make it two, Milly my love. You'll get to enjoy my company for a few days while I wait for the river to lower."

She crossed her arms and snorted as she slowly scanned him from head to toe. "I don't know how enjoyable it will be with you smelling like that."

"Then how about you show us to our rooms so we can wash off some of this travel?"

"Ronan can get you settled," Milly said, pointing her spoon at a lanky man who was busy pulling a fresh loaf of bread from the oven. "But make sure you soap those clothes while you're at it."

"Yes, ma'am."

"All our clothes got soaked in the river," I said, not wanting to upset the innkeeper by re-dressing in the same smelly garments as before.

Milly smiled. She wasn't what I would have called beautiful, or even easy on the eyes for that matter, but there was a warmth about her that reminded me of my mother. "That's fine, dear. I'm sure I have some extra changes on hand for such an occasion." She turned back to Hobb, and her demeanor hardened. "No food until you scrub that hide."

Hobb grinned and snuck a swift peck on her cheek. He hopped backward, barely dodging her spoon. "This way, my friends," he said, quick-stepping his way toward the kitchen door, where Ronan was waiting. "I guess we better get to cleaning."

The thought of getting out of my filthy clothes and into some hot, soapy water had me pushing my way past Hobb and my father in hopes of being the first into the tub.

Chapter 13

I WAS THE LAST in the tub, but it turned out to my benefit. Being last, I was able to take my time and relax. I didn't have to worry about being rushed in order to let the next in line get their chance. By the time I got out and dried off, the skin around my fingers and toes had wrinkled. It was the first real washing I'd had since leaving home. I hadn't realized how dirty I was until I got out. My bathwater was muddier than the river we'd swum through.

During our time in the tub, Milly had our clothes washed and hung on the lines outside for drying. She had somehow managed to rustle up some outfits that almost fit. It seemed she had quite the collection, thanks to guests who'd been unable, or unwilling, to pay. Instead of making good on their debts, they had left their belongings behind. The outfit I was wearing was clean but over-sized. I had to keep pulling up my trousers to keep from tripping. I hoped my clothes dried quickly.

I forgot all about it when we sat down to eat. Milly opened one of the private dining areas in the back so we wouldn't have to endure the nervous stares that came when a couple of Upakans entered a room. I wasn't sure if it was for our benefit or for her guests'.

"Milly, you've outdone yourself this time," Hobb said as he stuffed a heaping bite of stew into his mouth. "With food this good, I might reconsider moving over here."

Milly crossed her arms and started tapping her foot. "I've been waiting ten years for you to make good on it, and all I get are empty promises. I'm quite the catch, you know."

Hobb smiled as best he could with a mouth full of carrots and potatoes. "There's no denying it."

"I have plenty of other gentlemen callers who'd jump at the chance to snare me in their net."

Hobb choked, spitting part of a carrot on the table. "Are you trying to kill me, woman? What kind of talk is that to be having in front of guests?"

Milly shifted her attention to us. "Well, what do you think? Is it right to string a woman's heart along and never propose marriage? A woman has needs too, you know."

This time, it was my father who choked. "I, uh . . ." He beat his chest as if trying to force the food to go down. "I believe if a man and woman feel that way about each other, they should certainly discuss it."

"Hey, whose side are you on?" Hobb pointed his spoon at my father in warning.

"There, you see," Milly said with a look of victory. "You should listen to him. And now that you'll be around for the next few days, I'd say we have plenty of time to talk about it."

Hobb's face whitened. He dropped his spoon in his bowl. "I think I've lost my appetite."

"Well, I've got chores to attend to, so I'll leave you gentlemen to it." The innkeeper leaned over, grabbed Hobb by the chin, and twisted his head around. Before he had time to protest, she planted a hard kiss on his mouth.

I turned my eyes. I couldn't believe the way these two were acting, especially in front of others. I smiled. It was the most fun I'd had the entire trip, apart from jumping into the Shemoa to rescue him, and not forgetting our battle in Norshag.

After the meal, Father had Hobb sketch out a small map of the city to "keep us from getting lost while we have a look around." Father didn't say it at the time, but I was sure his *looking around* had something to do with our contract.

He had the ferryman include some of the major landmarks like the Justice Hall, the patroller offices, and anywhere the city's leadership might assemble. He even had him add the new magistrate's personal estate. Hobb said you couldn't miss it. It was the largest in Oswell and was located on a small hill near the center of town, overlooking the city. Every magistrate had lived there since the

founding of the city.

We left most of our weapons in the room and opted for our long daggers and knives. Nothing screamed *up to no good* like a couple of hooded travelers walking down the street, carrying enough weapons to go to war. We didn't want to draw attention while getting the lay of the land. That was one of the first rules drilled into us as trainees—avoid conflict on unfamiliar ground.

We hadn't been walking long before the magistrate's estate came into view. Just as Hobb had described, it stood like a watchtower keeping an eye on the citizens below.

"So, who's our contract?" I asked, a little nervous at not being told much about what we were doing up till now. To be honest, I wasn't exactly sure I wanted to know.

It was one thing to kill in self-defense, like what those crazy people in Norshag had forced us to do, but it was another to sneak into someone's bedroom and slit their throat. Our people had been doing it for generations, so I guessed I could too.

"This is going to be a challenging contract to fulfill," Father said, passing a wary glance my way. "In fact, it's the largest contract I've ever taken and the most difficult."

That piqued my interest. *The largest contract? And the most difficult?* I waited for him to explain. When he didn't seem to be in any hurry, I finally asked, "Who's the target?"

Father took a deep breath. "There's more than one."

I slowed. "More than one? How many more? Who are we getting paid to . . . you know . . ." I scanned the faces of the people
walking by to make sure they weren't listening in.

Father waited for us to pass a young couple, who were more
preoccupied with each other than anything going on around them.
"Our contract is for Magistrate Sirias—"

"Magistrate Sirias?"

"—and his entire family."

I stopped, all but tripping on my own feet. The breath caught
in my throat. *His entire family?*

"Breathe, Ayrion."

I suddenly realized my Father's hand was on my shoulder. I did
as he said and forced a slow breath, and then another. A cartload
of questions ran through my mind, but only one managed to make
it out. "Who would want to kill an entire family?"

Father pulled me to the side. "Here, sit down."

I took a seat on the outer lip of a nearby well. The bucket was
missing from the pulley, and the well didn't look to have been used
in some time.

This was what I had been training for since I was old enough
to walk, and yet, now faced with it, I wasn't sure if I could do it. It
was one thing to kill a man, quite another to kill his entire family.
"Don't you ever wonder why you're being asked to do it? What if
they don't deserve to be . . ."

Father sat beside me and stared at the people making their way
up and down the street, going about their lives, seemingly without
a care in the world. "I asked my father the same question when I

was your age."

I looked up.

"He told me, 'It's not our place to question why. We are merely the tool. A knife doesn't demand to know why it's being used. It merely responds to the wielder.'" He looked over at me. "In many ways, we are the same. You must learn to bury your emotions and become the tool. If not, they will bury you." Father patted my leg. "I'm going to need your help. It's one of the reasons I brought you along."

"But . . . but it's an entire family. What if they have kids?" My head lifted. "Do they have kids?"

Father nodded. "They have two. A girl about half your brother's age and an infant."

I moaned slightly and glanced at my feet, studying the prints my boots left in the dirt. "I . . ." I couldn't raise my head to look into what was sure to be disapproving eyes. "I—"

"What is it, Ayrion? Spit it out."

"I don't think I can do it." *There, I said it.*

"Do what?"

"I don't think I can kill them." There was a moment's pause. I waited for the rebuke, but my statement was met with only silence. I waited some more. Why wasn't he saying anything? He was probably too ashamed at having raised a son incapable of completing his contract. *Does he consider me a coward? Am I coward? Why isn't he saying anything?* It felt like I'd been staring at my feet for hours when Father's voice finally broke the silence.

"Good. Neither do I."

My head lifted. "What?"

My father smiled. It was the same proud look he gave me when learning I had completed the Tri'Nephrin in the first place. "I have no intention of killing them."

"You don't? Why not?" The question was sort of blurted out before I thought about how stupid it sounded. "I mean, you can't quit a contract once it's been taken. It'll be a mark against our family. And besides, you're the Cleaner. There's never been a contract you haven't completed."

My father cocked his head. "You sound like you're trying to talk me into it."

"No. I'm just . . ." I swallowed nervously. "I'm just worried about what will happen to us if we don't."

My father rested his hand on my shoulder once again. "Don't worry, Ayrion. I have every intention of completing the contract."

My mouth went slack. "Wait, what?" I stared into his face, trying to understand. "I thought you just said you weren't going to . . ." I finished the rest of the sentence with a whisper. "Kill them."

"I'm not."

I scratched the back of my head. "How are you going to fulfill the contract if you aren't going to fulfill the contract?"

Father stood. "Come. I'll show you."

## Chapter 14

BY THE TIME FATHER walked into our room at the Golden Tassel and gave me the nod, I'd nearly talked myself out of going. Just the thought of all the ways this could go wrong had my stomach in knots. One of the downsides to having an active imagination.

We had spent the better part of the day mapping out the magistrate's estate, making sure not to look conspicuous as we walked its perimeter at least half a dozen times. We had counted out the guards—their postings, their rotations, and their attentiveness to their duties. Father had pointed out which ones took their job seriously and which were there just for the pay.

From the top of a nearby building, we had studied the grounds—looking for weaknesses in the estate's protective wall, the best places to breach, and the route with the most natural coverage between the wall and the buildings.

Lastly, we had studied the home itself. It wasn't too difficult spotting which of the rooms were the residences, since none of the curtains had been drawn. The personal bedchamber of each of the family members was located on the second floor. I was grateful for that, considering some parts of the estate had four to five floors. Each room had its own separate balcony. I couldn't figure out how one family could live in something so big. A building like that back home could have housed at least half a dozen families.

We were as prepared as we were ever going to be. At least Father was. I, on the other hand, still didn't know the details behind what we were going to do. I had to trust Father would tell me when he was ready. Hopefully, before we got there.

I followed him down the back stairs of the inn and out through the servants' quarters. This time when we left our room, we took everything with us, everything except the horses, of course. We needed stealth, which would have been difficult to accomplish on horseback rather than on foot. The drawback was that I was forced to carry all my equipment, including my sword, bow, and quiver.

Like a shadow, I kept to his footsteps. It felt good to be back in my own clothes again and not constantly worrying about tripping over my pant legs.

It was well after midnight, and the city felt deserted. A stillness lay across each street like a heavy morning fog. I could hear my own heartbeat. We navigated toward the center of town by following a route of backstreets and alleyways Father had committed to memory that afternoon. It was the most direct route from Milly's to the magistrate's estate without having to cross any of Oswell's main thoroughfares.

The only movement we spotted as we clung to the shadows was the occasional mutt or alley cat searching for its next meal. It took us at least an hour to move through the maze of narrow side streets before reaching the section of the wall where we had decided to enter the estate. We waited for the sentries to make their sweep; each pass took nearly a quarter-hour.

The wall surrounding the estate was built of river stone. Even without the help of a nearby maple, we could have scaled it by hand, but since we had to get our packs over too, the tree made climbing a lot easier.

Once the guards had made their first pass, I followed Father across the street. I waited under the wide-limbed tree as he went up first. I handed him one of my packs and swung onto the first limb. We sat in the tree for a few moments as we scanned the grounds for patrols. Nothing moved. Father waited a minute more and then signaled. Staying as low as we could, we left the seclusion of the branches and climbed out onto the top of the wall and dropped over.

We landed behind a row of trimmed shrubs.

"Leave the bags," he said, keeping his voice barely above a whisper. "We'll get them later."

I hid my pack under one of the prickly bushes and waited for Father to do the same.

"Bring your bow."

I nodded. Father grabbed his and slung a large coil of knotted rope with a grappling hook over his shoulder. We wouldn't have to climb very far, but the grapple would definitely make it easier.

We worked our way around the shrubs to the first of several openings. We had chosen the west side, not just because it was where the family's bedchambers were located, but because it also provided the most natural cover. The north and south sides of the estate opened to gardens, but there was a small grove of trees that ran the full extent of the west side and stopped not a stone's throw from the balcony we wanted. It was the perfect cover for us, and poor planning for the defense of the grounds. I doubted that keeping a couple of Upakans from sneaking in to assassinate the owners had been a design consideration.

We crept through the trees, our footsteps silent on the thick carpet of grass. Once we reached the edge of the tree line, we knelt and waited. The area between us and the magistrate's home was open ground, no cover to hide our approach.

Voices loomed as a couple of guards meandered past one of the fountains in the courtyard. They were too far for us to hear what they were saying.

After what felt like a very long time but was probably not much more than a few minutes, Father motioned us forward. We stayed low to the ground as we rushed across the open yard toward the side of the building.

There was a noise on our right, and we dropped to the ground. I clutched my bow to my side but relaxed when I realized one of the guards was laughing. His companion elbowed him, and he clamped a hand over his mouth and turned.

I didn't move. I didn't even breathe. Had they spotted us? I twisted my head slowly and realized they weren't looking at us but at the magistrate's bedchamber. They were probably worried they'd woken him. When the two men finally turned back around and continued with their rounds, I breathed a deep sigh of relief.

Father was the first to move. He was up on one knee and signaling me to follow. As fast as we could, we raced the rest of the way across the yard, stopping at the wall below the second balcony. Like most of the other rooms in the house, the lights had been extinguished. Other than the torches lining the garden area, the only thing lighting our way was the half-moon, and that was shrouded in clouds.

We hid our bows in a flowerbed, and I kept watch as Father unraveled the grappling hook. Instead of throwing it, he laid the rope back on the ground and cupped his hands, making a motion I unfortunately recognized. He wanted to toss me.

I looked up at the balcony and smiled. After scaling Dragon Fang, this was hardly challenging. There was a railing circling the outer perimeter with spindles large enough to grab. I nodded that I understood and placed my foot in the cup of his hands while holding on to his shoulder for balance.

A single tap to his arm and he launched me into the air. I caught the spindle with my first hand and pulled myself up far enough to grab hold of the top of the railing. From there, I was able to swing my leg up. There was enough of a lip on the outside edge of the balcony for me to rest on without climbing over.

I waited for Father to toss me the hook, but he didn't. Instead, he started to back away from the wall. Seeing what he was about to do, I scooted over to make room. He backed up as far as he dared and made a dash straight at the building. He leaped at the wall. His foot caught one of the decorative ridges, and with a hard push, he sprang into the air. He didn't make it high enough to grab the spindles, but he did manage to reach the floor. I went to help him over, but before I could, he'd already pulled himself up and leaped over the railing. My father might not have been a big man, but he was stronger than he looked. I followed him up and over before the next patrol passed.

From our vantage point, I could see all the way to the outer wall. No shouts or cries of alarm rose from the guards below, so Father moved over to the doors and tested the handle. They were unlocked. With guards on patrol, I guessed the magistrate had no need to fear burglars, let alone assassins.

Father leaned in close and whispered in my ear. "You handle the wife while I deal with the magistrate. Make sure she doesn't scream." I drew my dagger, but my father shook his head. "No killing . . . at least not yet."

*Not yet?* I hadn't meant the gesture to mean I was going to kill her; I just figured an armed assailant was more threatening than an unarmed one. I nodded to let him know I understood, although I started to wonder by his statement whether I might have misunderstood his intentions. I had thought we weren't going to be killing anyone.

Father slid open one of the doors, and I followed him through the curtains. We moved to the side of the opening so the light from outside wouldn't throw shadows of our silhouettes across the adjacent wall. It didn't take long for our eyes to adjust.

The room was large, larger than our family room and kitchen combined. It was lined with furniture: tables, chairs, dressers, desks, and a whole lot of other things I had no idea what to call. The magistrate's bed butted against the wall on the far right, and there was a small fire still smoldering in the hearth in front of us. The warmth was welcome, especially on my hands and face. The days seemed to be getting colder as winter drew near.

We studied the two lumps in the bed on the other side of the room. Neither moved. As silent as the gentle breeze rustling the long curtains behind us, we crept across the room. My father took the side of the bed with the largest lump, and I took the other. The covers had been drawn to their chins and looked thick enough to need a sword to penetrate.

Slowly, we stood with our weapons at the ready. My heart was racing. I could see the slow rise and fall of the comforter covering the magistrate's wife. I couldn't believe I was standing over some strange woman in her bed, with the possible intention of killing her. Apart from the thrill of getting this far unseen, there was the disturbing chill up my back about what we had been hired to do: murder an entire family. I hoped my father was true to his word about not planning to kill them, though I still wasn't sure how he was going to fulfill the contract unless he did.

Father looked at me and made a simple gesture of cupping his hand over the magistrate's mouth. I nodded and made ready to do the same to the wife. Father had his long dagger out and at the ready.

My hands were shaking as I followed his example and slowly leaned in to grab the lady's mouth. I stopped just a few inches from her face and looked across the bed, waiting for the signal. A single nod from my father and we attacked.

I threw my hand over her mouth and pressed down as hard as I could. Her head sank into the thick pillow as her eyes ripped open. There was a brief moment of shock before recognition set in and she tried screaming. I could feel the warmth of her breath on my hand as I continued to hold my grip.

She started to thrash in the bed. It was getting harder to keep her down. Out of the corner of my eye, I could see the magistrate doing the same, until my father leaned in and showed him his blade. The magistrate went still. Using his example, I did the same and brandished my dagger in front of the woman in a threatening way, and she too went motionless.

"Do you recognize what I am?" my father asked as he leaned in close, close enough to let the magistrate get a good look at his face. The room was dark, but there was enough light coming from the fireplace to reflect in his eyes.

The magistrate nodded. He was smaller than I would have assumed. Upakan leaders earned their place because of their ability to fight, but this man seemed too scrawny to claim such a title as magistrate. I doubted he'd ever seen a single day's labor in his life.

"Good. Then you know why I'm here."

Again, the short, lanky man nodded. There were tears in his eyes as he tried turning his head to look at his wife, who was already crying. I felt sorry for them in a way. I wondered what it would be like to be awoken in the middle of the night by a couple of assassins ready to slit my throat. They had to know their lives were over.

"I have been contracted for you and your family."

At the mention of his family, the magistrate started thrashing once more. His wife did the same. I had to all but sit on her to hold her down.

"Quit moving or I'll bring your kids in here and let you watch them die in front of you."

The magistrate and his wife went deadly still, and so did I. "What? I thought—"

"Quiet." The tone of my father's voice was all that was needed to keep me from finishing. He turned back to the magistrate. "To-day's your lucky day, Magistrate." The poor man looked bewildered. I couldn't help but agree. "If any other of my clan had claimed this contract, you, your wife, and your two children would be lying in your own blood right now instead of whimpering in your sheets." Father lowered his blade slightly.

The magistrate's wife turned her head to see what was going on. She had calmed down enough for me to let go of her arms.

"Unlike many of my fellow Upakans, I tend to have a certain distaste for cold-blooded killing. But to be clear," Father said, lean-ing in far enough for the magistrate to get a good look at his face, "I have no qualms with killing the two of you right here if you test me."

Father waited for the man to acknowledge he understood be-fore continuing. "You have a choice. Either you can pack your things and leave quietly with us tonight, never to return, or I can fulfill my contract in a different way." He raised his blade once more, and the magistrate sank deeper into his pillow. "One way or another, your life is going to change tonight. The choice is yours."

Father lifted his hand slowly from the man's mouth.

The magistrate didn't say anything at first. He turned to look at his wife and she nodded, her tears still moistening my hand. The man looked at me briefly, then back to my father. "It appears I have no choice."

"I thought you'd see it my way." Father stepped back from the bed and motioned for me to do the same. I released the woman's mouth and stepped away.

"Pack whatever you value most, but pack light. If anyone sees you leave, I won't have a choice but to finish the job."

"We understand," the magistrate said, his voice shaking as he sat up and swung his legs over the side of the bed.

"Good. One more thing. I need your seal of office."

"It's in my study. Why do you need it?"

"Proof of completion. Now hurry. Dawn is coming, and we need to be out of the city before it arrives."

The magistrate hopped down from the thick mattress and turned to his wife. "Get the kids. I'll start in here."

Chapter 15

"WHAT IS TAKING SO LONG?" It was impossible to miss the impatience in my father's voice. "And where's that seal?"

"Oh, I almost forgot," the magistrate said as he pulled a small golden object out of his pocket and handed it to Father. "Hurry, Merilyn."

The magistrate's wife was even shorter than he was. Her hair was barely long enough to cup her cheeks. She waddled frantically from one side of the room to the other, collecting valuables and trying to get their two wide-eyed children ready.

"Where we going, Mama?" their daughter asked. She couldn't have been much older than five or six.

"Away," her mother said as she tucked her daughter's long auburn hair up under a colorful bonnet. "It's a secret. Now get your shoes on."

Father continued pacing in front of the hearth, stopping every so often to peek through the balcony curtains. Each time, he'd grunt and walk back over to the fireplace to continue his pacing.

The magistrate and his family spent the better part of an hour packing clothing, jewelry, and an assortment of other items they were going to have a hard time fitting into the three bags they had managed to find.

I wondered what it must be like to be forced to leave your home, your friends, and your life behind. To start anew with nothing more than what you could fit into a couple of bags. I glanced around the room at all the expensive furnishings and wondered what I would choose to take in such a situation. I was thankful I didn't have to find out.

"Are you ready?"

The magistrate took one more look at his family and nodded. He grabbed the girl's hand and started for the door that led to the hallway.

"Not that way." Father pulled one of the long curtains aside. "This way."

"That's the balcony," the magistrate said. "There are no stairs."

"I know." Father stuck his head outside, checking for sentries. "How do you think we got in here?" He motioned and I was the first one on the balcony. The magistrate and his family quickly followed. "Stay below the railing," he said, gesturing for them to get down.

They hunkered near the entrance to their bedchamber. "How

do you expect us to get down?" the magistrate's wife asked. "We have children."

As if in answer, Father looked at me. "Get the hook and toss it up."

I nodded and climbed over the rail. Father grabbed my arms and lowered me as far as he could before I finally let go. Once I had the grapple, I took aim and tossed it into the air. Father caught it and secured the rope end around the magistrate's wife. I kept checking over my shoulder for any sign of the patrols, but so far, they had remained out of sight. Father, with the magistrate's help, lowered the woman and her infant son over the side. I forced myself to remain calm even though I chafed at how long it was taking to get the family out.

My hands worked quickly to untie the knot so they could pull it back up. The little girl was next. Father had to pry her off the magistrate before he could lower her over the side. As soon as he did, she started to cry. Father didn't wait for her to hit bottom. He simply released the rope and forced me to catch her, covering her mouth when I did.

Her mother tried comforting her. "Everything's fine, Rosella. See, wasn't that fun? It was like a swing."

The little girl stopped her crying long enough to look at her mother, who was trying her best to smile. Rosella wiped her eyes.

Using the distraction, I managed to get the rope off the little girl and toss it back to Father. He grabbed it and secured the hook to the railing. The bags were the next to come. They dropped them over the side to where I was waiting to catch them before they hit the ground. I nearly collapsed under the weight of the last one, which must have held the magistrate's jewels and coin.

Before they could get the magistrate over the side, Father yanked the man back and motioned frantically for us to get down.

"Down, down," I whispered to the magistrate's wife as I pulled Rosella into the grass with me. I placed my hand over the little girl's mouth, checking to make sure the magistrate's wife had done the same with her infant. I held my breath as a pair of guards strolled by, near the tree line.

I took a deep breath and hoped Rosella didn't pick this moment to have another fit. The guards seemed to be taking their time as they passed on the way back to the front. I kept a smile on my face, hoping it helped encourage the little girl to stay calm.

It did.

Once the guards crossed into the gardens and out of view, Magistrate Sirias shimmied down the rope. He checked on his wife and grabbed two of the bags. I carried the third.

Father unhooked the grapple and lowered himself over the side. He dropped softly to the ground. "Grab your bow. We need to get to the trees."

We joined the others at the edge of the building. A couple of guards were walking across the front courtyard on our left, but their backs were to us. If we were going to go, now was the time.

"Keep the kids quiet and head for the trees," Father whispered. He motioned for me to lead the way, and I rushed across the open lawn, thankful for the thick clouds obscuring the moon.

By some miracle, all six of us made it into the trees without being seen. We reached the outer wall and followed the thick shrubbery around until we found the place where Father and I had hidden our sacks. I pulled them out from under the bushes.

Until this point, I hadn't understood why we had brought them, but now it made perfect sense. What better way to hide the magistrate and his family than to dress them in well-worn leftovers from Milly's stash? Who would expect to find the leader of the city dressed like a commoner?

"Here, put these on," Father said as he started passing out bits of clothing from the sacks.

"What, here?" The magistrate's wife looked aghast. "Out in the open for all to see?"

"Yes, we can't have you wandering the streets of Oswell dressed like that."

"Like what?" The woman glanced down at her clothing. "I'll have you know—"

"Quiet, Merilyn," her husband said, giving her a harsh look. "Just do as he says."

The magistrate's wife stomped her foot. "You should have had us change back in the room—"

"No sense carrying extra weight when we might not have needed them," Father said.

She paled when she realized what he'd meant, and started working on the top buttons of her nightgown.

Father turned my head to give them some privacy. I hadn't even noticed I was staring. It was the first time I'd seen a woman's undergarments, if you didn't count my sister's when we went down to the pools to swim.

We stuffed their fancy clothing in the bags, and Father scaled the wall.

Once at the top, he waited and watched.

"What's he doing?" the magistrate's wife asked impatiently. "Are we going or not?"

"He's waiting for the patrols to pass," I said. "They circle your estate every twenty minutes."

"How would you know that?" the magistrate asked.

"Because we spent all day today timing it."

The magistrate raised his brow but didn't say more.

"They're gone," Father said as he climbed back down. "Let's go."

Getting over the wall wasn't quite as time-consuming as lowering everyone from the second-floor balcony, but it wasn't exactly quick, either. Father showed the magistrate where to climb, and then he took both Rosella and her little brother over himself before coming back to help me with the magistrate's wife.

I was the last one over the wall. We didn't waste any time getting across the road and into the shadows of the narrow alleyway on the other side.

"We will need to stop for horses."

"Where?" the magistrate asked. He pointed back toward his house. "We have a stable on the estate. We could grab a couple—
"

"And how would we get them out the gate without your guards seeing us?"

The magistrate wrung his hands. "Right, I didn't think of that."

"Don't worry," Father said. "I know just the place. Besides, there's someone we need to collect before we leave."

I passed Father a suspicious glance. "You're not talking about . . ."

Father didn't say anything. He just smiled.

It took us an agonizing amount of time to cross the city. We stopped frequently to make sure we hadn't been seen, and kept a slow enough pace for the magistrate and his family to keep up. It was a wonder we made it at all.

My tension eased when we reached the stables at the Golden Tassel. I was happy to see the place. It meant we were getting close to completing our contract. All we had to do now was make it outside the city undetected, a goal I wasn't sure how we were going to accomplish. Father always seemed to have a plan, though. I hoped this time was no different.

"Get the horses ready," Father said before heading around the back of the inn. I knew where he was going. I almost wished I could go along just to see Hobb's face when he woke to my father standing over his bed.

"Come on." I motioned the others to the stable. We opened one of the doors and stepped inside. The stable was almost full. It looked like a number of new occupants had come to the inn since we'd left that morning. Spotting our horses in the back, I grabbed the first saddle and began loading our weapons and gear.

"What about us?" the magistrate asked as he watched me going about my work. "What are we going to ride?"

"Pick two and start saddling," Father said as he walked through the front. "You stuffed plenty of gold into that satchel of yours. You can leave payment for a couple of horses and their gear."

"What's going on in here, Narris?" Hobb said grouchily. His hair—what was left of it—stood on end, and he was still trying to get his left boot on as he fumbled through the doors. "It's bad enough waking to find an Upaka standing over my bed, but now you got me slinking off in the middle of the night like a common purse-snatcher?"

Father motioned him over. "Hobb, I'd like you to meet Magistrate Sirias and his family." He turned to the magistrate. "Magistrate, this is Master Hobb, ferryman extraordinaire."

Hobb choked, his mouth hanging open like he was about to stuff it with a helping of Milly's fruit pie.

"A pleasure, Master Hobb."

Hobb just stood there. "I, uh . . ."

"I assure you, that was my reaction as well when these two showed up in my bedchamber this evening," the magistrate said with a slight smirk.

Hobb shifted his attention back to my father. "What've you gotten me involved in?"

"Remember how you said that you owed us your life? It's time to collect."

Chapter 16

"IT DIDN'T TAKE LONG to grab saddles for the three extra horses. In fact, it took Hobb longer to clear the fog from his head than it did for us to have all five mounts ready to ride. I had just lifted Rosella up to sit in front of Magistrate Sirias when a confused voice behind me brought everything to a halt.

"What's . . . what's going on here?"

I turned around. It was the stable boy. He must have been asleep in one of the empty stalls at the back. With all the noise we'd made, I couldn't believe he hadn't awoken sooner. He tried wiping the sleep from his eyes as he stood there looking bewildered, perhaps wondering if this was all a dream. He was no longer wearing his yellow cap or bright necktie. In fact, he wasn't wearing much more than his skivvies.

"We have a long journey, so we're getting an early start of it,"

Father said as he made his way around the horses. He motioned with his head for me to get the others moving as he passed. He stopped in front of the stable-hand. "Be sure the owners of these horses receive this payment, will you?" He handed the boy a small pouch. "I think you'll find it generous."

I dared a quick glance over my shoulder as I walked two of the horses toward the front. The stable boy tried to smile, but I think he was too intimidated by who was standing in front of him to do much more than that.

"And here's a little something extra for you, lad. You did a fine job watching our gear."

Whatever Father had given him had certainly done the trick, as the boy's expression went from apprehension to excitement. "Thank you, sir," he said with a formal bow. "I'll be sure they get it."

Father closed the stable doors behind us and we mounted. I had always admired my father's ability to understand what motivated people.

"How are we going to get through the gates without anyone noticing?" the magistrate asked. He looked as antsy as his horse.

"We're not," Father said. "At least not all of us." That didn't seem to make the magistrate feel any better. It didn't make me feel any better, either. "We can't take a chance on you being seen, and a group this size would never make it through the gates in the middle of the night without raising suspicion."

"Aye," Hobb said. "They shut the gates at night, but there're also fewer guards standing watch. Besides, they're more worried about people getting into the city than those trying to leave it. I usually travel at night myself, especially during the summer months. But with this many, you can be sure they'll have questions before they let us go."

"Hobb and I will take the horses through," Father said. "We can tell them the extra mounts are for hauling his ferry out of the mud, which isn't too far from the truth."

"Not far at all," Hobb said with a stout grunt.

"While we are getting the horses out, Ayrion and the rest of you are going to meet us at the second guard station on the west wall. It's the only station that can't be seen by the others."

"Wait," I said skeptically. "You want me to take them?" I couldn't believe he was leaving such an important task solely in my hands. What if I made a mistake?

Magistrate Sirias cleared his throat. "The boy has a point. Wouldn't it be more prudent to have one of you along?"

"Ha. You won't see me scaling no city wall," Hobb said.

"Ayrion is a trained Upaka," Father said with every confidence. "He scaled the peaks of Dragon Fang with nothing but his bare hands and a pick. He'll be fine."

Sirias didn't say anything more, but I could see the uncertainty in his eyes. I couldn't blame him. His family's life depended on it.

"What do we do when we get there?" I asked, still not understanding why Father wasn't the one doing this instead of me. Maybe it was a test.

"You're going to lower them over the side, like we did on the balcony."

"But what about the guards?"

"From what we've seen, most of the stations are guarded by only a single sentry. Nothing you can't handle."

I hoped he was right.

"We'll ride as far as we can," Father said, "and then you'll have to make it the rest of the way on foot." With that, he turned his horse, and we left the Golden Tassel.

I watched the inn disappear behind us and wondered if I'd ever see it again. Maybe another contract would bring us back this way. I had a sinking feeling, though, that after word got out about the disappearance of the magistrate and his family, Milly wouldn't be all that prone to letting us stay there again. I pushed the thoughts aside. I needed to spend my time concentrating on how to get the magistrate's family over the city wall.

The streets were empty as we passed through the southwest side of Oswell. The buildings were much nicer than the ones in Norshag, and the air didn't smell so foul. Darkened windows stared at us as we made our way toward the south gate. Smoke from the chimneys rose into the dimly lit sky as the fireplaces were no doubt stoked against the chill of the oncoming winter nights. The thought had me pulling my cloak up around my shoulders.

The only noise to be heard was the clopping of the horses' hooves as they struck the worn cobbles. Their rhythm began to grate on my nerves. Each new strike drew us closer to our impending destination.

Father stopped us a couple of blocks from the city gates.

I slid off my horse and handed him the reins.

"Take Willis Lane," Hobb said, pointing to the next road up. "It ends at the wall. The guard station you're looking for will be on your right. Can't miss it."

Father handed me my bow. "You might need this."

I slung it and the quiver, along with the grapple and rope, over one shoulder. Behind me, the magistrate was busy consoling his daughter.

"I have every confidence in you," Father said.

I didn't know what else to say, so I said the first thing that came to mind. "I'll get them across."

He smiled. "Use your head. A simple solution is generally the best."

I nodded and watched as Father and Hobb disappeared around the corner with the horses. I still couldn't believe he was leaving me with such an important task. This had been the first time during this entire contract that my father hadn't been there with me.

"We should probably be going, don't you think?" the magistrate suggested, stepping alongside me. Beside him, his wife was carrying their youngest in her arms. The boy's eyes were closed, and his breathing was steady. I envied him. What it must be like to go back to a time when the only concern was my next feeding.

"Yes." I squared my shoulders. I had to look like I knew what I was doing. We headed for the street Hobb had indicated and started down. We couldn't travel very fast on foot, especially with Rosella clinging to her father's leg, but I urged them to keep going. I needed to make sure we had plenty of time to deal with whatever awaited us at the guard station. I glanced up at the sky, but the clouds were still covering the moon. I wondered how much time we had before dawn. It couldn't have been much.

After what felt like hours, I caught my first glimpse of the stone wall ahead. Our pace had slowed—Rosella kept stopping to point out every little thing she saw, and her parents' demands for rest were growing more frequent. Only once did we see someone else, but like us, they were in too much of a hurry to even look our way.

A loud crash to our right had me tripping over my feet to stop. The others did the same. The magistrate stepped on my foot in the process, but I hardly had time to hop around when a large vase flew out of the second-story window of the house next to us and shattered a few feet from where we stood.

"I told you, if you ever came home drunk again, it would be for the last time!" an irate woman said. There was another loud crash, followed by a dull groan. We didn't stick around to see what happened next. The magistrate lifted Rosella and we took off. I glanced over my shoulder, half expecting to see the woman's husband flying out the window, but he never did.

"This way," I said, motioning the others to the side of the street. We stopped just shy of the last home. The windows were dark and shuttered like all the others. I peeked around the corner. Like Hobb had said, the guard station was about two streets away. A staircase wound its way up to a small platform at the top of the wall, large enough for four or five men to stand on.

At present, there were two.

"What do we do now?" the magistrate asked. He leaned over me to get a better look.

I studied the scaffolding leading to the platform. "*We* aren't going to do anything. It's my job to get us up there, so that's what I'm going to do."

"But there're two of them."

"Only two? Hardly seems fair." I wanted to slap myself when I realized I sounded just like Flon. I grimaced. "Just stay here. I'll signal you when I'm done."

The magistrate grabbed my arm. "You're not going to kill them, are you? They're just doing their job."

"I won't. At least, I'll try not to." I was starting to like the magistrate. He might not have been the most intimidating figure, but he seemed to genuinely care for the people. I wished we hadn't been contracted to get rid of him. He probably would have been good for the city. "Here, watch this." I handed him my bow and quiver.

"Aren't you going to need that?"

"Not if you want me to get us up there without killing anyone. Besides, the bow would only work if there were only one guard. By the time I got my first shot off, the other guard would sound the alarm. Wait here."

I edged my way around the corner of the building, making sure to keep to the shadows even though the guards' backs were to me. With one hand on the grapple to keep it from bouncing against my hip, I was able to close the distance quickly. I stopped across the street from the base of the stairs and laid the grapple against the building.

The platform leading to the top of the wall was taller than it had looked from two streets back. I could barely see the guards' heads from where I crouched. How was I going to reach the top without them noticing? And once I did, how was I going to incapacitate them without one of them sounding the alarm?

I studied the wall. It was well built. At least twenty-five to thirty feet in height. The stones had been laid in a way that would have made scaling it difficult at best, and the grapple would make too much noise. I turned my attention to the scaffolding instead. The network of boards that constructed the underbelly of the platform would be easy to climb. In fact, if I'd had the time, I might have tried it anyway just for the fun of it. Still, the problem was how to crawl out from under the platform and over the railing without being seen.

Then the answer dawned on me. It was so simple, I wanted to laugh. Why did I care about being seen? I was a thirteen-year-old boy. Why not act like it?

Lowering the hood of my cloak, I walked across the street and started up the stairs. I climbed as quickly and quietly as I could, stepping only on the outside edges of the boards and not the centers where it would be more likely to creak. I paused a few steps from the top and peeked over the edge. The guards still had their backs to me. The shorter of the two was about Father's height but stockier. The second was at least a head taller and quite lanky. The brass warning bell hung from a large hook on the right side of the platform. Beside it was a mallet. Whatever happened, I had to make sure the guards never reached them.

Unable to think of any other reasons to remain hidden, I took a deep breath and continued up, purposely tripping on the last step to announce myself. The men turned and grabbed for their swords as I stepped onto the platform.

"What do you think you're doing up here, kid?" the shorter guard said as he released his grip on the blade. "Why aren't you in bed? You live around here?"

I lowered my head to keep them from seeing my eyes, pretending to be interested in something on the other side of the wall. "I just wanted to see what it looked like from up here. My friends dared me to take a look."

The taller man chuckled and slapped the shorter. "It's all right. Let him have a look. Not much longer and he'll be old enough to stand watch himself."

"I suppose," the first guard said as he gave me a suspicious look. "But make it quick. I don't want your mama comin' after me 'cause I let you up here."

"Yes, sir," I said, sounding as eager as I could. I headed straight for the far side of the platform where the bell hung, positioning myself between them and the alarm. I glanced over the wall at the surrounding trees, wondering if Father and Hobb had managed to make it out with the horses yet. "How does this work?" I asked, picking up the large mallet. I pretended to swing at the bell.

"Whoa! What do you think you're doing?" the taller guard asked as he headed in my direction. "That's only for emergencies. Don't go swinging that around."

The other guard shook his head. "Told you he'd be trouble."

"Here, give me that." The taller man stopped in front of me

with a frown as he held out his hand.

"If you insist." I spun on my heels and slammed the ball end of the mallet against the side of the guard's head. The man's eyes rolled up, and he collapsed at my feet.

"What's this?" The short guard drew his sword and charged. I met him halfway. He swung, and I jumped to the left, but before I could use the mallet on him, the first guard came to enough to grab my leg, and I went down.

The short guard made a mad dash for the bell. In a panic, I grabbed one of his legs on his way by and kicked the other out from under him. He landed a few feet from the wall, his sword skidding across the platform and off the end.

I managed to climb on his back. I could have knifed him, but I knew the magistrate would be furious, and the man was only doing his duty. So instead, I tried to get my arm around his neck to choke him unconscious, but the guard was much stronger than I was and he threw me off.

I landed against the side of the wall. There was a sharp pain in my arm where I hit, but I managed to flip over anyway and grab his left boot. I pulled with all my might as the guard fought to make it to his feet. I was about to kick his other leg when the boot suddenly came off and I rolled backward. I scrambled to get to my feet, already knowing it was too late, when a loud crack broke the silence and the guard collapsed in a heap beside the end of the platform.

I looked up. My father was standing there, holding a half-broken board. "I figured you could use some help," he said with a smile.

What was he doing there? "I thought—"

"What? You thought I'd actually leave you to do all the work yourself?" Father smiled and dropped the plank. He walked back over to the stairs and motioned for the magistrate's family to join us. "I wanted to see how you handled yourself under pressure."

"Poorly," I said, rubbing my sore arm.

"On the contrary. You got your charges to the wall. You devised a plan, and you executed it. And you did it with one hand tied behind your back. If you had merely wanted to kill these men, your task would have been much easier. But you didn't."

"Being the Cleaner is harder than it looks," I said, realizing now what my father must have gone through each time he'd taken a contract. He was right. Killing these men would have made my life a lot easier, but then I would have had to be willing to live with it.

Father rubbed the top of my head. "I'll have to tell you the story of my first contract. I'm sure it will cheer you up."

Behind us, Magistrate Sirias was the first to reach the top of the platform, his youngest in his arms. His wife was just behind him with Rosella close on her skirts. The little girl held the grapple, half the rope dragging behind her. "I carried it all the way by myself." She made a noticeable grunt as she held it out for me to take.

I gave her a warm smile. "You're pretty strong for a girl." She smiled back and reached for her father's leg.

"It's time we go," Father said. He walked to the wall and glanced over the side. There was no sign of Hobb or the horses, but that didn't mean they weren't there.

I grabbed my gear and slung it over my shoulders. Father helped me onto the wall, and with one foot in the rope hold, he lowered me over the side. It was a quick trip. Once at the bottom, I stepped out of the noose and tugged on the rope.

The woods behind me were quiet. I kept picturing a large razorback sneaking up behind me, but every time I turned, there was nothing there.

Above me, the magistrate's wife clung to the rope with one hand and her infant with the other as they lowered her slowly toward me.

"You're almost there," I said encouragingly. I could see the fear in her eyes. "There. You can straighten your legs. You're at the bottom."

She did, and I untied the rope, tugging it twice.

Rosella was next, and then her father.

After everyone else was down, Father left the rope hanging over the side, but instead of keeping the grapple fixed to the back of the wall, he placed it at the top. A dangerous move. If it slipped, he'd fall. To keep from causing the hook to jerk about, he used the soles of his boots and his gloves to slide down the rope instead of doing a hand-over-hand descent. He was impressive to watch.

"Stand back," he warned. Once his feet reached the bottom, he whipped the rope away from the wall and the grapple fell.

"That's a neat trick," a familiar voice said behind us. "I'll have to remember that the next time I decide to climb Oswell's wall in the middle of the night." Hobb walked out from the surrounding trees, leading all five horses. "How'd everything go on your end? I don't hear the city bells, so I take it we're in the clear?"

"Appears so," Father said as he helped the magistrate and his family mount.

"What now?" the magistrate asked.

Father swung into his saddle. "Now we ride. Dawn is nearly here, and we need to be as far away from this place as possible."

I tilted my head. Between the clouds, the stars had faded from view and the sky was shifting to gray. Father was right; we didn't have much time. I turned my horse and, with a gentle prod, urged her forward.

Chapter 17

THE JOURNEY back to Hobb's Crossing was a tiring one, considering we didn't stop other than to rest the horses and catch a few hours' sleep. Father wanted to put as much distance between us and the city as we could.

Once we reached the river, I rode south with Hobb and the magistrate's family to the next crossing while Father stayed with the ferry. It took us nearly two days, but we finally made it back around to Hobb's Crossing.

The river was narrow enough for Father to shoot an arrow across with a thin line. The line was connected to the ferry's guide rope, allowing us to pull both across to our side. From there, we tied the rope to the horses on our side and towed the ferry out of the mud, dragging it and Father across the river.

Hobb said he wasn't too worried about stretching the guide rope back across anytime soon since he didn't get much traffic that way as it was. He was still contemplating the idea of moving closer to Milly.

"Where will you go?" Hobb asked Magistrate Sirias as we all sat around the hearth that evening in the main room. We had just finished a hot meal of rabbit stew, and the kids were fast asleep in front of the fireplace.

"We've got family in Makeda—"

"Then you can't go there," Father cut in, leaning forward in his seat. "Everyone needs to believe you're dead. The last place you should be is with people who know you. Word travels."

The magistrate lowered his head. "Of course you're right. I didn't think about that."

"Your family hated me anyway, Sirias." His wife seemed pleased by the news.

"I guess we'll head south, then. I've always wanted to see the coast. Maybe I can find something in shipping. I'm very good with numbers, you know."

Merilyn nodded. It wasn't an enthusiastic nod but one of serious deliberation.

Hobb took a sip from his mug and wiped his mouth with his sleeve. "What are your plans, Narris? The two of you heading back to that Defiler-forsaken land of yours?"

Father gave Hobb the eye. "Watch it. You're talking about my home."

"Only an Upakan would want to call that cursed place home. I guess it's fitting, though."

"How so?"

"'Cause only the toughest sons of faeries would ever be able to handle it." They both chuckled and Hobb raised his tankard in salute before taking another long drink.

We stayed another day, helping Hobb with damages from the storm while the magistrate and his family decided where to go. Father offered what knowledge he could from his extensive traveling, but there wasn't much more we could do beyond that. Eventually, it was time to go. We packed what provisions we could, wished everyone a fond farewell, and turned our horses west.

"It'll be good to get home," I said as I twisted in the saddle and watched Hobb's Crossing slowly disappear behind us. "I'm going to miss them."

"Who?"

"Hobb, Milly." I turned back around. "Even Magistrate Sirias and his family."

"Yes, that's the difficult part about making new acquaintances. Soon enough, you'll have to leave them behind."

"I'm thankful we have our family. I don't like saying good-bye."

"We are blessed. For better or worse, Upakans stick together."

The trip home was far less exciting, though I did get to see the destruction caused by our run-in with the razorbacks. The grassfire had burned a swath all the way to the Slags and ran for miles in either direction. It was a desolate-looking place. No birdsong, no croak of the frogs, not even the chirp of the crickets. All life had been burned away, leaving only ash in its wake.

Once through the lower plains, Father took us on the longer route around the southern tip of the mountains instead of through the Squeeze. Neither of us wanted to see Norshag and its town of crazy mountain people again.

The forests to the south of Norshag were beautiful, even with the loss of leaves. The woods were full of life as the animals prepared for the coming winter. Beyond the forest, though, the terrain hardened. The closer we came to the southern tip, the more barren it grew.

Mount Ash stood tall and alone in the distance. The road ahead passed between the enormous volcano and the southernmost peaks of the Northern Heights. For at least two days, the air burned our throats and stung our eyes as the thick cloud overhead rained ash down on us and our horses.

Another few days passed, and I was looking forward to being home and sleeping in my own bed. My heart raced as we crested the final rise and caught our first glimpse of the ruins in the valley below. The broken stone had never looked so good.

"It's about time." I snapped the reins, urging my horse to quit her dawdling. "Hurry. The pools are calling to me."

Father laughed as he caught up. "Your mother is calling to me, those warm arms and soft lips—"

"I don't want to hear that," I said, feeling embarrassed.

Father laughed.

We rode down the hillside and through what was left of the outer wall, which was little more than chunks of stone scattered in piles as far as the eye could see.

I hadn't thought about it until we started working our way through the rubble, but I was about to leave the sunlight for the dimness of our city below. It had been weeks since I'd worn my shaders. I wondered how difficult it would be to readjust to the caverns.

We left the horses with the stable hands. After Father paid what was owed, we carried our gear back to the tunnel entrance. It had been nearly a moon since we'd passed this way. Somehow, the experience made me feel older.

One of the guards there to greet us had been on duty the day we had left. The other one was new.

"I see you made it back in one piece," the guard at the desk said as he scribbled something in his ledger. He glanced at me. "You as well." He sniffed, as though he hadn't expected me to return, or perhaps not in one piece.

I smiled and straightened my shoulders. "Did you doubt it?"

The guard didn't say anything. He finished his writing and placed the quill back in its jar. "Anything to report?"

Father shook his head. "Other than another completed contract, no." He handed the guard the official seal of Oswell that he'd collected from the magistrate. "Make sure Fanon gets that. Proof of completion."

The guard nodded and laid the stamp aside. "Everything looks in order. Welcome back, Narris." He looked at me and grunted. I figured that was as good a welcome as I could expect.

Father put his arm around my shoulders, and we headed across the cavernous foyer. We stopped at the mouth of the tunnel, and he lit one of the torches. The darkness ahead seemed harder for my eyes to pierce after having spent the last month in the sun.

I was growing impatient, making sure to huff loudly enough for my father to hear me as we made our way down the south tunnel. I had to keep slowing my pace so Father could catch up. I couldn't wait to tell the others about everything that had happened to us. It was a tale worthy of song. We'd battled fiery serpents, fought bloodthirsty cutthroats, suffered the Slag's stench, swam the icy waters of the Shemoa, moved through Oswell unseen, completed the largest contract Father had ever undertaken, and then escaped over the city walls without anyone knowing we were there . . . Well, other than Hobb, and Milly, and not to forget the stable boy and the two guards we'd knocked unconscious. Either way, it was definitely a contract worthy of a hefty price. I wondered if Father would give me any of it for my part.

Father opened the front door to our home, and I rushed through in front of him, tossing my bags to the side as I ran past. "We're back!" I proclaimed, a wide grin on my face as I braced myself for what I was sure would be a big hug from my mother, and possibly Rianna. I didn't figure Jorn would be all that eager to hug me.

Mother stepped from the kitchen into the main room with Rianna right behind. One look at her face and my smile withered.

"What's wrong?" Father asked.

Mother wiped her hands on her apron. "Flon has chosen to fight Ayrion for his final test."

Father dropped the gear bags on the floor. "Flon wants Ayrion to be his challenger? That's ridiculous. What idiot would choose to go against Ayrion for their testing? Only the winner is allowed to advance. What's the boy thinking?"

"It wasn't Flon's idea," Mother said, still looking a bit shaken.

"Well, whose was it?" Father asked.

"It was Brim's."

## Chapter 18

"FATHER STARTED TO PACE, something he did whenever troubled or in deep thought. At the moment, it seemed he was both. "That doesn't make sense. Brim's smarter than that. He wouldn't choose Ayrion as his son's challenger with something as important as his advancement on the line. That would be foolish."

"Not as foolish as you think," Mother said as she moved farther into the room and leaned against one of the dining room chairs. "The Primary came by the house personally. He didn't look happy to find you and Ayrion were out on contract. He made it very clear that unless his son won the challenge, our family could forget receiving any future contracts."

"Brim doesn't have that kind of authority." Father struck the top of the table with his fist. "Blood and fire! Why does he keep coming after us?" He finally stopped pacing and looked at me. "Ayrion, I hate to ask this of you. I know how much you worked to earn it. But you'll need to let him win. We can't afford to lose any more work."

I stared at them, not knowing what to say as a thousand reasons ran through my mind as to why I couldn't let him win. The top of the list being that it would mean I would lose my chance for advancement and have to wait another whole cycle before I could test again.

Besides, it was Flon. He deserved to fail. He deserved a whole lot worse. He hated me, and I hated him, but at least my abhorrence came from a legitimate source—his bullying, which stemmed from the fact that I was better than he was and everyone knew it. I took a deep breath and slowly released it, feeling my chest deflate, along with the last of my pride. I nodded. "I'll let him win."

Father walked over and placed his hand on my shoulder. "I know how hard this is. It's never easy to lose, especially to someone like Flon. But we need to pick our battles wisely." He stared at me for a moment. "Understand?"

"Yes." I did understand, but it didn't mean I had to like it.

"I'm proud of you, Ayrion."

The earlier excitement about our arrival had all but died, leaving in its wake a sense of dread as we all stood there staring at each other in silence.

Father finally broke the unwelcome stillness as he released my shoulder and grabbed two of the travel bags we'd left at the door. "Where's Jorn?" he asked, looking around the front room.

"He's in class," Mother said. "He'll be home later."

Father laid the two satchels on the table and stretched. "Well, your man's been gone for nearly a full moon. I expect some attention over here."

Mother raised her brow. "I could say the same."

They met in the middle with a firm embrace and a hard kiss. I turned my eyes about the time Rianna engulfed me with a big hug. "Welcome back. Wish it was under better circumstances. So, how did it go?"

"Yes," Mother said as she pulled away from Father's arms. "How did it go? Did you complete the contract?"

"We did," Father said, looking none too happy at having his affection cut short.

"And?" Mother asked.

"And what?"

"And are you going to tell us about it? You've been gone for nearly a full moon. Surely, something worth sharing happened during that time."

Father smiled and then gestured for us to join him around the table. He was a natural storyteller. He knew exactly how to draw us in, how to enhance the story without completely breaking from the reality of what had truly happened—namely, that we had almost died on three different occasions.

I enjoyed watching Mother's and Rianna's faces as they listened intently to the exciting story Father wove of our quest: the dangers we had faced, the friends we'd made, the places we'd seen, even our run-in with the huge razorbacks. It was a proud moment for me.

It was almost enough to take my mind off Flon and the upcoming challenge. Almost.

I did notice that Father left out some of the more gruesome details, such as our battle in Norshag. He also didn't reveal anything about helping the family escape. He simply said the contract had been fulfilled and he was going to collect the payment for it in the morning.

After spending the rest of the afternoon unpacking our gear, I grabbed some soap and a drying cloth and headed for the pools.

"Hold up; I'm coming too," Rianna said before I had made it halfway out the door.

I grabbed one of the lanterns hanging by the front door. My eyes hadn't completely adjusted, and I needed the extra light. After a long walk through the north tunnels, we stepped into the main cavern, and the roar of Triple Falls enveloped us. I'd forgotten how much I missed the noise. It tended to drown out all other distractions.

"Come on. I'll race you in," Rianna said as she headed for the water below.

We were tripping over our own feet the entire way down as we attempted to strip while we ran. We left a trail of clothes behind us. With nothing but our underclothes, we hit the edge of the first pool and leaped in.

The warm water had never felt so good. I didn't want to come up. I rubbed my hands thoroughly through my hair and let the water rinse out the dirt before bursting to the surface to inhale a mouthful of air. Rianna was already swimming around the outer edge of the pool, pushing off the rock and stroking as hard as she could. It was her routine. She always made one full lap on entering.

I was halfway around my first lap when I stopped at the sound of voices behind us. I turned, half expecting to see Jorn coming down to join us for a swim. We weren't so lucky.

Flon, along with three of his friends, stepped from the mouth of one of the smaller tunnels. Like his father, Flon stood head and shoulders over the others. He was already taller than my father and more muscular, thanks to the Primary seeing to his training personally.

"I heard you were back," Flon said as he and the other three began collecting our clothing on the way down. I had a feeling he wasn't doing it to be nice. He held Rianna's top to his nose and took a long whiff.

"Give me my shirt back, Flon," Rianna hissed.

Flon smiled and I felt a chill run down my back. It was anything but pleasant. It was the smile of someone who had just cornered their prey and was about to pounce. "You smell good, Rianna. My offer still stands for Mal'jinto. It'll probably be the only offer you ever receive as long as you claim relation to that menace," he said, pointing at me with her shirt.

"I'd rather die unbonded than to be forced into bed with the likes of you."

Flon's face reddened. He twisted her clothing in his hands. "Any girl in our clan would kill to get an offer from me."

Rianna sneered. "Kill themselves, you mean."

I wanted to laugh, but I didn't.

Flon's anger was momentarily diverted as his attention shifted to me. "Have you heard the news?"

It didn't take a scholar to know what he was referring to. "Yes."

"Good. Then I'm sure you'll behave accordingly."

"If you're referring to me putting you on your backside in front of the clan? Sure, I'll behave accordingly."

Flon raised his finger in warning. "You try anything stupid and I'll make sure the next time you're chained to the whipping post, Dorin doesn't stop until he's emptied you of every last drop of your blood."

Flon's cronies chuckled.

"You hurt him," Rianna said, "and I'll cut off your shrunken twiddle and you'll never bond with any girl."

Flon looked like he was ready to throw himself in the water after her. Instead, he turned and stormed out, followed by his cronies, but not before taking our clothes and drying cloths with them.

Needless to say, our trip home was more than a little embarrassing.

## Chapter 19

THE DAY OF THE BIG FIGHT was here. I woke early, ran through my morning workout down at the pools, ate breakfast, helped Mother with the chores, and spent every last waking minute stressing over all the ways this fight could go horribly wrong.

It wasn't like I hadn't fought Flon in the ring before. I'd done so numerous times. But this was the first time I'd been required to lose, to let this pompous excuse for an Upakan beat me; worse yet, to let him do it in front of the entire clan.

Flon had chosen me on purpose. He knew he could get his father to force me to lose. Not only would that assure him a promotion to the next stage in his training, but he could also make me look the fool in the process.

Also, the Primary would want Flon's win to be legitimate. That could only be accomplished by challenging a strong opponent. What kind of victory would it be for Flon to face off against a less-worthy fighter?

When it was time to leave, my family escorted me to the center of what the Orpa Clan claimed as their section of the city. The fight was to be held in the arena. Other than the ruins on the surface, it was the largest open area available that would allow for the seating of the entire clan. The enormous chamber had once been home to some kind of assembly room for the Keldoran Senate, back before the great quake. Now it had been converted for the use of public gatherings, which typically ended up being some kind of match.

All eyes focused on my family as we passed through the crowded foyer and down the hall toward the back, where the arena was. Hushed whispers, and some not-so-hushed whispers, filled the air around us as people slowly stepped aside to let us by.

I followed Father through the open doors. The arena was nearly filled, and the sound of a hundred conversations reverberated off the stone walls. I could almost smell the adrenaline. My hands were shaking, so I balled my fists. I glanced at my mother, but she didn't see me. She was preoccupied with helping Father find a place to sit.

Jorn looked at me. "I hope you break his face." It was the most support he'd shown me in some time.

I smiled.

Father had elected not to tell Jorn about the Primary's threat. At ten, Jorn wasn't the best at keeping secrets.

We were on the second level. There were at least a dozen steps leading down to the main floor. Torches lined the outer walls, spilling their light onto the stone risers that encircled the fifteen-foot ring at the bottom. The inside of the ring had been covered with packed sand carted in from above.

"This way," Father said. There was an opening on the first row for the immediate families of those scheduled to fight. Thankfully, as Primary, Brim sat on the opposite side of the ring on an elevated platform for the members of the Peltok. He enjoyed setting himself apart from the rest of the clan. This was one time I was glad he did.

Father pointed to a vacant section in the front row, and we took our seats. Those sitting nearby scooted down. From the looks on their faces, it had less to do with common politeness and more with not wanting to be associated with me.

Flon was seated on the other side of the ring, just below the Peltok's raised platform. His entire family flanked him on all sides, like a wall, protecting their favorite son from harm. He smiled at me when he saw me looking. It was the smile of someone who already knew he was going to win.

"Don't look at him," Rianna said, placing her hand on my leg. "You're only giving Flon the satisfaction of knowing how much this hurts." She was right, as usual, so I looked away.

It didn't take long for the rest of the seats to fill.

Ness, the third member of the Peltok, stood and walked to the edge of the platform. She held out her hands and the audience quieted. "A challenge for advancement has been made by Flon, son of Brim." The crowd applauded, the natural acoustics amplifying the noise. "He has chosen as his challenger Ayrion, son of Narris. And his challenge has been accepted."

Father patted my leg. It was meant to be an encouraging gesture, but it only intensified the reality of what was about to happen.

"Will the two fighters take their places?"

"Remember," Father said as he leaned in to keep from being heard. "You know what to do. I know you don't like it, but for the sake of keeping food on the table, make sure he wins." He winked. "I'm proud of you."

Mother smiled, but I could see the tears building at the corners of her eyes. It was another reason why she generally didn't attend these sorts of events. Rianna squeezed my hand, and Jorn made a fist and imitated punching his face.

I stood and walked to the edge of the ring. Like Flon, I removed my boots and socks, then my shirt. A murmur rose from those behind me when I did. My scars from Dorin's whip were there for all to see. I didn't know why I was so embarrassed by them. Most trainees showed off their scars, but since mine were given to me rather than earned, I wasn't all that proud of displaying them.

I left my clothes lying beside the stone partition that separated the sand from the rest of the floor and stepped into the ring. The rules were simple. Once you stepped in, you couldn't leave until a contestant either won or lost, or the judges ruled it a draw.

Not wanting to be forced to watch my defeat twice, I placed a barrier in front of my magic, blocking its use. Like the whipping post, I didn't want to see visions of what was to come. Besides, I preferred not to use my magic in the ring anyway. I wanted my victories to be legitimate. Not saying there weren't times I used it to my advantage to take Flon down a peg or two when he needed it, which was more often than not as of late.

At some point during the fight, I was going to have to turn it back on. I would need to use the visions to see how to make Flon's victory look real without doing too much damage to my own reputation. For that, I needed magic.

I was the first in. The crowd cheered as they anticipated the fight ahead. Normally, seeing a seventeen-year-old fight a thirteen-year-old wouldn't have made for a very exciting match. In fact, many would have looked on it as something to be ashamed of for the older fighter, but everyone knew I had never lost a fight. They also knew about the rivalry between me and Flon and how that would play out in the ring.

I watched as Flon took his time with his shirt, making sure to flex his muscular frame as he did. I didn't know if he was trying to intimidate me or play to the crowd. Knowing him, both. He laid his shirt on top of his boots and took a moment to stretch before turning and waving to the audience. The Primary started to clap, which of course meant the rest of the audience had to follow along. I rolled my eyes.

After a few more minutes of pandering, Flon finally decided to step across the barrier and face me. There was a momentary look of uncertainty on his face. It was brief, but it was there. I was sure those watching didn't notice, since it was immediately replaced with his typical smugness. I smiled on the inside. He was nervous.

"I'll try not to make you look too bad," Flon said as he worked his way slowly around the outer perimeter of the ring, his voice projected for the crowd to hear.

"Don't worry," I said with the same amount of volume. "You'll never get the chance."

Flon snarled, but that brief look of uncertainty reared its head once again before being replaced with anger. A quick glance over my shoulder toward the council let me know that Brim was anything but pleased by my response as he leaned forward in his seat and stared me down. The look in his eyes said that he wanted to bash my head in with a very big mallet.

I continued to pivot from where I stood at the center of the ring, watching Flon as he circled. He was head and shoulders over me, but as my father was quick to point out, "size doesn't always matter." In Flon's case, I knew it to be true. What normally made for great intimidation also took away from his speed and agility.

I was faster, more flexible, capable of dodging and weaving in a way that someone of his size and bulk could not. The downside was that most strikes would prove far more damaging to me than to him, which meant I needed to be extra careful. The state Flon was in, I was pretty sure he wouldn't stop with just a single takedown blow. While he had the chance, he was going to do his best to make an example of me. I might be forced to let him win, but I'd be hanged before I let him humiliate me in the process.

I was getting tired of spinning around. "Are you going to keep circling me like a constipated nanny goat, or are we going to fight?" I wanted to get him riled up, and since Flon was never one for being mocked, it was a sure way to force his hand.

The tactic worked. Flon's face hardened, and his eyes narrowed. The veins in his forehead and neck bulged as he threw caution to the wind and charged. He roared all the way across the ring.

I ducked and spun to the right. His fist flew over my head. The force of the swing let me know he was out for blood. He didn't just want to humiliate me. He wanted to kill me. If it wasn't for the laws written in the Shal'Noran, preventing any of the Upaka from taking the life of another, Flon would have certainly done his best to try.

He turned and punched with his other hand. This time, I blocked, letting his swing spin him farther to the left than it should have. He was still too caught up in the rage to notice. I could have broken his leg while he was off balance. It took a lot not to. Instead, I hit him in the back with a quick strike to the kidney. It wasn't a serious blow, but I knew the pain would stick with him.

He flinched and pulled away but then turned with a powerful backswing, forcing me to retreat or get knocked to the side. Once more, he came at me, this time with a series of punches and kicks. He was playing to the audience. A stupid mistake that I was going to take advantage of. I blocked and dodged each strike, finally dropping with a sweep to the legs that sent him flying face-first into the dirt.

He rolled and was back on his feet before I could get to him. He started circling once again. This time, I joined him. Both of us watching, studying, looking for a weakness to exploit.

"What's wrong, Flon?" I said mockingly. "You seemed to be

favoring your left side. Next time, don't leave it open."

Again, he charged, this time without the roar. He punched with his left, feinted, and kicked with his right. I blocked the first, side-stepped the second. "You're slowing down," I chided. "You sure you don't need a break?"

He growled and spun low, trying to sweep my feet as I'd done to him, but I was too quick and jumped over his leg. I blocked the next punch and threw a couple of my own. He blocked and countered. I whipped a kick at his chest, and he spun to dodge but tripped. I didn't hesitate that time. With my right leg, I pivoted to land a hard kick to the side of his ribs, only to find he had feigned the stumble. Halfway into my kick, Flon turned and caught my leg. He punched me hard in the stomach, and I went down.

I could hear the Primary shouting from his seat. The crowd seemed to echo his enthusiasm as they cheered all the louder.

I had cracked a rib for sure. Every breath felt like a knife being slid into my chest.

No sooner had I hit the ground than Flon was leaping into the air toward me. I rolled and he landed on one knee, expecting to crush me, but by the time he struck dirt, I was up and spinning around. This time, my foot didn't miss, and I caught the side of his face before he managed to get his guard up.

Flon's head whipped to the right, and a couple of his front teeth went with it.

The crowd went silent, except for my father. I heard him shout behind me and I smiled.

Flon screamed as he ran at me. His eyes were on fire. He'd lost all sense of reason. Blood ran down his chin.

I tried getting out of the way, but he threw a fistful of sand in my face. I flung my hands up to protect my eyes, but without my magic, I was too late. I hadn't seen it coming soon enough to counter. Now I couldn't see anything. I angled far enough to the side to keep from catching the full brunt of Flon's frame, but he hit both my legs with one arm and I went down. Blinding your opponent in an advancement fight was considered cowardly. It seemed Flon didn't care.

I tried to roll free, but he was quicker than I expected and caught me by the back of my pants, nearly jerking them off when he yanked me back to the ground. He crawled over me and started punching. All I could do was throw up my arms to protect my head. I could hear Rianna screaming somewhere off to my left and Brim shouting from his pedestal on my right.

If there was ever a time to resort to magic, it was now. I released the barrier and it flooded through me with an overwhelming surge. The visions struck all at once, leaving me disoriented as I watched Flon's fists continue coming.

"What do you think you're doing?" he said as he fought with everything he had to land a solid hit to my face. "I'm supposed to win. You embarrass me like that again and I'll make sure your family suffers." His words were soft, just loud enough for me to hear over the noise of the crowd.

I did my best to divert his hits, but he was much stronger than I was, and no amount of magic could stop that. If I didn't do something, Shal'Noran or no Shal'Noran, he was going to kill me. I only had one move left. Flon, in his rage, had straddled my body to keep me from wiggling free. What he didn't consider was that in doing so, he had left one very important area open.

With no other option, I grabbed Flon by his low-hanging parts and squeezed with all my might. I'd never seen anyone that size jump so high or squeal so loud.

The Primary was out of his chair in an instant. I thought he was going to jump into the ring, but one look at the crowd and he slowly sat back down. I knew I'd crossed the line on this one.

Flon lay on the other side of the ring, writhing as he protectively held his shrunken twiddle, as Rianna had called it. I was too busy trying to catch my breath and test my ribs to worry about finishing the job, not to mention I was supposed to be letting the oaf win. I wiped the blood from my mouth and crawled back toward the stone partition, where I attempted to clear the dirt and sand from my eyes as I waited for whatever was coming.

I didn't have to wait too long. Flon pushed his way to his feet. He turned and looked at me. I didn't see the rage that had been there before. I didn't even see embarrassment, which I found a little surprising given the circumstances. All I saw was an eerily calm composure, a lack of all emotion. It was like looking into the eyes of a dead man.

He started across the ring. He didn't run, didn't yell, didn't even snarl. He simply walked calmly over to where I stood and stopped within arm's reach. The crowd was so loud, I could no longer distinguish the voices of my family from the rest.

I knew it was time. I couldn't put it off any longer. As much as

I wanted to make sure Flon never reached his advancement, I didn't want my family suffering for it. The Primary's influence was too powerful.

"I'm ready," I said, looking for some sign of understanding in Flon's face. So far, nothing. "Go ahead; let's get this over with."

I raised my fists. Flon did the same. I scooted away from the partition, circling back to the center and waiting. I hoped he knew how to improvise, because I wasn't sure what I needed to do to make this look convincing. Flon closed on me.

I started with a punch to the chest. He blocked. I kicked at his ribs. Again, he blocked, but this time, he countered with a punch to the gut, then to the head. I blocked the first but pretended to miss the second and jerked my head to the side just in time to make it appear like he had landed a solid blow.

I spun around and stumbled backward, as though the strike had left me spinning. That was when Flon made his move. I saw it coming and immediately blew out all the air in my lungs and tightened my abs. This was going to hurt. His fist struck me in the gut, and I cried out as the force sent me backward a couple of steps. The pain from the cracked rib made my eyes water.

He kicked at my head, and I ducked and spun to the left, but not before I let him catch me in the arm with his elbow. I bore it, but the force of the hit caused my arm to spasm. I stumbled to the left, making it look like Flon's earlier punch to the head had done more damage than it really had.

Flon kicked me in the back of my legs, and I went to my knees. This was it. The moment he'd been waiting for, and I'd been dreading. He wrapped his big arm around my neck and lifted me up. He stank of sweat and blood. I held onto his arm to keep from being strangled as he twisted one of my arms behind my back, holding me there for everyone to witness. He slowly turned, presenting me to the crowd.

Brim was at the edge of his seat, a wicked smile on his face. He didn't seem to be looking at his son, though. His gaze was too high. He was staring at my father.

The crowd went wild with excitement at seeing their favorite son come back from what they thought had been a sure defeat. I knew this was it. At least I wouldn't be losing in complete disgrace.

Flon was behind me now. I could feel his breath against the back of my neck.

"Well, what are you waiting for? Get it over with."

Flon leaned in and whispered in my ear. "I told you if you embarrassed me again, I was going to make you suffer, and you didn't listen." He turned and looked at my family. "I think your sister will make a nice prize, don't you?"

Something in me snapped. Before Flon could finish choking me out, I leaned my head forward as far as it would go and then rammed it back into his face.

Flon shrieked, but his arm around my neck let go and I staggered forward, gasping for breath. I reached the far side of the ring and turned to see where he was, but it was too late. He was already flying through the air with his feet aimed straight for my head. I didn't have time to duck.

His heels connected with the front of my face, and I felt something in me break. It was a pain like I'd never felt before, and then nothing. Suddenly, I was standing at the side of the ring once again trying to catch my breath.

Realizing it had been another vision, I turned in time to see Flon coming at me once again. My body took over. This time, I didn't try to dive out of the way. Instead, I tucked my shoulder up under his legs and pushed upward. He flipped in midair. His legs went up and his head went down.

There was a loud snap when he hit the dirt, and his body went limp.

The audience went silent.

I was almost afraid to look down. Flon lay there, staring at me. I thought his eyes had seemed lifeless before. Now they really were. His head was bent unnaturally to the left.

I knelt beside him and gently shook him. "Flon? Flon?" Fear took over.

"What have you done?" Brim shouted as he leaped into the ring.

Before he could reach me, my father was there, pulling me away from the body. "Get back, Ayrion." He dragged me to the other side of the ring and away from Brim.

"No! No!" The Primary dropped to his knees and cradled Flon's head in his arms. Flon's mother screamed and was out of her seat, running for her son, with half their family behind her.

The other two members of the Peltok quickly made their way down the platform stairs. They stood to the side and watched in silence. The crowd did the same. No one moved. Most were probably too afraid, considering what had just happened.

Mother, Rianna, and even Jorn met us at the edge of the ring.

"What do we do?" Mother whispered.

"I don't know." There was fear in my father's voice. It was something I'd never heard from him before.

"I didn't mean for this to happen," I said, my whole body shaking. "I wasn't trying to kill him."

"What were you thinking, Ayrion?" The scolding from my father hurt worse than anything else. "I told you to let him win."

"I was, but . . ."

"But what?"

"But he threatened to force Rianna to bond with him."

"Over my dead body," Rianna said, half-spitting the words. "If you ask me, he got what he deserved."

The wailing of Flon's mother intensified, bringing our conversation to a stop. Those members of Flon's family who were surrounding the body suddenly parted as Brim stepped through. He got one look at me and headed across the ring. There was no questioning what he intended to do. It was written all over his face.

My father pushed me back against the partition and stepped between me and the Primary. "It was an accident, Brim. We all saw it." He raised his hand for the big man to stop.

"Get out of my way, Narris, or I'll put you in the dirt beside him."

Before the Primary had made it across, my mother and sister hopped the partition and joined Father in forming a barrier in front of me.

"You don't want to do this," Father said as Brim stopped barely an arm's length away. My father's right hand angled to grab one of the knives I knew he kept hidden up his sleeves.

There was murder in Brim's eyes.

The other two members of the Peltok rushed over. Ness was the first to speak. "Primary, might we have a word?" She kept her voice low so she wouldn't be heard by the surrounding audience. "You don't want to do this. There are too many people watching."

Brim paused long enough to notice all the eyes staring at him. He took a deep breath and pointed directly at me. "I want him in front of the council . . . immediately!" He looked me in the eyes, and my knees trembled. Brim snarled, then turned and marched back across the ring. The other two council members left as well, but not before Ness passed me a brief but sincere look of pity.

I gulped. Of all the ways this could have gone wrong, I would have never imagined this being one of them.

Chapter 20

"ᙖANISHMENT? For what? For winning?" My father was beside himself with rage. "The laws of Shal'Noran don't apply here, Brim, and you know it! Flon's own actions brought this about. Now, I hate that the young man was killed, but my son can hardly be blamed for what was clearly an accident."

I stood beside my father in front of the council, Mother to my left. It was all I could do to keep my hands from shaking as I watched my future unravel before me like one of my mother's poorly knit socks.

Brim leaned forward in his seat at the center of the platform and sneered. "If I'm to be forced to live without my son, then so will you."

"This isn't justice. It's vengeance!"

"Your son's a menace to our way of life!" Brim said, pointing straight at me. His eyes read of fury. "Be thankful I'm not ordering his execution."

"That's exactly what you're doing. You banish him and you're taking away his life, his family, his home."

"Which is exactly what he did to mine!" Brim hit the arms of his seat, coming halfway out of it when he did.

For an Upakan, being banished was worse than execution. We were shunned everywhere we went. We were outcasts who survived by living apart from the rest of the world, in a place no other society would dare. A barren wasteland.

I knew there was nothing my father could say that would change Brim's mind. He'd just lost his son. The only thing Father was going to accomplish was to give the Primary the means to banish the rest of my family along with me.

At this point, I didn't see much of a future here for me anyway.

Before my father could say anything more, Brim leaned forward. "Arguments are over." He glanced at the other two members, and each nodded. Ness's nod was at least reluctant. "The sentence stands. Ayrion will leave the Lost City by dawn. Any attempt to return is punishable by death." He looked past us to the armed men at the back of the room. "Guards, take Ayrion to the cells. Let him spend his last day enjoying the solitude of what awaits him."

"You can't do this!" My father started to rush the platform, but I grabbed his arm and held him back. "You can't banish him without giving him a chance to collect his things or say good-bye."

Brim hopped to his feet. "Did I get the chance to tell my son good-bye?" The hatred on his face was enough to silence my father.

Mother pulled him back.

The Primary stepped down from the dais, his cold eyes barely glancing at me as he passed. I watched as he and the other members of the council left the room.

"There's nothing you could have done," I said, hoping to ease my father's rage. "It was my fault."

Father turned and pointed directly at my chest. "Never think that. None of this is your fault." There were tears in his eyes.

Mother wrapped her arms around me, sobbing as she did, but the guards pulled us apart. "No. You can't take my boy."

Father held her as she wept. "I'll pack your stuff tonight," he said. "We'll have everything ready for you by dawn."

The guards dragged me from the room and from the faces of my parents. They led me down to the prisons in the lowest levels of the Justice Hall.

The keeper of the cells unlocked one of the doors and shoved me inside. "Enjoy your stay, as brief as it is." He chuckled, and the three men left, taking the torch with them.

Darkness enveloped me, a fitting end to the circumstances of my life. If there was a higher power at work, He must have really had it in for me. I pressed myself against the back wall of my cell and slowly slid to a seat on the cold stone. I pulled my knees to my chest, wrapped my arms around them, and began to cry. I was surprised by how easily the tears came. Warriors weren't supposed to cry, but no matter how much I wanted to stop, they just kept coming. I sat there and contemplated what I was about to face, the possibility of never seeing my family again, forced to wander through Aldor with nowhere to belong.

It was during that time of uncertainty that Magistrate Sirias and his family came to mind. I thought it ironic. It wasn't two weeks before that I had pondered what it must have been like for them to be forced to leave everything they knew behind. And here I was, about to share in their fate. I suddenly wondered where they were and if they wouldn't mind taking me with them. I dismissed the idea as soon as it came. The last thing they would ever want would be to drag along the very person who'd put them in that situation in the first place.

I rested my head against the wall and closed my eyes. Sleep never came. It was the longest night of my life. I cried until the tears would no longer come. I tried a couple dozen times to consider what I should do once I left the Lost City, only to have each attempt shattered by more crying as I thought of what I'd be losing.

By the time I heard the key twisting in the door's lock and the latch being thrown back, I was completely drained of all emotions. When the guards stepped inside and tried rustling me to my feet, I found I could barely stand. I winced at the sharp pain in my side from the injured rib. I felt like I'd just undergone another session with Dorin and his whip. It took a moment for the blood to circulate back to my legs as they dragged me into the corridor between cells and marched me up the long flight of stairs to the Justice Hall.

I stepped outside the hall and onto the open landing that led down to the street below. Instead of finding my family there waiting to see me off, it looked like the entire clan had shown up to witness my banishment.

"Ayrion is forthwith banished from the Lost City," Brim said as he came to a stop alongside me. He projected his voice across the cavern for all to hear. "Any attempt to return is punishable by death."

Brim leaned over and lowered his voice so only those standing there could hear. "As you spend the rest of your miserable life alone with no home or family, you remember my son. I pray what time you have left will be long and excruciating."

The Primary took a step back and nodded for the guards to continue.

The street below was lined on both sides with the members of our clan. Brim had made sure that my banishment was as public and humiliating as possible. With what strength I had left, I held my head high. There was no way I was giving him the satisfaction of my breaking down in front of them. I was thankful I had cried out all my tears last night. It allowed me to present a stoic face as I was marched through the throng of watchers.

The crowds eventually thinned the closer we got to the tunnels leading up to the surface. So far, I hadn't seen my family. I started to panic as we headed into the shaft on the left. What if Brim had forbidden them to see me? What if he had made sure they couldn't give me supplies to survive on?

We reached the end of the tunnel and stepped into the open foyer. I held my hand up to block the light. The two guards motioned for me to continue, but instead of following, they turned and headed back down the tunnel, shaking their heads as they went. With the threat of death hanging over me if I attempted to return, they apparently felt there was no need to stand watch.

There was a small gathering waiting about halfway across the empty hall. The tears I had been holding back began to flow as soon as I recognized the faces. It was my family. I ran to greet them. "I didn't think you were coming. I figured the Primary had ordered you not to see me."

"Oh, he tried," Father said, laying one of my carry bags down beside my bow and quiver. "But I still have some influence. He doesn't know we're here."

Mother and Rianna rushed me at the same time, both squeezing as hard as they could. It was wonderful. Even Jorn attempted a hug.

"Can't you come with me?"

My parents looked at each other. Mother had tears in her eyes.

"We were up all night discussing it," she said. "But—"

Father sighed. "But there is a reason the Upaka live in the ruins of a dead city. We are shunned everywhere else. If we left with you, there would be no work, no way to buy food. No one is going to give someone like me a job, but they might be willing to take on a thirteen-year-old boy. The hard truth is, son, that you would stand a much better chance on your own."

I didn't know which was worse: having to hear the words, or knowing he was right.

Mother didn't say anything, she simply held me.

Father nudged the travel sack at my feet with his boot. "I've left you half the money from our contract. You earned it. If spent wisely, it should get you to Aramoor with enough left over to live on until you can find some form of work or apprenticeship."

"Aramoor?"

"It's the largest city in the five kingdoms and your best opportunity to find work. It's also large enough to stay hidden in if the need arises. I was giving this some thought last night. I suggest you stay with Hobb for a little while. He'll be able to offer some assistance. At the least, he can help you rustle up a horse and some supplies."

I was suddenly feeling very thankful for the instruction the ferryman had given me in tracking. I was going to need it to survive.

"You might try finding passage working on one of the barges traveling south down the Shemoa River. They could take you all the way to Aramoor if you're lucky."

I didn't know what to say. My mind was racing with everything he was telling me, as well as an endless number of other possibilities.

"Ayrion, I want you to have this." Father pulled off his signet ring and placed it in my hand.

I looked at it. It felt heavier than I had imagined. "I can't take this. It's yours."

"I don't need a ring to tell me I'm a warrior. I already know it." He closed my hand around the black onyx band with our clan's white rune. "I want you to have it."

I tried sliding it on my finger, but it was too big and fell off.

Father knelt and looked me in the eyes. "Every time you see this ring, I want you to remember your family. I want you to remember who you are. No matter what the council says, you are an

Upaka. And the day this ring fits your finger is the day you'll be old enough to claim your right as an Upakan warrior."

I wiped my eyes and looked at it. I'd longed for the day I would claim my own ring, but this was hardly the way I wanted to get it. I wanted to thank him, but my throat tightened as I fought back the tears. Before I could try again, my father wrapped his arms around me and held me tight. I didn't want him to ever let go.

After some very emotional hugs and kisses from my mother, Rianna, and even Jorn, we started for the front doors. Father led the way, letting Mother and Rianna walk beside me. Both were holding on to me, not wanting to let go. For the first time, I wasn't embarrassed by the display of affection.

Father made sure I had my shaders with me. I pulled them out and hung them around my neck.

"You be sure to wash every week," Mother said, cupping my face as fresh tears ran down her cheeks. "I know how you get. You're too much like your father." She broke into sobs. "I love you, my sweet boy."

Rianna hung on my neck. "I'll think about you every day, especially down at the pools. Don't break too many girls' hearts out there."

I hugged Jorn. "Take care of the others while I'm gone," I told him. "I know you'll make a great warrior one day."

Jorn smiled. He started to say something, but when nothing came out, he punched me in the arm and stepped back.

Father gave me his hand. "You've got a good head on those shoulders, Ayrion. Be sure to use it. Don't let others intimidate or misuse you. The world is a hard place, but if there was ever anyone I thought strong enough to make it, it would be you. And who knows; we may yet meet again. I'll be looking for your face with every new contract I take."

He took a step back beside Mother, and we all stood there in silence, memorizing each other's faces. I wondered how long it would take for them to fade. Taking a deep breath, I strapped on my sword, hung my bow and quiver around my neck, hefted my large travel sack over my shoulder, and lifted my shaders into place.

With a smile on my face, I turned and waited for the guard to open the door and then stepped into the early morning light. I knew I couldn't turn around—it would be far too painful—so I focused on putting one foot in front of the other. I wanted my family to see how strong I was. Maybe that would help them not worry so much about me when I was gone.

I didn't stop until I reached the top of the hill outside the ruins. With tears streaking both cheeks, I turned and stared down at the home I was no longer welcome to share, the life I was no longer welcome to live, and the family I would most likely never see again.

With a broken heart, I turned my back on the Lost City and started walking.

Chapter 21

EVEN THOUGH I WAS now quite familiar with the eastern route through the Squeeze, I had no intention of taking it. The last thing I needed was another run-in with the *good* townsfolk of Norshag. If I'd learned anything over the last month, it was to not tempt fate twice.

Instead, I headed south.

The landscape didn't change much. As long as I kept the Northern Heights on my left and Mount Ash on my right, I knew I was headed in the right direction.

It didn't take nearly as long for my eyes to adjust to the light as it had during my excursion to Oswell. By the second day, I was able to remove my shaders altogether. The road ahead was flat, and patches of dried field grass dotted the landscape on either side. It was a sea of nothing. At least, it was what I imagined a sea of nothing would look like, considering I had never seen a real sea.

Father had been to the Rhunarin Ocean once during a contract in Aramoor. He'd said it was the most amazing thing he had ever witnessed—water as far as the eye could see. Boats bigger than our house. I'd made it my mission to see this ocean for myself once I reached Aramoor. It helped keep my spirits up.

The constant moving during the day held back the chill in the air. I was never so thankful for the sun as when the first rays of dawn broke through every morning and warmed my face. It was still too early for snow, but the nights were cold. With no trees in sight, I had to scrounge for loose brush to light a fire in the evening. By the time morning came, the embers and their warmth were long gone.

I'd walked for four days without any sign of human life. It appeared that the rest of Aldor had no desire to visit this part of the world. With the destruction left by the volcano, and the only civilization for miles being Upaka, it was no wonder travelers were few.

By the fifth day, I had reached the southern tip of the Northern Heights. The ground was rocky, and the air burned my lungs as the plume from Mount Ash shifted in my direction. Every now and then, the old mountain would grumble and remind me it was still there.

It was one of those ground shakes that had me breaking camp before first light. Spending so much time out in the open was weighing heavily on me. I felt exposed. I wasn't sure what the opposite of claustrophobia was, but I found myself really missing the

enclosed tunnels beneath the Lost City. The sensation was much stronger this time with my father not there to take my mind off it with another one of his tales of adventure.

After a quick breakfast of cheese and half an apple, rinsed down with some water collected from a stream the day before, I glanced at Father's map to get my bearings. The map not only showed the major landmarks and roads between kingdoms, it also marked the best places to find water. So far, it seemed accurate.

I rolled my heavy blanket up and placed it on top of my pack. Normally, I would have worried about blisters on my back from the straps, but considering I was wearing three shirts and my heavy cloak just to keep warm, I didn't think that would be much of a problem. The shirts came off one at a time as the day warmed, and usually by the end, I was down to a single woolen tunic and my cloak.

Before the sun had reached its crest, I was nearing the end of the first leg of my journey. Up ahead, the road on which I was traveling merged with a larger one running east to west. The deep ruts on each side let me know that heavy wagons frequented the spot. I stopped at the crossway and looked behind me, wondering if I would ever be this way again, or if this was to be the last time I would ever see the great mountains.

I took my time eating lunch. It wasn't like I had somewhere pressing to be, and my feet needed the rest. Before I had finished, I noticed a thick cloud of dust hovering over the road to the west. I was going to have company, and judging by the size of the cloud, it was a large group.

I looked around for a place to hide, but there wasn't one. Even the sporadic patches of tall grass were gone. It appeared I didn't have much choice but to wait for whoever it was to pass.

It didn't take long for the caravan to reach me. By the time they did, I had my bow out and strung and hanging loosely from my shoulder. Half a dozen horsemen surrounded four wagons, each laden with heavy crates and barrels. Two of the wagons were covered in heavy canvas. The dirt caked on the men's clothing spoke to the amount of traveling they'd seen.

"Whoa there," the first driver said as he brought his team to a halt. I was enveloped by a thick cloud of dust and silt from the road, forcing me to hold my breath till it passed. "Mite young to be wandering about these parts." The man speaking was heavyset, with a full beard braided halfway down. He took a good look at me once the dust passed. "Never mind," he said, spitting to the side. "You're one of them." He motioned with his head back in the direction I'd just come. "A bit far from home, aren't you?"

I looked at the hard stares from the other men and straightened my shoulders. "I have business in Oswell," I said, letting the tips of my fingers stroke the top of my sword. I kept the other hand resting firmly on my bow. The horsemen stayed close to the wagons, protectively so. Their swords were sheathed, but there was a wariness in their eyes I didn't trust. I was suddenly curious as to what they had hidden under the canvas.

"Do you, now? And what kind of business could an Upakan youngster have in Oswell? A little scrawny to be doing much killin'." A couple of the men snickered.

"My business is my own," I said, not wanting to appear weak.

"Ah, to be sure," the head wagoner said as he stroked his long beard. "It's a wise man who knows when to keep his mouth shut." He relaxed against the back of his seat and let the reins fall in his lap. "Of course, it's a wiser man still who knows not to travel these roads alone." He smiled, and it wasn't the friendly sort of smile that leaves you wanting to smile back. It was the sort of smile that made you reach for your sword.

My hand tightened on my bow. "I appreciate the warning."

The man's smile vanished. "It wasn't a warning."

I cocked my head. "Pardon?" My back began to prickle, and my mouth was suddenly as dry as the dust swirling around my ankles, a clear indicator that something was wrong.

"What's the matter, boy? Was I not plainspoken enough for you? Whoever decided to leave you out here did you no favor."

I looked around. "I . . ." For once, I had no idea what to say.

"Like I said, not too wise."

Frantically, I ran through my options. Fighting them was out of the question. Even with the aid of magic, there were too many. I doubted they even felt the need to draw a sword, considering how outnumbered I was. My only advantage was that I appeared to be the only one carrying a strung bow.

"I don't want any trouble," I said, backing away slowly, generally the first response anyone in trouble does without thinking. I was in full self-preservation mode.

"Well, son, that's a good thing. 'Cause, to be honest, I don't want any either. So, you just hand over that travel pack of yours and empty your pockets, and we'll be on our way."

Clearly, my luck hadn't changed. Out here in the wild, losing your gear was a death sentence.

"I need my stuff to get to Oswell," I said with little hope that talking to the man was going to have any effect. But for some reason, I felt compelled to try. Like a victim begging for his life, it left a sour taste in my mouth, but better my mouth than my gut after being run through with one of their swords.

I counted their heads once again—six riders, four wagoners. Maybe it would be best just to give them my stuff. There was at least a chance I could survive without it.

"Your needs matter little to me," the bearded man said, eyeing my pack. "All I care about is what you have stuffed away in that satchel and the price it will fetch at market." His expression grew serious. "Like that ring." The wagoner shifted in his seat as he leaned forward. "Where'd you get it? Looks valuable."

The breath caught in my throat, and my hand reached for the center of my chest. I hadn't realized my father's ring had come untucked from my shirt. It must have been when I was looking at it during lunch. I might have been able to survive without my gear, but there was no way they were taking my ring.

I tucked it back into my shirt and took another couple of steps back, glancing over my shoulder. There was a small outcropping of rock leading up to the foothills behind me, but I'd never reach it on foot. They'd run me down with their horses before I could make it even partway. Hand-to-hand combat was out. My only chance was to put as much distance between them as I could and use my bow.

"Don't be stupid, boy. Just hand over the stuff, and we'll be on our way."

I turned and ran. I unhooked my bow from my shoulder and pulled the first arrow.

"Well, what are you all waiting for?" the wagoner shouted at the others behind me. "Go get him!"

As soon as I heard the horses' hooves, I turned and drew the bowstring to my chin. There was no point in running farther; I'd gone as far as I could. With a deep breath, I took aim and released.

The arrow flew true, and the lead horseman dropped. Before he hit the dirt, I had the next arrow out and nocked. I aimed again. They were nearly on me. The string thrummed, and the man on the right fell.

This wasn't going to work. I'd only get one more shot off before they had me, and then it would be over. I bit my tongue, fighting to maintain focus. What could I do? I had to do something. Out of desperation, I changed tactics and drew the final arrow to my chin, but instead of aiming for the horsemen, I aimed for someone else.

I released another arrow and it flew over the riders and straight for the wagons.

The head wagoner screamed as the shaft buried itself in his side. He nearly tumbled from his seat as he juggled the reins and the arrow at the same time. "Fall back! Fall back!" I could hear the fear in his voice. The crack of a whip echoed off the rocks behind me, and the wagons took off.

I reached for another arrow, but by the time I'd pulled it from the quiver and turned, the remaining riders had turned and were heading for the wagons. I could still hear the bearded man's mournful wails as the cloud of dust once again rose in their wake, hiding the bandits from view.

I couldn't believe it had worked. Apparently, a well-placed shot to the lower abdomen had been enough to convince the man he didn't want to stick around and take the chance of catching another. It seemed people who preyed on others were nothing but cowards.

My hands were shaking by the time I placed the arrow back in its quiver and went to collect the other two. Clearly, there was no honor among highway thieves such as this, since they had left their fallen comrades behind, along with whatever possessions they had on them.

I stared at the two men, their eyes lifeless as they looked up at me. I waited for the stabbing pain of regret to reach up and suffocate me as it had with Flon. But it never did. Flon's death had been unexpected, an accident. As much as I'd wanted him to suffer, I hadn't wanted to kill him.

With these men, I knew what I was doing, but somehow, the feeling didn't overwhelm me like it had before. Maybe it was because I didn't have a personal connection with them, or maybe it was because I knew they had every intention of stealing my possessions and leaving me to an excruciating death in the wilderness.

I pulled my arrows from their chests and rummaged through their belongings. They certainly wouldn't have use for their stuff

now. No sense in letting it go to waste.

The two thugs must have been paid very well for their services or had stolen from other poor souls along the way, because each had a thick purse brimming with more than just coppers. Even more valuable than the coin were the two horses the men had left. I tied my gear to the first and mounted the second. My travel time had just lessened considerably.

Maybe my luck was turning.

I glanced at the two bodies, sprawled out in the sun, and felt a twinge of guilt at not burying them. But considering what they had intended to do to me, it was no more than they deserved. I tied the second horse to the first, and with a snap of leather, we headed east.

Chapter 22

THE JOURNEY AROUND the lower foothills, through the forests south of Norshag, and across the open plains below the Slags proved uneventful. After my near miss with bandits, this was a welcome relief.

I spent my days enjoying the beauty of the countryside as I carried on a number of meaningful conversations with my new companions. The horses seemed to enjoy the attention and didn't complain about me talking too much.

Having put Hobb's instruction to the test, my meals consisted mostly of fresh coney, along with a boar I had managed to track using what the ferryman had shown me of their rubs and wallows. I even speared a few trout out of a passing stream, but when I swallowed a bone that took nearly an entire day to wiggle free, I decided to stick to land animals from then on.

It was a good feeling, not being dependent on others. I could do what I wanted, when I wanted, and how I wanted. I wished my parents could have seen me. Even still, as much as I enjoyed the time to myself, I found it rather lonely. I found myself dwelling on the direction my life had taken.

It was the first time I didn't have an answer for the future. My life had been planned since I was old enough to walk. I was to be a warrior, like my father.

I lifted the chain from under my shirt and stared at my father's ring. The black onyx band was just a reminder of what I had lost. I let it fall against my chest. Everything had fallen apart, like a shape in the clouds, there one moment and gone the next, and there was nothing I could do about it.

It was during one of those broodings that my horse whinnied and came to a stop, forcing me to grab the saddle or be dumped off. Looking up, I noticed we had finally reached the Shemoa River, which was a pleasant surprise. I hadn't expected to make it this far for another couple of days.

I let the horses graze off the tall grass while I pulled out the map to see where along the river we were. I knew I was somewhere south of where I wanted to be, since I had taken a lower trek through the grasslands to keep from running into another razorback. The problem was that all the bends on the map looked alike. I had no idea where I was.

I put the map back in its pouch and turned the horses northward. We traveled the edge of the river for most of the day before finally spotting Hobb's Crossing ahead. A trail of smoke rose in the distance, letting me know the ferryman was home.

Seeing the old place brought back some cheerful feelings as I rode through the front gate. The ferry was back on this side of the river and tied to the dock below. Hobb had replaced the broken boards on the railing where I had ridden through to save his life.

I swung down and stretched before tying the horses in front of the house. Something inside smelled good. Grabbing the brace of coneys I'd killed earlier that day, I climbed the steps to the porch. I'd planned on using them as a peace offering.

Clearing my throat, I knocked on the front door and took a step back. I couldn't help but smile as I waited for Hobb to open it. I'd been practicing all day what I was going to say when I got there: *Surprise! Guess who. Bet you didn't expect to see me again.*

No one answered.

I knocked again and waited. Apparently, either Hobb was too busy to answer, or he wasn't inside.

With a frustrated grunt, I slung the rabbits over my shoulder and made my way down the steps and around back. Inside the stables, a single horse was in its stall, but there was no sign of Hobb, so I headed for the small guest quarters Father and I had stayed in the last time we'd been there. The front door was cracked, and I could hear something going on inside. The closer I got the more I realized it was singing. Well, as close to singing as Hobb could get. I'd heard wild animals out on the plains that sounded better than the racket pouring out of the cracked doorway.

As quietly as I could, I slid the door open and peeked inside.

Hobb was in the corner sweeping behind one of the beds. It reminded me of the time we'd snuck into the Golden Tassel and scared Miss Milly. The thought brought a mischievous smile to my face.

With as little noise as possible, I made my way across the room. I didn't recognize his song, but as loud as he was belting out the melody, he wouldn't have heard me if I had ridden my horse inside.

Hobb was just leaning over to sweep his latest pile into the pan when I reached out and grabbed his sides.

"Gotcha!"

"Ahhh!" Hobb jumped straight into the wall, scattering the pile of dirt. "What the flaming blazes?" He swung his broom around and I ducked. "Who . . ."

I stood there grinning proudly like a trainee having passed his first round of tests.

"Ayrion?"

"Yep! It's me!" Hours of practicing what I was going to say went up in smoke with a simple *Yep. It's me.*

"Boy! I oughta tan your hide with this broom."

"Imagine if I'd been here on a contract."

Hobb wiped his forehead. "I prefer not to." He looked around the empty quarters. "Where's your father? For that matter, why are you here? You just left a few weeks ago. Surely, you haven't received another job in Oswell already."

"Father's not here. It's just me." I pulled the tied coneys from my shoulder and held them out, hoping to put Hobb in a better mood.

One look at the rabbits and he lowered the broom with a brisk sigh. "Well, come on up to the house and you can tell me all about it. I reckon you'll be wanting a place for the night?"

I nodded, not sure what else to say. If he found out I was looking to have the place for a bit longer, he might tell me to move on.

"Fine, fine," Hobb said as he walked across the bunkroom, carrying the rabbits by their feet. "I'll have supper ready shortly. You know where the stables are, so see to your horse and make sure you wash up before you come. Should be ready by then." With that, the ferryman was out the door. I noticed he left the broom and pan with me.

After stabling and unloading my gear in the bunkhouse, I headed down the steps to the river and washed up. The water was too cold to stick my head under this time, so I used a cloth to wipe my neck and under the collar of my shirt. I'd have to do a better job of it tomorrow; I was too tired and saddle-worn to worry about it today.

I left the dock and walked up to the house. The sun was just beginning to set in the distance, leaving a rather gaudy display of colors in the swift-moving sky. I took a moment to enjoy it. Somehow, watching it from the security of Hobb's front porch as opposed to the backside of a horse out in the middle of the Keldoran Plains made me appreciate it even more.

The smell of stew caught my attention, so I knocked on the front door.

"Come in," Hobb said. "No need to knock."

I opened the door, wiping my boots on the baseboard before stepping in. The inside of Hobb's house hadn't changed at all. A few more pieces of long lumber decorated the entranceway, along with half a bedframe, but other than that, Hobb's home felt as warm and inviting as ever.

The smell of fresh-cut wood was intoxicating. It was one of the small pleasures I had discovered since leaving my underground estate. There seemed to be a never-ending source of new smells just waiting to be sniffed out.

"Take a seat. Stew's ready."

I sat in the same seat I had used the last time we were there. I could have taken the one at the opposite end of the table to better see Hobb, but somehow, it just didn't feel right.

Hobb dished me out a bowl and handed it over.

"Smells delicious," I said as I placed the steaming platter in front of me. I took another whiff before picking up my spoon. "Let me guess . . . rabbit."

"Fish."

My spoon hovered between my mouth and the bowl. "Fish?"

"Well, mostly. There's also some leftover pieces of pork, pheasant, tree rat, and hedgehog." He motioned for me to continue. I wasn't sure I wanted to. "Go on. It won't kill you. I cleaned out the pantry to make room for fresh stock."

At this point, I was too hungry to care. He could have told me it was week-old river eel, and I'd probably have stuffed my face till I popped. Apart from the various textures, I couldn't tell much of a difference, and by the end of the meal, I'd eaten at least three bowls' worth.

"You Upakans have quite the appetite."

I looked up after licking out the rest of my final helping. "Maybe we're just not used to food that tastes this good."

"Living where you do, I imagine not," Hobb said as he dropped his spoon on his platter and left the table. "I reckon cave lizard can get old mighty fast." He smiled as he took his seat by the fire and lit his pipe.

I couldn't tell if he was trying to be funny. Washing the meal down with the rest of my watered-down ale, I carried my chair over to join him.

"Tell me a story, Master Ayrion." Hobb leaned forward and held his pipe out to me. "Puff?"

My parents had always warned me that taking up the pipe would slow me down. That it could do me harm. But I didn't want to look like a child, so I took it, stuck it in my mouth, and inhaled.

Not even Master Dorin's whip had burned that bad.

I dropped the pipe and nearly lit the floorboards when the embers fell out on impact. I coughed so hard, I thought I was going to lose my insides. My eyes watered like they had the day Flon had killed one of my wolf cubs. What was worse, instead of helping me, Hobb leaned back in his chair and bellowed with laughter, smacking his leg hard enough to leave a welt.

I stumbled out of my seat and downed half the pitcher of ale before the burning subsided. I was lightheaded from the drink, but at least my throat wasn't on fire.

Hobb was still laughing when I made it back to my seat. I

couldn't tell which of us was crying harder. Anyone stupid enough to do that willingly deserved the punishment that came with it.

"That's the funniest thing I've seen in years." Hobb wiped his eyes. "Oh, boy, I needed that." He looked at me and laughed some more. "Here," he said, handing me a piece of cloth. "Wipe your nose."

He leaned over, picked up his pipe, and stamped out the embers with his boot before refilling the tobacco from a pouch he wore around his neck. With a thin piece of kindling, he lit it once again and puffed a couple of rings into the air. "So, how about that story."

"Wha . . ." I had to take another swallow from the glass I'd poured to clear my throat. "What do you want to hear?"

"I want to hear how it is an eleven-year-old boy ca—"

"Thirteen."

"What's that?"

"I'm thirteen."

"My apologies," Hobb said with a slight bow of his head. "How a *thirteen*-year-old boy came to be wandering across the Keldoran wilderness all alone." He leaned forward and whispered, "Is this one of those rites of passage to manhood I've heard tell about?" He didn't wait for me to respond. "'Cause let me tell you, son, the first time you notice a woman . . . that's when you know you're a man." He leaned back in his chair and took a short pull on his pipe. "That's also the day you know that your life will never be simple again."

I opened my mouth, but Hobb beat me to it. "Just look at me.

One day, master of my own life; the next, selling it all off to go live comfortably in town." He shook his head. "Women. Funny creatures, they are. Like pixies. They put thoughts in your head and make you think they're your own." He took a longer draw and released it slowly, watching as the wispy strand rose into the rafters.

"What do you mean, selling it all off?" I asked, leaning forward in my seat.

Hobb sighed and placed his elbows on his knees. "I agreed to marry Milly."

There was a long moment of silence.

"That's great," I said, then looked at his sour expression. "Isn't it?"

"I thought it was, until she decided it would be better for me to move into town and help her with the inn than for her to move out here and help me with the ferry." Hobb raised his hands in frustration. "What do I know of keeping an inn? I'm no cook and cleaner."

"You're good with your hands, though," I said, trying to find something positive. "You've kept Hobb's Crossing running all these years. The Golden Tassel is just a large way station."

Hobb leaned back in his seat and stared at the fire. "Aye, that's true. Those sheds of hers are in pitiful need of repair, not to mention the work on that barn she calls a stable." He sat there pondering a moment before shaking his head and turning to look at me. "How'd we get to talking about my problems? I wanted to hear your story." He gestured at me with his pipe. "Where were we?"

I wondered where to begin.

"I was banished." The words sort of jumped out of my mouth before I could stop them.

Hobb moved his pipe to the other side of his mouth and continued chewing. "Banished, huh?" He puffed some more. "What for?"

My hands were clasped together in my lap. "For killing someone."

Hobb stared at me a moment, then broke into another round of laughter. "I thought that's what you people were paid to do."

"I killed our clan chief's son."

His laughter stopped. "Oh. What do you plan on doing now?"

I shrugged. "Father said to come find you. You're the only person out here that I know."

Hobb scratched the back of his neck. "Well, I would have been happy to take you on here. Creator knows I could have used the help, and company, but . . . with me looking to sell the place and move in to Oswell, I'm not sure what to tell you. I could see if Milly's got room there for you, maybe some work, but to be honest, I don't think Oswell would be a good fit for an Upaka. Too much bad blood living this close to the Lost City—"

"I'm planning on going to Aramoor."

"Aramoor?" Hobb leaned forward and tapped the embers from his pipe into the fire. "Yes, that could work. A city that size would be easy to get lost in. Lots of foreigners coming in and out of the port. Probably a lot more willing to turn a blind eye to one of your kind." He looked at me. "No offense, of course."

I smiled. "Those were the same reasons Father told me to go there as well. He said I should try getting passage on one of the boats heading south. That I could take the Shemoa all the way to Aramoor."

"Aye, she flows right into the city, but those rivermen are a tough breed. And with winter coming, the last of the ships would have already taken off. The river ices during the colder months. It's too dangerous to take shipments down. You'd have to wait till spring." He pointed at me with his pipe. "I'll tell you what. I've got plenty of work still to do around here. Should take me all winter to finish. You help me get this place ready for sale, and I'll see to it you get passage downriver." Hobb stuck his pipe in his mouth and held out his hand. "Deal?"

I stared at it for a moment. Spring. That was at least a good four months off. Did I want to wait that long, or could I possibly find someone willing to take me now? Of course, did I want to travel downriver with my fingers and toes frozen and my teeth chattering like a tree rat?

I smiled and took his hand. "Deal."

Chapter 23

M Y TIME SPENT WITH Hobb over the next few months proved to be better than I had a right to expect. It was strange not having the burdens of Upakan society weighing me down. Like a heavy stone tied to an exhausted swimmer, the constant need to be the best at everything I did had been drowning me. For once, I didn't have to worry about training a certain number of hours every day, never knowing if the next set of testing was going to land me in front of the Peltok or not.

Not to say my time with Hobb was idle. We worked hard every day. I laid my head on my pillow each night feeling like I had accomplished something of worth. By the time spring arrived and the last of the winter ice thawed, we had rebuilt part of the guest quarters, added a couple more stalls to the stables, and cleaned both the inside and out of the main house, which in my opinion took longer than the rest combined.

It had been a good feeling to look at the old river station and see the difference we'd made since my arrival. My own blood and sweat had been added to the mix. I hoped he found a buyer. As much as he'd helped me, he deserved it.

We rode the three days from Hobb's Crossing to the town of Cretollo, passing the time with tales of Hobb's years spent on the water. As a young man, he had worked as a deckhand on several ships sailing the Shemoa before finally settling down, and Cretollo was the first city in which he had been apprenticed.

Riding into the city, he remarked on how little things had changed. Docks lined the river, stretching out to ships of all shapes and sizes for the loading and unloading of goods. There were boats small enough for just a single occupant, and others large enough to have one or two *sails*, as Hobb called them.

These were the first boats I'd ever seen, other than Hobb's ferry and the drawings in some of my books. The thought of riding on one had me pushing my horse even faster. We tethered our horses outside one of the shipping warehouses and walked inside.

The open room was packed full. The smell of fish and sweat hung in the air, but underneath it was a hint of spice and vinegar, no doubt part of the cargo being loaded.

Tables were lined near the back and side walls, each bearing the colors of the ship and captain they represented. The captains were busy filling their books with customers looking to either ship goods, order goods, or book passage. Hobb pointed out that most of the ones standing in line were shopkeepers looking to restock their supplies now that the winter ice had broken. There were at least five other customers in line behind us, waiting to see this particular ship owner.

I studied the flow of the warehouse and its people as Hobb set about purchasing my ticket. I hadn't been paying much attention to his conversation until I heard him raise his voice.

"You owe me, Tillman."

I stopped watching some of the customers and stepped over to see what was going on. Hobb had a dangerous edge to his voice. Across the table, a short, nervous man, with a pointed nose and narrow eyes, stared at us over his spectacles. There was a thick ledger open in front of him on the desk, filled with numbers in neat, organized columns.

"Impossible, I tell you," Tillman said with a high-pitched voice, brandishing his quill like a weapon. "The boats are already full. Passage was booked in advance. What do you want me to do, tell a paying customer that I'm revoking their passage to make room for a nonpaying one?" He looked in my direction, but only briefly, and not in the eyes.

I could see that Hobb and my father were right. I would never be able to fit into a smaller community. All because my eyes were different than theirs. I tried donning my best smile, the same one I'd saved for when Mother found a scone or two missing from the plate and rightly assumed it was I who took them.

Just like everything else in my life, it didn't work.

"Tillman, this is nonsense." Hobb's face was getting redder by the moment. "I passed your boats heading in, and they aren't half-filled yet. You've got plenty of room." He leaned across the table. "I ferried your goods upriver last year while one of your boats was down for repairs." Hobb pointed at the captain. "You owe me."

The little man bit the nails on his left hand, looking at the growing line behind us. "Hobb, you know I would. But . . . but . . ." He glanced around nervously and leaned forward. "If I let one of them on board," he said without looking directly at me, "I'll lose my other passengers." He lowered his voice even more. "You know how people feel about . . . White Eyes."

"White Eyes!" a lady behind us said, having done her best to eavesdrop. "You're ferrying Upakans?" Her head darted back and forth as if expecting an assassin's blade to pop up at any moment. She grabbed one of her bags. "I'll be seeking passage elsewhere," she said with a huff. "Don't want my throat slit in my sleep."

Tillman stood halfway out of his seat. "But, madam—"

The woman made a garish scene of gathering the rest of her baggage before prancing over to another line.

"See there, Hobb," Tillman said, pointing at the lost passenger. "Look what you've done. I won't take no Whi . . . Upakans on my boats; I don't care what I owe—"

"I'll take him," a gruff voice said on our right. A grim-faced man sitting two tables down turned and looked our way. His eyes were hard, as was the rest of him. A dark, well-groomed beard covered a strong face, coming to a soft point below the chin. His skin was as tough and weathered as old boot leather, no doubt from too many hours in the sun, and he wore a long brown trench coat that reached to the floor where he sat waiting behind his table. The line in front of his booth wasn't nearly as long as the other captains'. In fact, there was no one there at all.

"Over my dead body," Hobb said, pulling me close. "Don't think I haven't heard the rumors, Treygan, about your boat and where you take it. Half your shipments never make port, and those that do tend to be lighter than when you started out."

"All the more reason to have an Upaka on board, wouldn't you say?" the man said, pointing in my direction. The wide cuffs of his sleeves rose when he did, revealing a long scar on his right arm. "And let's be honest: no self-respecting captain 'round here is going to let one of the White Eyes on board his ship, not even a runt like that one."

I balled my fists, but he had a point. As fast as Tillman's line had cleared at the very mention of Upaka, this Treygan fellow was probably my only chance of getting to Aramoor. "Maybe we should take his offer," I said, glancing behind me as the last of the people in our line quickly scattered.

Hobb laid a hand on my shoulder. "Treygan can't be trusted, lad. Something ain't right with his shipments. Some say his boat is cursed. Best we find passage elsewhere."

"Where?" I asked, looking around the warehouse.

Hobb turned and scanned the room as well, but the eyes of the other captains told us we'd get no better welcome than we did with Tillman. Hobb sighed, then turned and pointed at the mousy man in front of us. "I won't forget this, Tillman. Your crews will pay handsomely to dock at Hobb's Crossing from now on." It might have been an empty threat on Hobb's part, since he had every intention of selling, but Tillman didn't know that. Hobb stormed out of Tillman's line. "Come on," he said as he grabbed my pack and started for Treygan.

"Wise choice," Treygan said with a smile as he leaned back in his seat. He didn't look like a man you wanted to cross.

Hobb dropped my pack beside the table and grunted. "Well, what's your price?"

Treygan looked me over while digging at the dirt under his nails with his belt knife. The blade had a beautiful sort of curve to it, and the handle looked to be made from bone. It looked human, and the way the captain spun it in his hand let me know it wasn't just for show. "You any good with that?" he asked, pointing the knife at my bow.

"Try robbing me and you'll find out," I said, not wanting to show fear.

Treygan laughed and laid the blade down in front of him. "He's an Upaka, all right. I'll take him."

"What do you mean you'll take him?" Hobb asked. "We haven't settled on a price."

"I'm short on crew at the moment—"

"Now, there's a surprise," Hobb said as he leaned on the table.

Treygan scowled, then looked at me. "You a fast learner, boy?"

I looked at Hobb, then back at Treygan, and nodded.

"Then I'll bring you on board as a deckhand. You can work alongside the other rivermen, and as long as you can keep up with your duties, you'll get a cot, three hot ones, and a share of whatever we haul at the end."

Hobb adjusted his belt. "Well, that's not saying much, since half the time, your ships barely make it to port at all."

"I'll take it," I said before Hobb could stop me. I wasn't going to find passage anywhere else, and it would be best not to antagonize Treygan about it before I boarded his ship, or it would be all the harder for me later on. Besides, at this point, I'd have done it for free as long as it got me to where I needed to go. I was Upakan, after all. Learning new things was mandatory, and with magic like mine, I'd be running the river in no time.

"Done," Treygan said, his meaty hand slapping the table. "Grab your gear and I'll have Bones take you on board and show you around." He looked past me to the other side of the room. "Bones!"

From the back of the warehouse, a dark object bobbed up and down as it moved through the crowd. I was taken aback when I realized it was the top of a man's head. His skin was as dark as the soles of my boots. I'd read about some of the dark-colored tribes who lived on the southern island, but I'd never seen a member of one before.

The man with the dark skin looked like he hadn't eaten in weeks. He was nothing but skin and—

"Bones," Treygan said. "I've just hired a new deckhand. Take him on board and give him the grand tour."

"Aye, aye, Captain. As you wish." Bones turned, and his clothes whipped around with him. If not for the rope around his waist, his trousers would have been lying on the floor. They were as baggy as the bottom of a fat woman's skirt. He looked at Hobb. "Well, get a move on with ya. Sun's burning in the sky."

"Not me," Hobb said. "The boy."

Bones turned, got one look at me, and shook his head. "Captain, it's bad luck to have one of them on board." He drew an *X* on his chest and then spat to the side.

"Hang your superstitious nonsense," Treygan said. "I'm the captain, and if I say he's coming with us, then he's coming with us."

Bones spared a wary glance my direction, then looked back at Treygan. "Aye, aye. Your ship, your say. I just don't want to be failin' in my duties as first to speak my piece."

"Well, as first, it's your duty to put our young deckhand to work. Stow his gear below with the rest of the shipment."

"Aye, Captain," Bones said, then turned to me. "This way."

The look in his eyes let me know this was going to be a long trip.

Chapter 24

$H$OBB WALKED WITH me from the warehouse down to the docks. It was a short walk, but the closer we got, the louder it became. Wagons and flatbeds laden with crates, barrels, and loose containers lined the street as far as I could see, their drivers shouting orders as they pulled their teams up in front of the walkways leading to the docks.

Men dressed in the same loose-fitting clothing as Bones scurried up and down the piers loading and unloading the cargo. Many of the rivermen had tied their pants to just above the calves with long socks stretching all the way to the knee. I couldn't understand why until I watched them scale the ropes up to the tops of the masts. The shorter legs kept their pants baggy enough to move unencumbered. I wondered if I would be required to do the same.

The rivermen were a colorful lot. Most wore vests or heavy

overcoats. Some had hats that billowed in the wind, and others, scarves that hung loose about the neck or were tied around the forehead. Many had pierced ears, some had pierced noses, lips, and even brows.

"Are you sure about this, Ayrion?" Hobb asked as we stood at the head of the first dock, looking down the long row of ships. "You're welcome to come back with me."

A couple of piers down, Bones waited for us to say our good-byes.

"I wouldn't be accepted in Oswell any more than I am here," I said. "I need to get farther away from the Lost City."

"Well, you certainly can't get much farther than Aramoor," Hobb said with a huff. "I don't like the thought of you traveling alone." He cleared his throat. "I've enjoyed having you around." His voice broke and he took a moment to compose himself. "If I'd ever had a son . . ." He didn't seem to know how to say what he wanted, but I thought I understood. I smiled. It was probably one of the nicest things anyone had ever said to me.

"He would be a lucky boy."

Hobb knelt and wrapped his big ferryman arms around me. They were strong and comforting. It reminded me of my father's final hug. I hugged him back. "You be careful, you hear," Hobb said. "Keep your eyes open. I wasn't foolin' when I said there's something off about Treygan and his crew." He waited for me to nod before continuing. "And remember, if you ever have need, you know where to find me."

"I'll be careful," I said, not wanting to let go.

By the time we did, I had to wipe my eyes. I was glad to see I wasn't the only one.

"Here," Hobb said. "Take this." He handed me a small pouch of coins. "It isn't much, but it should help."

"I can't take this—"

"You can, and you will," he said, with a stern look that let me know not to argue. Hobb stood to his feet. "I wish you well, Ayrion. May the Creator guide your steps and keep you safe as you walk them."

I wasn't sure if I believed in the Creator, but I appreciated the sentiment nonetheless. I tucked the small coin pouch in my trouser pocket and hugged him one last time before turning and walking the wide planks leading past the front of the ships.

He was still waving when I glanced back over my shoulder. Would this be the last time I saw him? The last time I shared a bowl of coney stew or sat by the fire while he smoked his pipe? My emotions threatened to get the better of me, and I dried my eyes on my sleeve.

I didn't look back again.

"Watch it, now," Bones said.

I jumped to the left to keep from colliding with a single-wheeled hauler racing across the planks in the opposite direction. The sailor never faltered. He would have run flat over me without stopping. Each of the haulers was stacked with goods as tall as the men wheeling them. I kept waiting for two to collide, but they never did.

Bones motioned us on. Even among the chaos, there seemed to

be a semblance of order. Those coming off the ships took the right side of the boardwalk, closest to the water. Those coming from the warehouse took the left.

The river was much wider here than it was at Hobb's Crossing. I couldn't believe how many boats had made berth, another term Hobb had taught me during my stay. He had wanted to make sure I knew as much about sailing the river as I could before making this trip. At the time, I hadn't been sure I'd cared to know, but now that I found myself in the unexpected position of having to join a ship's crew rather than being a passenger, that knowledge was going to be extremely useful.

With each ship we passed, I looked up and wondered if this would be the one. Some I hoped weren't, because of their small size and sad shape. Others made me hold my breath in anticipation, only to sigh when we didn't stop.

Bones marched down the dock like a man not to be ignored—head up, stride steady, eyes straight ahead. The other rivermen gave him a wide berth. Those sitting on the wall to our left whispered among themselves as we passed. I couldn't hear what was said, but the sniggers and head-wagging didn't leave much need. Was it because Bones was part of Treygan's crew? Or because of the color of his skin? Maybe the people around here weren't any more used to seeing a dark man than I was. It appeared Bones and I had more in common than I thought.

Up ahead was a gap in the boats. Two piers lay empty between the ship floating at the end and the rest of them. It was as though the other captains had purposely kept their boats moored as far from it as they could. Of course, that was the one we were heading for.

What was it about this ship and its captain that had every other vessel afraid to go near it? Then again, maybe it wasn't that they were afraid. Maybe they were simply ostracizing the captain for some reason. That thought lifted my spirits a little. It would mean I had something in common with Treygan as well.

The empty space between the ships gave me a chance to get a good look at Treygan's vessel. It was large enough to have a sail but not large enough to need two. The wood was dark, much darker than the other boats. There was a sleek design to the hull that the others didn't have. It appeared to have been crafted more for speed than strength.

"What's this?" a short, stout man asked as we rounded the bow of the ship and started down the dock. He stood at the top of the gangplank, wearing a long white apron that flapped in the breeze, giving him the distinct appearance of wearing a short skirt. Like many of the others, he had piercings in both ears. He also had the longest mustache I'd ever seen. Both sides hung below his chin. "Since when did the captain start taking on passengers?" he asked as he walked down the gangway to meet us. He looked me over and grunted. "And a White Eyes at that." He made the same *X* on his chest that Bones had and spat over the side.

"Captain's orders," Bones said. "This be our new deckhand."

"Deckhand?" The shorter man laughed. "If he were any smaller, we could turn him upside-down and use him for a mop."

I smiled, hoping the jab was in good fun, and held out my

hand. "I'm Ayrion."

The short man wiped his hands on the front of his apron and folded his arms. "It be a sad day when we be forced to take on the likes of this one."

"Move aside, Kettle," Bones said. "The captain's what runs this ship, and he says we take him."

Kettle puffed out his chest but eventually moved aside to let us pass.

I nodded politely as we did and followed Bones up the gangway, receiving a sneer from Kettle for my efforts.

The ramp lifted slightly with the swaying of the ship, forcing me to shift my balance to keep from tripping. It was a strange sensation, walking across something that was constantly moving. I had a feeling it was going to take a while to get used to.

We were met on deck by an older gentleman with thinning white hair. Along with his very bushy eyebrows, he had a thick truss of whiskers that stretched clear down to his waist. It was neatly braided and tied off at the end with colored beads. Like many of the other watermen, he wore a vest over his baggy shirt, and the cuffs of his pants fell to just above the ankle, revealing a thinning frame.

"Welcome aboard, son," the old man said as he pulled an ornate pipe from his mouth and pointed down the plank with it. "Pay no never mind to Kettle. He'd scoff at his own reflection if he ever had occasion to see it."

Kettle growled and then headed down the dock, grumbling the entire way about no one listening to common reason.

"The name be Tressle," the old man said with a bow, "but everyone just calls me Pops." He swept his hand around in a flourish. "This be the *Wind Binder*. She's the fastest ship from here to the Rhunarin, and possibly beyond. I don't care what those other sad excuses for captains tell ya. There's no ship's been built that can catch her."

"My name's Ayrion, sir. I'm happy to make your acquaintance."

"No need to be so formal, son," he said with a dismissive wave. "Will ya be staying with us long, Master Ayrion?"

"Captain's brought him on as our new deckhand," Bones said with about as much enthusiasm one would expect from someone tasked with keeping an eye on an Upaka. "So, I reckon he won't be with us long. Take him below and stow his gear. I've got things to tend to before we sail."

"Aye, aye, First, it'll be my pleasure." Pops stuck his pipe back in his mouth. "This way, my lad. Watch your step, now. The rigging can reach up and grab your leg when you least expect it. Are you at all familiar with your way aboard ship?"

"A little."

"Well, this be the main deck we're standing on now. And that up there," he said, pointing toward the bow, "that be the foredeck, right above the captain's cabin. Don't want him catching you going in there without permission. Last mate to try it, the captain threw overboard." Pops slid the cap off his head and held it over his heart. "He swam like a rock, he did. Of course, it didn't help that he had one tied to him when he went in."

There was a moment of awkward silence as what he'd said sank in.

"Anyways." Pops placed his cap back on and pointed to the left. "That be the quarterdeck over there." There was a set of stairs on either side leading up to the top. "That's where the navigator sets the ship's course."

We maneuvered through stacked crates and barrels that had been secured to the deck. Pops brought us to a stop in front of a door at the back of the ship . . . or *stern,* as Hobb would have corrected me. I had memorized the lay of most ships from drawings Hobb had made, showing me where everything was located and how it was used.

"This wouldn't be your maiden voyage, would it, lad?" Pops asked as he opened the cabin door to reveal a good-sized sitting room with a couple of long tables, chairs, and a small kitchen area. On our right was a set of stairs leading below deck.

"That obvious, is it?" I asked, following him in.

Pops grabbed a lantern from a hook on the wall. "Don't worry. You'll get your bearings soon enough. This here be the mess," he said, motioning toward the eating area. "Kettle's ship's cook, if you hadn't guessed that already." He started down the stairs. "If there be one person you don't want to get on your bad side, besides the captain, it be the ship's cook. The last riverman that did ended up with a . . . well, probably best I don't tell you what was in his bowl, but needless to say, it were the last time he disrespected Kettle."

"Great. I'm already off to a good start," I said.

"Don't take it personal. Kettle treats us all the same. It be when he *isn't* complaining that you need to worry."

Pops waited for me to reach the bottom and then held up the light. "Those be our berths," he said, pointing to the left at a group of hammocks that had been tied between beams.

"Pick up your feet," Pops said as he continued down the keel of the ship. We stopped in front of a large chest near the far wall. "You can stow your gear with mine." He pulled a rusty key from inside his tunic where it hung around his neck. "Don't worry none. It be as safe as the royal vaults in the king's palace, I assure you." He placed the key in the hole at the front and turned. It clicked, and he opened the lid. The chest was only half-full, leaving enough room for me to lay my gear.

I hesitated. Everything I owned in the world was in my travel pack—my clothing, bedroll, climbing picks, weapons, thin coil of rope, and a fire pouch. Everything except, of course, for the coins I'd lifted off the dead highwaymen. I had them tucked in my boots, along with my cut of Father's contract. Pops seemed like a decent sort, but could I really trust him not to go through my stuff? Then again, did I have much of a choice? Where else could I put my gear that it wouldn't be rifled through by the crew?

"I keep her locked at all times," Pops said, sensing my reluctance.

I finally nodded and placed my pack inside.

Pops shut the lid and locked it again before tucking the key under his shirt. "Right. Let's get topside. Captain will be wanting to shove off soon enough. Best we be ready for it when he does."

I followed Pops back up the stairs, sparing a quick glance back across the half-filled hull. It appeared there was going to be plenty for me to learn on this trip—what to do, what not to do, who not to offend, and places to stay out of if I didn't want to take a short swim to the bottom of the river.

Chapter 25

I STEPPED OUT OF THE MESS and was met by an icy gust of wind, cold enough to make my teeth chatter. The harshness of winter might have passed, but that didn't mean its remnants couldn't still cut you to the bone.

"Is this the new deckhand?" a heavyset man with bright red cheeks asked. In his hand was a compass that hung from a gold chain attached to the lining of his coat. He began to fidget with it when he caught sight of my eyes. "Oh, my." The man shook his head. "This won't bode well at all. Mark my words."

"Here be our navigator, Bray," Pops said. "But we call him Needle. It's a compass joke. Plus," he said, leaning in a little closer, "he be pretty handy with a needle and thread. His wife be a seamstress."

Needle huffed.

"Needle, this be Ayrion," Pops said, placing a hand on my shoulder. "He'll be with us till we reach Aramoor."

Needle continued shaking his head and flipping his compass. "Not good. Not good." With that, he climbed the stairs to the quarterdeck and took his place by the tiller.

"Pay no mind to him," Pops said. "Never seen a more nervous sort in all my days. But he be one of the best navigators this side of the Razor Spine."

It seemed I wasn't going to be making friends easily among this crew. I decided it would be best to keep my head down and stay out of everyone's way. I was at least glad for Pops's willingness to acknowledge me without the immediate prejudice that the rest of the crew appeared to have.

"Out of my way, boy," a girl said behind me, right before I was shoved into the side of a barrel labeled TURNIPS. She glowered as she passed. She looked about my sister's age, with long hair the color of dark honey that hung down her back. It waved like a pendulum as she strutted toward the bow of the ship. She must have been a new passenger, because her outfit was much too rich for her to be one of the crew.

She wore dark leather trousers tucked into boots that widened at the calf. Her shirt was bloodred, and her overcoat reminded me of the greenest of summer leaves, accented with gold buttons down the front and on the cuffs.

As pompous as she appeared, I couldn't look away.

"Wouldn't let the captain catch you gawking," Pops said.

"Why's that? Who is she?"

"That's Ismara. Captain Treygan's daughter."

"Oh."

She climbed the foredeck, turned, and looked right at me. Her eyes were hard, much like her father's. The last thing I needed was another complication to deal with, so I shifted my gaze to keep from staring. I could still feel her eyes boring into the back of my head, which made me even more determined to stay as far away from her as possible. Like Hobb had said, "Keep your eyes open and your mouth shut."

Good advice for all occasions.

"So, what are my duties?" I asked, anxious to do something besides stand there and shiver.

"Ah." Pops raised his finger. "A better question would be: what *aren't* your duties?"

I didn't like the sound of that.

"Your duties are whatever you're asked to do, and since you don't have the experience to handle ship maneuvers yet, then my guess is you'll be spending most of your time with—"

"With me," Kettle said, a sour look on his face as he walked over and tossed a spare apron at me. "This should fit well enough. Last person to wear it was Toenail, and he was barely four and a half foot with his hat on."

"Not now," Bones said as he stepped off the top of the gangway. "Captain needs him at the warehouse. We've got a shipment that needs loaded."

At the sound of a shipment, heads across the deck popped up from whatever task they'd been on.

"What sort of cargo, First?" a man behind me with a booming voice asked. I hadn't seen him before, which was surprising, considering his size. His skin was strangely pale for a boatman. Nowhere near as pale as mine but certainly enough to make him stand out from the others. The wide-brimmed hat blocking the sun from his face made him look even bigger.

"That's Whitey," Pops whispered. "Biggest man on the ship. Nothing he loves more than a good brawl. Probably why the captain brought him on board."

"The sort that pays more," Bones said, "due to it being rushed."

"If there was ever a ship or crew that could meet a deadline," Pops said, chewing on his pipe, "it be this one."

"Aye," the others agreed.

"We was worried we was going to be hauling supplies again," Whitey said with relief.

"Don't you fret. We'll be shipping supplies to the mining camps as well," Bones said. "But because of what happened last time, we'll be picking up the cargo at an undisclosed location."

"What's that mean?" Kettle asked as he snatched the apron from my hands.

"It means the captain's keeping it to himself."

Kettle tugged on his long mustache and groaned. "Seems that's about all we be hauling nowadays. Not much profit in shipping supplies to people who can barely rub two coppers together."

"Not good," Needle said, looking down over the railing above the cabin. "Not good at all."

Whitey pushed his large hat back on his head and wiped his

brow. "How's a waterman to earn an honest living 'round here if we don't have cargo and passengers to ship? We won't survive another year like last."

Bones didn't say anything. One by one, he scanned the faces of the crew. "A shipment's a shipment. Count it lucky we still have that. Maybe we'll pick up more downriver. This is only the first stop."

"We all know there ain't much chance of that happening," Kettle griped.

"There's the docks," Ismara said over the others, having been monitoring the conversation. There was a sharp edge to her voice, almost as sharp as the sword she was pointing at the gangway. "You're free to leave at any time."

"And where would we go, young missus?" Whitey asked. "We's already been tainted by association. The other captains know us and won't be bringing us on board."

"That's not my concern," she said. "But unless you want me to report this insubordination to the captain, then I'd suggest you get back to work."

A few mumbles could be heard across the deck, but the crew finally did what she said and went back to their responsibilities. She looked at me for a moment as if deciding whose side I was on, then walked back to a small table to study whatever was on top.

"Pick up your feet, boy," Bones said as he turned and marched back down the ramp. "Captain's waiting."

Realizing I was just standing there staring at Ismara, I turned and ran after him.

It wasn't a good sign that the crew was already complaining before they'd even set sail. Trouble was, I could understand their grievances. They seemed to be facing the same sort of problems my family was back home: shunned to the point of not getting enough work to live off of.

In a way, I felt right at home with this crew. They might not have wanted me there, but we were all misfits in our own way. I just wished I understood where the resentment was coming from and why no one wanted to do business with them. So far, I hadn't seen anything that would justify it.

Chapter 26

**I** HEARD RAISED VOICES coming from the warehouse where the captains had set up their booths. I followed Bones in. Half a dozen men pressed against Captain Treygan's table, and they didn't look like they were seeking passage.

The captain stood behind his table, calm as a summer's night before a storm. The way he continued flipping his bone knife and smiling gave the impression he didn't have a care in the world. His mouth might have curved upward, but his eyes did all the talking. The cold, calculating look let me know that if it came down to it, he wasn't going down without a fight.

"That's my contract, Treygan, you flaming swine, and you know it!" one of the men said. By the cut of his hat and the sash tied around it, he was a captain. Not to mention the way the other sailors seemed to be guarding him.

"And how is it my fault that Elis didn't get his crops harvested in time?" Treygan asked nonchalantly.

"It's not my fault," a shorter man between the two said as he anxiously wiped his face with a dirty rag. He wore a pair of overalls with patches on the knees from having been worn longer than they should have. "The snows stretched longer than expected, Owen," he said to the other captain. "It couldn't be helped."

I followed Bones in as he pushed his way around the side of the crowd to reach Treygan. Raising my cowl, I stood far enough out of the way not to be noticed, watching to see what would happen next. I'd left my sword and bow back on ship, not expecting to need them to cart sacks down to the docks. But that didn't mean I was unarmed. My hand slid to my side, where my dagger rested, just in case.

Elis wiped his forehead once again, sweat pouring off his brow, uncommon for such a chilly day. "My contract states that if I don't get this load to market by the first Eighthday of Nùwen, I forfeit half my collection." He pointed at Treygan, his hand noticeably shaking. "His ship's the only one that can make it in that time." He glanced at the other captain. "I'm sorry, Owen, but my hands are tied."

Owen placed his hand on his waist, mighty close to the hilt of his cutlass. "Better to lose half than all by shipping with this crook."

More of Owen's men gathered around the table. Captains around the room stopped their business to see what was going on. Most of their lines had already dwindled, some to get a closer look, others to leave while they still could.

I worked my way through the crowd, weaving between the men as they pressed closer. As small as I was, no one paid that much notice as I scooted in behind the other captain.

"A contract's a contract," Treygan said, sporting another one of his arrogant smiles. The man had either the heart of a warrior or the brains of a mackerel. At this point, both were going to lead us into some very hot water, and soon. "Paper's already signed." He raised the parchment up for everyone to see. "Besides, Elis is right. There's no ship can match the *Wind Binder* for speed."

Treygan looked past Owen and caught my eye. Somehow, he'd spotted me when no one else had. What I saw in his eyes had me pulling my dagger from my belt.

"I say it ain't worth the paper it's signed on," Owen said defiantly. Those standing around nodded in agreement.

I looked around. What small crew we had was waiting on board for the wagons to roll up and be unloaded. They had no idea what was taking place in here. Bones wasn't about to leave his captain's side, and I wouldn't have enough time to run and get them. By the time I could make it to the ship and back, the captain and first would be bathing in their own blood.

Treygan eyed Owen's men.

Bones leaned in and whispered something in the captain's ear. Probably telling him to use some sense and just let the other captain have the cargo. It wouldn't do us much good if we were too dead to ship it.

Owen leaned over the table. "Hand over that contract, Treygan," he said, soft enough that the captains at the other tables couldn't hear, "or I'll take your ship like I did the others."

*Others?*

Half a dozen of Owen's men reached for their blades.

One of the lessons you learn early as an Upaka is that whether dealing with an army, a militia, or a pack of rowdy rivermen, there is always a leader. They are the one you want to subdue first. Cut off the head, and the body will usually die.

In close combat like this, with my speed and training, I had the advantage. I stood a good chance of making it out of the warehouse and taking down a number of Owen's men in the process. I doubted I could say the same for Treygan and Bones.

"Last chance, Treygan," Owen said as he drew his cutlass and placed the tip on top of the table. "Turn over that contract or I'll pry it from your bloody— Nyaaah!"

Owen froze as I lifted my dagger between his legs. He gasped and stood on his tiptoes.

"Tell your men to move back," I said, as low and menacing as I could muster, "or I'll castrate you right here."

"Sh . . . sheathe your weapons and move back!" Owen said, his voice suddenly high-pitched for a man of his stature.

Owen's men looked at him like he was crazy, and when they didn't respond fast enough, he shouted at the top of his lungs, "I said back the blazes up! All of you!"

Up until that point, they hadn't noticed me standing there with my dagger tickling the captain's masculinity. It wasn't that I enjoyed playing with the man's fruit, but I wasn't tall enough to reach the front of his neck from where I stood.

Treygan drew his sword and stepped around the table. Owen continued balancing frantically on the balls of his feet as he dangled over the tip of my blade.

"We're leaving," Treygan said, "and you're coming with us." He raised his blade to Owen's throat.

Now that the captain had him, I lowered my dagger and stepped back. As soon as I did, Owen twisted around far enough to get a look at me. He looked surprised at first. I didn't know if it was because I was Upakan or because he'd been bested by a thirteen-year-old, but either way, the fire in his eyes said enough.

"I'll not forget this, boy!" he spat.

I didn't respond. Unlike Treygan, I had no desire to rub it in the man's face by smiling, or dancing, or sticking my tongue out at him.

Treygan spun Owen back around. "Once we're aboard, loaded, and set sail, I'll think about releasing you. Until then, you'll remain silent and ponder all the reasons why threatening me and mine has landed you in this predicament." Treygan's smile returned as he pushed Owen toward the head of the warehouse, where a mob of angry sailors stood waiting. "Tell them to keep their distance or watch me open your throat."

Owen gulped. "Stay back!"

"But, Captain—"

"You heard me! Stay back or I'll flog the lot of ya!"

The rivermen moved back, allowing us just enough room to pass.

If stares could kill, we'd have been dead thrice over as we made the long trip down the docks toward the *Wind Binder*. By now, the rest of the crew had caught on that something was happening and had made it halfway to the warehouse with Whitey in the lead. The other rivermen were quick to move or risk being tossed in the river. Surprisingly, Ismara was right there beside him, sword in hand, as she threatened to open half the sailors from tip to stern.

With their help, we made our way slowly back to the ship.

"Kettle." Captain Treygan motioned the cook forward. "Take Captain Owen on board and show him every courtesy, will you? The rest of us have some loading to do." Treygan turned to me. "Go with him and make sure the captain doesn't attempt something stupid."

I followed Kettle up the gangway. He kept his blade to Owen's back, directing him onto the ship. "This way, Captain," Kettle said as he marched Owen toward the bow. "We want to make sure you're good and comfortable. Now up the steps." He patted Owen's backside with the flat of his blade.

Owen flinched, but to his credit, he kept going.

I took the opposite stairs and was waiting for them at the top.

"Right this way, Captain," Kettle said as he moved him to the front railing overlooking the boardwalk. "Now stand there and look pretty for your men."

"Once I'm free," Owen said, "I'm going to cook you alive and serve you to the crew."

"Then I guess that doesn't leave me much reason for letting you go, now, does it?"

I could feel the sway of the ship beneath my feet. Below us, the rest of the crew unloaded Elis's wagons and carried the sacks and barrels on board. My stomach felt uneasy. I found myself swallowing to keep it in check. I hadn't felt this way on Hobb's ferry, so why was I now?

With half the hands from the other ships standing just off the boardwalk, waiting for the signal to attack, our men didn't delay in getting the ship ready to depart.

After the mooring lines were loosened, a longboat was lowered to tow the *Wind Binder* out far enough to set sail.

The men from the other ships followed us to the end of the dock, but no one dared attack as long as Kettle had his sword at Captain Owen's gut.

Pretty soon, we were far enough away from shore to unfurl the sail. Once the longboat was raised and tied off and its rowers back on board, Needle shifted the tiller at the stern, and wind filled the sheet with a strong-enough lurch for me to have to bend my knees to keep from falling over.

"How's our guest?" Captain Treygan asked as he reached the top of the stairs behind us and made his way across the bow. Whitey was right behind him.

"Ready to leave, I'd say," Kettle said with a chuckle. He lowered his sword and stepped away to let the captain by.

I took a step back and had to catch myself. Something about the rocking of the ship had my head spinning. It was already affecting my stomach. I grabbed the railing and took a deep breath. Out on the docks, Owen's men scrambled to get their boats ready to sail, anxious to come after us.

Treygan spun Captain Owen to face him. "As promised, Captain. You're free to go."

"Go where, you jacktoad? You've already set sail."

"Aye, the water might be a bit cold, but I'm sure a sailor of your caliber can make it to shore if he tries." Treygan nodded at Whitey.

"What are you—"

He'd barely gotten the words out when Whitey picked him up and tossed him into the river.

Owen shouted the entire way down.

The crew cheered as they leaned over the side and watched him break the surface, spitting water and curses as we passed. He threatened to kill each and every one on board, kill their families, their friends. I even thought I heard something about favorite pets.

"That's the funniest thing I've seen in years," Ismara said as she joined me at the edge of the ship. She smelled of leather and jasmine, a strangely alluring combination. I would have enjoyed it more if I hadn't been feeling so sick.

She looked at me and her smile disappeared. "What are you staring at?"

"Nothing," I said, quickly shifting my gaze out toward the last of the warehouses as we picked up speed.

"Don't give our young deckhand such a hard time, Ismara," Treygan said. "He's the reason I'm still standing here."

"What, him?" she asked, her brow raised in disbelief.

"I can see why the Upaka are so effective," Captain Treygan said. "You've made an enemy today, lad. But you've also made a friend." He held out his hand.

I took it, then leaned over and emptied my guts onto the deck.

"I take it back," Ismara said, laughing so hard, I thought she'd send herself overboard. "*That's* the funniest thing I've seen in years."

## Chapter 27

$\mathcal{M}$Y FIRST FEW DAYS aboard the *Wind Binder* were miserable. I spent most of them hanging over the side of the ship, emptying out what little Pops could force me to get down. I didn't know it was possible to lose so much despite having eaten so little. My balance was completely off. For someone whose entire life's training depended on balance, the experience was alarming.

Pops said the quails would pass once I found my legs. I prayed he was right.

After Captain Treygan's acknowledgment of the part I played in his rescue, the crew seemed more willing to accept me. Not to say they welcomed me with open arms, but at least the cold shoulders and threatening stares stopped.

I even managed to get a smile or two from Kettle as I helped him prepare the meals. Or he could have been smiling at me burning my hand while stirring the pot of one of his latest concoctions.

The farther south we traveled, the warmer the days became. Pops found me an old pair of trousers and shirt that he had Needle alter so they would fit. He even gave me an old knit cap of his to ward off the evening chill. I couldn't say that I preferred the loose-fitting clothing, but if it meant saving my own clothes from wear, then I was fine with it. The trousers only fell down once. Thankfully, no one—especially Ismara—was there to see.

We passed a number of small fishing villages as we journeyed down the Shemoa. They were little more than a few scattered homes with thatched roofs, and small boats along the bank casting nets. None was large enough to have even a single dock, let alone a full port. On the fourth day, we stopped outside of a small but thriving community called Melforn on the east side of the river.

The captain ordered us to drop anchor a little way offshore. He said we wouldn't be there long enough to waste money on docking fees, but I thought he was more worried about Captain Owen and his ships trying to catch up. Last place we'd want to be was tied to a dock with nowhere to go if they did.

Treygan ordered the longboat lowered. He asked that I accompany him, along with Whitey and Ismara. I jumped at the chance to get on solid ground again and was the first one in the boat. However, I did stop long enough to change back into my regular outfit and grab my sword.

The row to shore wasn't difficult. I did start off the trip facing the wrong direction, which Ismara was quick to point out. It seems you have to face backward to row forward. Whitey shook his head, and the captain smiled. All it took was a couple of solid strokes with the oar and I let my magic do the rest as my body repeated the movements.

The water was smooth now that the wind had settled to a light breeze, and my arms hardly felt strained by the time we finally reached shore. We landed the longboat upstream, out of direct sight of the docks. Whitey and I pulled the boat up far enough on shore for Ismara and Captain Treygan to hop out without getting their boots wet.

The captain straightened his hat. "Whitey, stay with the boat. Ayrion, you're with me."

"Ah, but, Captain, I wanted to—"

"Don't argue. I want you with the boat. Can't afford to lose it."

Whitey looked like he'd had the wind knocked out of him as he lowered his head. "Aye, Captain."

"I'll bring you one of those fig tarts you like so much," Ismara said.

My mouth hung open. It was the first time I'd seen her be nice to anyone.

Whitey smiled and removed his hat. "Thankya, missus."

I followed Treygan and Ismara up a small rise, my sword bouncing against my thigh as we climbed. At the top was a dirt road, which appeared to wind its way back around toward the docks.

The walk to the warehouses was a short one, but instead of going inside, the captain took us left at a cross street, and we headed away from the river through the narrow streets leading into the busier part of town.

Melforn was certainly no Oswell. It wasn't even a Cretollo. It was, however, crowded, but only because it seemed the city had decided to expand on top of itself instead of outward. Buildings that looked to have originally been built for two stories had three and sometimes even four. The smell of it had me wanting to pinch my nose. It stank of hard sweat, urine, and wet dog, a combination strong enough to overpower that of even the river. Every now and then, I'd catch a whiff of jasmine emanating from Ismara and I'd move a little closer.

We stopped just off the main street leading into town, which consisted mostly of shops, eateries, and a couple of inns. The inns didn't hold a candle to the Golden Tassel. No flowers in the windows, only shutters with missing teeth. They reminded me of Flon after I'd landed that kick to his face.

A sudden bout of sneezing pulled me away from my momentary lapse into a past I was trying to forget. The smell of cinnamon and cloves filled the narrow street we had turned down.

"In here," Treygan said as he entered a shop on our right. The sign on the front read SEMPRIL SPICES. "Have a look around but don't touch anything." He seemed to be looking at me when he said it. "Oh, and keep an eye on her." He nodded in Ismara's direction.

I sneezed once again, trying to take small, shallow breaths to ward against the aromas in the shop.

The captain must have taken it as an affirmation, because he left us there and headed for a door at the back. He knocked twice and waited. A moment later, the door opened, and an older woman peeked out. She took one look around the shop and ushered him inside.

"I catch you staring at me again," Ismara said once her father was out of earshot, "and I'll cut your eyes out."

"But your father just said—"

"I don't care what he said. I can look out for myself. I don't need some little White Eyes gawking at my backside. How old are you anyway? Ten?"

"Ten? I'm thirteen."

"Oh, pardon me," she said with a flippant wave of her hand.

"How old are you?" I asked. She couldn't have been that much older.

"None of your business," she said with a snarl. "Old enough to know better than to ask a lady her age."

"If I see one, I'll be sure not to," I said under my breath.

She spun around. "What was that? You want me to remove your tongue as well as your eyes?"

I huffed and left her there to peruse the shelves near the back.

"Where do you think you're going?" she asked.

"Away from you. Or did you prefer me to keep watching?"

She rolled her eyes. "Just stay close."

"Where am I going to go?" The shop was hardly big enough to spit across. The spices were strong, making my eyes water. Some—like the cinnamon, nutmeg, and ginger—smelled nice, but others—like the black pepper, cumin, and garlic—had me holding my breath and moving to another section of the shop.

"Why all the secrecy?" I finally asked when the silence had grown unbearable. "What are we doing here?"

"We're here 'cause the captain says to be here."

This time, it was my turn to roll my eyes. "Aren't you the dutiful daughter," I said sarcastically. "You're not the least bit curious?" I certainly was.

"If I tell you, will you shut up?"

I nodded.

"We're scheduling a pickup for supplies."

"What kind of supplies? Spices?" I dreaded the thought of spending every day on board a ship that smelled like this shop. I also couldn't imagine a reason for a secretive meeting to ship spices.

"Hardly," she said, and nothing more.

Either she didn't want to talk about it, or that was all she knew, so I decided to change the subject. "Did your father own other ships besides the *Wind Binder*?"

She placed the lid back on the jar and turned around. "That's a strange question to ask."

"It was something Captain Owen said while we were in the warehouse—"

"Owen's no captain. He's nothing more than a river pirate."

"In the warehouse, he threatened to commandeer the *Wind Binder* like he had the others. What *others* was he talking about?"

Ismara took a deep breath and slowly released. "Father used to own the largest shipping business on the Shemoa. We had a slew of ships. None as fast as the *Wind Binder*, but decent. In fact, you saw a number of them at Cretollo."

"What happened?"

"Owen and his pirate thugs happened. They used to plunder the shipping lanes between Aramoor and Duport, but when word got back to the king, he sent a whole fleet to dispatch their ships. After watching his ships sink to the bottom of the deep, that pathetic excuse of a sailor decided it would be more profitable to be the one doing the shipping. So, he left the seas and worked his way up the Shemoa, strong-arming the rest of the smaller shippers out of business.

"Pretty soon, he was second only to Father. That's when he started bribing and threatening all the merchants along our route, forcing them to stop shipping with us. Evidently, that still wasn't enough, because then he hired men to raid our ships at random ports along the river. It got to where we never knew which dock was safe to tie off at.

"Most of the rivermen and captains sailing with us decided the risk wasn't worth the pay, so they left. Owen bought out the rest of our ships, leaving only the *Wind Binder*. He's been trying to get it ever since."

"Why don't you go to the authorities?"

Ismara snorted. "What authorities? There's no official trade guild out here on the river like there is in Aramoor. Out here, the local authorities look the other way since their pockets are lined with Owen's gold. The crew we have are the ones who've been with us long enough not to sell out."

Before she could say more, the door at the back opened and her father walked out. He stuffed what looked like a coin pouch and a small piece of parchment into the inner pocket of his coat and tapped the outside as if to make sure it was safe before heading for the front door.

"Let's go."

I followed them out, but instead of heading back the way we'd come, Treygan took a different route. I wondered if we were on our way to pick up the supplies Ismara had mentioned. What kind of supplies could we be shipping that required so much secrecy? I was considering the various possibilities when the smell of fresh bread caught my attention.

"Go on," Treygan said to Ismara as we stopped outside a shop with a sign hanging over the door that read ORVILL'S BAKERY. "But be quick about it. And take Ayrion with you. He looks like he needs something sweet to chew on."

Ismara groaned but motioned for me to follow anyway.

The bell above the door rang as I stepped inside the stone block building. I took one whiff and never wanted to leave. The air was heavy with the smell of dough, cinnamon, cheese, and a mixture of fruit so divine, I thought I'd died and stepped into the afterlife.

At the back of the shop stood a large brick oven where an older gentleman with white splotches on his clothes was busy sliding in his next batch of dough. In front of him was a long counter that ran diagonally, holding a variety of fresh-baked loaves. They were organized by size, shape, and color, starting with the fine white on the left to the dark rye and black wheat on the right. The price of the loaves dropped the farther down the counter you went.

On the right was a selection of sweet breads, pies, and tarts. They came in two sizes: one large enough to serve a small family, and one small enough to fit in the palm of your hand. Both looked wonderful. I could almost taste the fruit filling just looking at them.

While I drooled over the desserts, Ismara walked up to the counter where a young woman was waiting to serve us. "I want four of the smaller tarts," Ismara said. "One with almond fig, one with cheese, one apricot, and . . ." She turned to look at me. "What do you want?"

"What kind is this on the end?" I asked, noticing the rich bluish cream rising from the top.

"That's blueberry."

"I'll take it." Blueberry had always been my mother's favorite.

The young lady grabbed one of each and rolled them in wax paper, tying it off with string.

"That'll be a silver and three," she said.

Ismara pulled out a small pouch and counted out the coins.

The lady thanked her, and I held the door as we left. Ismara was already untying the string before she had made it back to the street. One by one, she handed out the tarts.

"Ah, sweet cheese," Captain Treygan said with a smile. "You remembered. Let me guess, apricot for you."

Ismara smiled as she bit into hers. "Of course."

Treygan turned to look me. "And what did you get?"

My mouth was full, but I managed to get the word *blueberry* out despite that.

My tart was finished before we hit the next street over. I made sure to lick each finger in case I'd missed any by accident. It was nearly as good as the ones Milly had made for us at the Golden Tassel.

It didn't take us long to retrace our steps back to the docks and, from there, upriver to where we had left the boat. Whitey was sitting inside with his hat pulled over his head.

"I'm not paying you to sleep on the job," the captain said, tossing a rock that hit Whitey in the stomach.

Whitey awoke with a start and nearly tripped on the side of the boat as he hopped out. "Sorry, Captain. It was such a beautiful day, and with the water lapping against the back of the boat, I just couldn't help myself."

"I've half a mind not to give you this, then," the captain said, tossing the wax wrapping at the big man.

Whitey caught it and ripped it open with a wide grin. "Thank you, Captain." He stuffed the entire tart in his mouth in one bite.

"Don't thank me. Thank Ismara. She's the one who got it."

"Thankya, missus," Whitey said, lifting his hat.

Ismara smiled. "My pleasure, Whitey." I wondered how long it would take for her to warm up to me like that.

The captain helped Ismara in and then found his seat. Whitey shoved us back into the water and then hopped in.

"Where to now, Captain?" Whitey asked.

Captain Treygan reached up and patted the outside of his coat where he had placed the paper and pouch from the spice shop. "Back to the ship," he said. "We have one more stop to make."

## Chapter 28

B Y THE TIME WE had the longboat tied and the anchor
raised, the sun had set low enough on the horizon for the sky
to fill with color. It was going to be another beautiful sunset, one
that I was going to miss since Kettle needed me to help him prepare
the evening meal: stewed fish in butter and beer, beans, and bis-
cuits with a slice of cheese.

"Where's the captain and Needle?" I asked, noticing that the
two men hadn't come in to eat with the rest. "And why haven't we
cut sail and dropped anchor?" The butter slid from one side of the
pan to the other as the ship rocked under the breeze.

"You ask a lot of questions," Kettle said with hint of frustration
as he handed me another bowl and motioned for me to fill it.

"Isn't it dangerous to run at night? What if we hit a shelf and
pitch the ship?"

"You worry about dishing up that food," Kettle said. "Let the captain worry about the ship." He looked up at the rafters and sneered. "We be picking up another shipment."

Like Ismara, he didn't say anything more about it, and for the sake of peace, I didn't press.

After the meal was finished and I'd helped Kettle clean up what was left, I climbed to the top of the bow and watched the silhouette of the land on either side pass us by. I wondered how much of it I would miss seeing while taking the river instead of going by horse. By horse, the travel south would have been more difficult and time-consuming, probably adding a month or two to the journey. Then again, after making enemies of a few ship captains, and all the secrecy around the so-called shipment we were picking up, the extra travel time was looking mighty reasonable.

"Beautiful, isn't she?" a voice said behind me, causing me to flinch.

Ismara walked across the deck and joined me at the front. She leaned her elbows on the railing and watched the waves break against the ship. It was the first time she'd paid any real attention to me.

"So, you've finally decided to acknowledge I exist?"

She released a long breath from her nose. "Father told me to. But if you're going to act all pouty about it, I'll just leave." She turned with a huff and started walking back across the top deck.

"What's beautiful?" I asked.

She turned and stared at me for a moment before retracing her steps back to the edge. "The river," she said with a solemn sort of reverence. "I was born here. Will probably die here." She stared ahead, the wind blowing her hair behind her like a ship's flag, releasing the scent of jasmine in its wake.

"I was born underground," I said, hoping to carry her comment into a deeper conversation while she was acting remotely civil.

"What was that like?" she asked. "I can't imagine living without the sun on my face and the wind at my back. I get claustrophobic every time I go below deck. If it gets too bad, I come lie on the deck and stare at the stars."

We both tilted our heads and looked up at the brightly lit heavens. It was an amazing sight.

I realized this was the first time I'd been this close to a girl when I wasn't bending her arm behind her back, or wrapping my elbow around her neck, or punching her in the gut and throwing her to the ground. It was the first time I'd ever paid attention to anything besides the stance of her feet, or the position of her body, or the height of her guard. Now I was noticing other things, like the thin line of her waist and the curves that rose above it, the way her lips would pout whenever she was annoyed, even the way she arched her back to look at the stars. They were things that could land me in the river if her father were to ever find out.

"We have a river as well, back home," I said, more excitedly than I had intended. "It's underground. And there's a cavern called Triple Falls where the water flows off three shelves into a bunch of pools at the bottom. There's crystals in the rocks that glow bright enough that you don't even need a lantern. And the water is always warm because it runs near the lower magma tunnels." I would have kept going, but I ran out of breath and then realized I was rambling. "Sorry, didn't mean to throw all that on you—"

"No. Sounds wondrous. You feel about your home like I do about the river."

The thought of home left a knot in my throat.

"Why the long face?" she asked.

I took a deep breath and sighed. "Homesick, I guess."

"Why are you out here by yourself?" She tilted her head. "No offense, but you seem kind of young to be on your own. Or is that the way Upakans do it? 'Cause you seem to act older than you look."

"Thanks . . . I think."

I went on to explain a little more about the circumstances leading up to my eventual banishment. And like any good storyteller discussing his life, I was of course the hero of my tale, the outcast who was unfairly treated, judged, and imprisoned—all of which was true. I left out any mention of magic or the part it played, and I ended with my journey from the Lost City to Cretollo and my desire to reach Aramoor.

"Sounds like you left at a good time. I wouldn't want to live with a tyrant like that either. Why didn't the rest of your family come?"

I went on to explain how Upakan society worked, and that the only place my people could survive was clustered away from the rest of the world.

"You've seen how the crew treats me," I said. "They don't show it as much as they did at first, but most still get jumpy whenever

I'm around. If you ever doubt it, just watch how fast Needle's compass gets to spinning whenever he sees me." It was a nervous tic our navigator succumbed to every time he felt the least bit anxious.

Ismara laughed. "You got a point."

"It'll be easier for me to melt into a larger city than it would be for my whole family."

She shrugged. "Guess you're right. Still seems unfair, though."

"Fork ahead!" Bones shouted from behind us.

"Looks like we're nearly there," Ismara said, scanning the river ahead.

I followed her gaze and noticed there was a split that branched off to the left. I was surprised Bones had seen it. Even with my Upakan eyes and the moonlight, it was difficult to spot through the heavily forested region we were passing through.

"Hard to port!" the captain shouted.

"Hold on," Ismara said as she grabbed hold of the railing.

I did the same, and the boat began to tilt out of the water as the bow cut to the left.

"Raise the sail!" The captain's orders were met with a flurry of activity as Bones and the other men scurried to loosen the rigging and raise the sheet. The captain and Needle watched as they pulled down on the ropes that lifted the sail. The large sheet rose slowly to the top of the mast, where she remained once the ropes were secured below. The Wind Binder slowed as we headed away from the main branch of the river and into the darker region beyond.

The evening breeze faded the farther into the trees we went. Pretty soon, it wasn't there at all. The sudden silence had the hairs on the back of my neck standing as we slithered down the narrow passage. I hoped the water was deep enough that we didn't get stuck.

"Where are we going?" I asked, my voice low against the eerie silence. The tree frogs and the occasional hoot owl seemed to be the only things awake to witness our passing.

"We're meeting a supplier," Ismara said apprehensively.

"Does it have something to do with whatever the captain was doing back in Melforn?"

She nodded. "I need to get ready."

Before I could ask what she needed to get ready for, she was halfway across the deck.

I stood there for a moment or two longer, wondering what kind of supplier would be meeting us out in the middle of nowhere and in the dead of night. Knowing I wouldn't get an answer while staring at the water, I left the bow and followed her down to find Pops. Maybe he'd be willing to tell me what was going on.

By the time I made it back to the main deck, Pops was just stepping out of the mess cabin door. He was carrying my sword and bow in one hand and quiver over the shoulder, which he extended when he saw me coming.

"What are you doing?" I asked.

"Here, you'll need these."

"For what? What's going on?"

Before he could answer, the captain leaned over the railing above us. "Drop the anchor. We'll take the boat from here."

I heard the splash of the anchor as it hit the water and felt the ship slow as it dragged the bottom, eventually coming to a stop. Whitey helped Bones lower the longboat over the side and then joined the rest of the men as they readied themselves for whatever we were about to do.

Pops had an old sword strapped to his side. Bones wore a set of kamas at his waist; not a weapon typically seen around these parts, but very similar in shape to my pickaxes. Beside him, Whitey had a sword, a brace of knives, and a large bludgeon to boot. Both the captain and Ismara wore a sword on one side and a dagger on the other. Even Kettle had one of his long kitchen knives tucked in his belt and carried the axe we used to chop wood for the stove.

The only boatman not carrying a weapon was Needle. The navigator was too fidgety to handle a weapon. He'd likely injure himself, or one of us, if ever forced to use one.

"Needle, Pops, you have the ship," Treygan said as he swung over the side and climbed down the rope ladder to the waiting boat. "The rest with me."

"Here, don't forget these," Pops said as he handed me my quiver of arrows.

I slung it over my shoulder. My sword hung at my side, and my dagger pressed against my back, where it rested in its sheath. The only weapon I wasn't carrying was my boot knife, but since my boots were already weighed down with my coin pouches, I opted to leave it behind.

Looking down at the rest of the men in the boat below me, I couldn't help but feel like we were going to war. They left a spot open at the front for me to sit. Since I was the only one carrying a bow, I wondered if that had been on purpose.

I held my bow in my hand and kept my eyes open as we moved quietly through the water. No one said a word. This part of the river was even narrower than at Hobb's Crossing. I could have thrown a stone from one side and hit the other.

The rhythmic chop of the oars as they stroked the water was the only sound to be heard. Around us, the trees rose like the walls of a city protecting its occupants from unwanted guests. The deeper we went, the more I began to feel like the unwanted guest.

Behind us, the *Wind Binder* disappeared from view as we rounded the bend.

"There's light ahead," I whispered over my shoulder before pulling my cowl up to shield my eyes.

"They're already here," the captain said from the other side of the boat. "Good."

Ahead on the left bank, two men stood with torches lighting a small path leading out of the forest to the waterfront.

"We were beginning to wonder if you were coming," one of the men called out as we angled the boat toward the bank. The grip on my bow tightened as we neared.

I didn't wait for us to reach the opening before I hopped out and onto the bank a few feet away. If this was some sort of attack, I'd be hanged if I was going to float right up to it. I nocked an arrow and waited to see what the two men would do.

They glanced at me apprehensively. "What's this, Treygan?" the man closest to me asked. He was shorter than the captain, with a balding head and a full beard that covered a thin, angular face.

"Have you changed your mind?"

"No," the captain said, sounding a little annoyed. "This is Ayrion, newest member of my crew."

The two men took a moment to look me over. "Not much to him," the second man said. He was even shorter than the first, with brown hair and bushy whiskers that ran down the sides of his face. He looked more like an underpaid farmhand than someone we'd be meeting out here to collect a secret shipment from. "Can he hold his own?"

"Don't reckon you want to find out," the captain said with a wink in my direction. He pointed at my head. "Show them."

I lowered my hood.

As soon as the torchlight touched my face, the two men took a step back. "You have a White Eyes on board your ship?"

"Aye, and I'll thank you to watch your tongue. Don't believe they take too kindly to that name."

The two men glanced my way, looking even more worried, if that were possible. The shorter one nodded apologetically in my direction. It still amazed me how something as simple as the color of one's eyes, or lack thereof, could have such an effect. If mine had contained even the slightest tint, they wouldn't have looked at me twice.

"To be honest," the taller one said, "it'll be good to have him with us."

"With us?" Treygan looked at the two men. "What are you talking about, with us? We're here to pick up our regular supplies. I was told in Melforn they'd be ready when we got here."

"There's been a slight change of plan," he said with a nervous gulp as he looked at his comrade.

Treygan took a step forward, and the two men retreated. "Shipment or no shipment, you better start talking, or this is the last time you'll be receiving help from me and mine."

"We don't speak for the others," the shorter man with the side whiskers said. "You'll have to talk with them."

"What others?" Treygan asked, turning to look at the surrounding trees.

The crew did the same.

Bones took a step closer to the captain, causing the two men to retreat even farther. They looked just as nervous at seeing him as they had me, which wasn't much of a surprise, since his eyes were about the only thing you could see in the dark.

I scanned the forest and couldn't see anything amiss, but that didn't mean there wasn't something or someone there. So far, I'd received no warning from my magic.

"Come," the men said apprehensively. "The supplies are this way. You can talk to someone who speaks for us. Come."

Treygan drew his sword and pointed it directly at the guides. "By the Creator, you try anything, and I'll gut you like a fish and feed you to the eels."

Kettle had his axe up and ready, his head darting back and forth as he spun at every snapped twig. Ismara had both her sword and dagger out, while Whitey gripped his thick bludgeon with both hands.

Captain Treygan motioned for me to join him and then

pointed at the two men. "Lead the way."

I followed behind Bones and the captain with Whitey and Is-mara behind me and Kettle bringing up the rear. My bow remained nocked as I listened and watched for any sign of ambush. So far, the forest was quiet, other than the padding of our boots in the dirt.

I wanted to laugh. Here I was, on the other side of Keldor, trudging through some unnamed jungle in the middle of the night for a secret rendezvous to collect some mysterious supplies while following the lead of a supposed cursed captain and crew. I was starting to wonder if I'd ever reach Aramoor alive.

The trail led us to a small road where a couple of wagons were waiting, along with what looked like a dozen men, all heavily armed.

"Captain!" I drew my bow.

Whitey and Kettle pushed their way to the front to protect Treygan and Ismara.

"Stay your hands!" a heavyset man with a reddish beard hollered as he raised both arms. "You're among friends!"

I turned my bow in the man's direction. "Captain?" I waited for the word.

Treygan took a step forward. "Horis?"

The big man on the other side of the road smiled and took a step forward as well. "Didn't know if you'd recognize me after all these years."

The captain quickly waved us down. "Lower your weapons, men." He walked across the road, and the two men hugged like old friends who hadn't seen each other in years, which appeared to be the case.

I lowered my bow but kept the arrow nocked in case things went sideways, which for me, they usually did.

"Horis, you ol' scoundrel!" The captain released the man with a hearty laugh. "I heard you'd kicked it years ago."

The redheaded man put his fists to his sides. "Takes more than a little gout to put me under the soil."

Treygan took a step back and looked at the men standing around the wagons. "Mind telling me what's going on here? I came expecting to pick up some blankets and food, and instead, I'm met with an armed contingent."

*Blankets and food?* With all the secrecy and suspense bleeding off this crew since we'd gotten back from Melforn, I'd half-assumed we were picking up a shipment of gold or something. What was so important about blankets and food?

"Are we delivering supplies or not?" Treygan asked.

Horis's face grew pensive, and he patted the cutlass at his side. "We're gonna deliver more than that, my old friend. We're gonna kill every last flaming one of them and then burn that place to the ground."

Chapter 29

I T HAD TAKEN FOUR TRIPS to unload the wagons and ferry everyone back to the ship. The wagons had been stacked with blankets, clothing, and food. Wherever they were planning on taking this stuff, it was enough to serve a small outpost.

Once the last of the supplies had been unloaded, Treygan ordered a meeting in the mess. I hoped it was to give an explanation as to what was going on, because I was feeling completely left out.

"I'm tired of waiting, Treygan!" Horis pounded his fist on one of the tables in the mess. "You know better than most what goes on in those camps. It's high time we did something about it. I'm tired of smuggling in a few blankets and clothing." He drew his cutlass and held it in the air. "It's time they taste the cut of our steel."

The men with Horis raised their arms and shouted. The rest of our crew sat there and listened. I scratched my head. *Give who a taste of our steel?*

"There's not a man here," Horis said, gesturing to the filled tables, "who hasn't lost someone to the Cylmaran slavers. I ask you, where are you going to find a more willing group of fighters than those what's fighting for family and friends?"

"It's not their willingness I question," Treygan said. "It's their ability to swing a sword and not hit me in the process."

One of Horis's men in the back stood. "I'd be happy to give you a go." He was the biggest of the new members, every bit the size of Whitey but with a much harder face. He looked ready to fight anyone and everyone at the table.

"Sit down, Worg," Horis said with a worried frown.

"I say I want no part of this," Kettle grumbled. "Why should we be risking our necks for those that's no relation of ours? There's no profit in dying."

"Coward's words, those are!" Horis countered.

Kettle came to his feet and shook his meat cleaver at Horis. "I be no coward, and I challenge any man here who says otherwise."

"Enough." Captain Treygan stood and motioned for Kettle to sit back down. "There are no cowards here." It was given as an open statement, but he was looking at Horis when he said it. "I vouch for every member of my crew. We've been through some of the worst, and they've stuck by me. And Kettle has a point. For those who haven't had family and friends taken, it's easy to see why they wouldn't want to get involved, especially when it could mean putting their lives on the line."

Treygan turned and addressed our table. "But I ask you to imagine what you would do if the slavers had come and taken one of your own. A mother. A wife. A sister. A brother. How many of you wouldn't walk into the Pits of Aran'gal and spit in the Defiler's eye if it meant a chance to get them back?"

No one spoke, but their hard stares said plenty.

"The Cylmarans have been crossing our borders for years, taking our people to work in their mines. My parents were killed by slavers. Horis had a brother taken." Treygan shook his head. "After what I've seen, I can't help but think that my parents were the lucky ones."

"Aye," Horis said, his voice determined. "We plead with the crown and they do nothing. They're more worried about the southern border than they are about those of us living up here at the foot of the Black Hills. If they aren't going to lift a hand to help, then I say it's high time we helped ourselves. The guards at the camp are sparse during the winter months while the mines are closed. If we strike now before they can send reinforcements, we stand a good chance of taking the camp.

"What's more," Horis said, looking directly at me. "We have an Upaka with us. No one alive is more capable of getting in and out of places without being seen. At least, so I've been told." He stared at me as if waiting for me to confirm his statement.

*Great,* I thought, *let's just volunteer the Upaka when it comes to doing something stupid.*

"I won't make this an order," Treygan said, putting a foot on the bench and leaning on it. "So, if you decide this isn't your fight,

I won't think less of you. But for me, it's personal. I will say this: those that do decide to throw their lot in will receive a share of whatever spoils we find."

Kettle didn't say anything, but I could see a hint of gold flicker in the cook's eyes as he leaned forward in his seat, suddenly taking interest.

"The mines are at least two to three days south of here," Treygan said. "So, you still have time to make a decision before then. We'll remain anchored tonight. Best you get some rest before we set sail."

At this, Bones and Whitey escorted our guests down into the hold. There weren't enough hammocks, but there were plenty of blankets to go around.

I waited for the others to make it down before following. I was looking forward to crawling into my hammock and catching some much-needed rest. I'd made it to the third step when someone tapped me on the shoulder. It was Ismara.

"Father . . . I mean, the captain wants to see you."

What did Treygan want? Probably to talk me into joining this suicidal mission. I followed her out of the mess and across the main deck toward the captain's cabin. I waited outside the door as she opened it and mumbled something to her father inside.

"Send him in," I heard Treygan say.

Ismara opened the door the rest of the way and stepped aside. A single lantern swung from a hook near the door, bathing the cabin in warm light and shadows, as a couple of candles lit the top of a round table at the center of the room. The space was cramped even without the addition of a writing desk, two standing shelves, a couple of chairs, and a chest big enough for me to sleep in. By the look of it, I'd half-believe the stories of pirates and their booty were true if the chest hadn't already been open, revealing nothing more than some folded clothing, a couple of quilts, and a few books. Moonlight poured in through the bay windows at the back, adding its pale light to the table's candles.

"Have a seat, Ayrion," Treygan said as I stepped in a little farther. The captain was standing with Horis, looking at a stack of papers.

Ismara closed the cabin door and walked to another that stood open on the left. "Good night, Father," she said.

"Good night," he replied, not bothering to look up from his work.

She smiled at me and closed the door behind her. It didn't occur to me until after I heard the latch to her door click shut that the polite thing would have been to say good night as well. *Too late now,* I thought.

I took my seat and waited, wondering how it was that I continued to go from one bad situation to another. Enough time passed while the captain and Horis discussed possible infiltration scenarios without acknowledging my presence that I wondered if they had forgotten I was there.

I cleared my throat. "You wished to see me, Captain?"

Treygan dropped his quill and looked across the table at me. "We seem to have a problem. One that I hope you can provide us an answer to."

I leaned forward slightly. "How so?"

"Come, take a look."

I joined the two on the opposite side of the table in staring at a large hand-drawn map. It was quite detailed. I recognized some of the features as being locations along the Shemoa River.

"This here is the branch that leads into the Black Hills and toward our destination," he said, using his finger to trace the course through the mountains. "Right here," he said, tapping a circular area, "the water opens into a large cove completely surrounded by rock. On the far side, there's a narrow passageway that leads from the water back through the mountains to the Cylmaran mines, and where we need to go. There's only one way in."

I studied the map. The river looked wide enough for the *Wind Binder* to sail down, and half the boats in Cretollo could have anchored inside the cove.

I saw the problem. "You can't get in there without being seen?"

Horis smiled. "There's no way to sail a ship the size of the *Wind Binder* in without raising alarm," he said, leaning wearily on the table.

"How did you do it before?" I asked.

"Before?" Horis asked, looking at me as though I'd caught him off guard.

"You mentioned that you had taken other shipments in."

"Yes, well, we were using longboats then, toting blankets and food, not a small militia."

The captain removed his hat and laid it on the table. He scratched at the cloth tied around his head. "Most of my previous trips have been to try bribing the guards to release some of the miners. If we raise enough money, they sell us some. Our stop in Melforn was to collect payment and a small list of names in hopes they were in a generous mood. We use the supplies to get close enough to pay the ransoms. The Cylmarans care more about the size of their purses than anything. They can always send more of their own citizens to go work the mines. I think the main reason they cross our borders is in hope of capturing someone who we'd be willing to pay gold to get back."

"Why doesn't your king do something about it?" If a group of thugs had ever invaded Upakan land and tried kidnapping some of us to use as slave labor, there wouldn't have been anything left of them before the week was out. Of course, no one would have been stupid enough to ever try such a thing in the first place.

"He's your king, too," Treygan said with a chuckle.

I knew the High King was the figurehead for the five kingdoms, but the Upaka were considered outsiders and content to remain so.

Horis sighed. "Elondria is a big nation, lad, and it's surrounded on all sides. There's no way to protect every part of its border. No, I'm afraid we're on our own."

"Putting that aside," Treygan said, leaning over the table to look at the map, "the trouble with this rescue is that we have but one longboat. If we were to try ferrying our crew from the ship to the dock at the back of the lagoon, it would take us half the night."

"Not to mention we'd have to make multiple trips without raising suspicion," Horis added, stroking his ginger-colored beard.

"The only way this will work," Treygan said, "is to sail the

*Wind Binder* into the lagoon and come ashore. But—"

"There's no way to do that without being seen," I finished. I studied the map some more. "How often do these Cylmaran ships dock and unload supplies?"

The two men looked at each and shrugged.

"Is it possible they might mistake us for one of their ships, at least long enough for us to take the docks before they sound an alarm? We don't have any markings on the ship. No flag to show our allegiance—"

"Aye," Horis said, "but the Cylmaran ships do. They'd spot us before we made it halfway across the cove. They have watchers here and here." He pointed at the mountains on the left side, near the dock. "Even if we manage to sail through in the middle of a storm where they couldn't see us until we reached the dock, the sentries would spot us and sound the alarm before we could ever make it to the camps."

I looked back down at the large piece of vellum once more. It seemed a hopeless cause.

"So, why do you need me?" I asked.

The captain smiled. "How are you at climbing?"

I laughed.

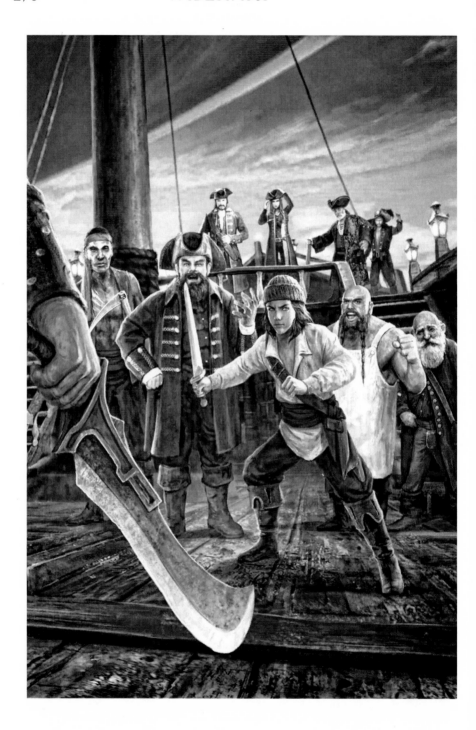

Chapter 30

HE TRIP INTO THE Black Hills took longer than expected. The wind had turned as a storm coming in from the south forced us to raise the sails, cutting the speed we'd previously enjoyed.

I stepped onto the deck to the sound of steel clanging in a familiar rhythm. The crew was gathered around the main deck, watching a couple of fighters trading strikes. As short as I was, I couldn't see who was fighting, so I climbed the steps to the quarterdeck and joined the captain and Needle at the railing.

From this vantage, I was granted the perfect view of Ismara dueling one of Horis's men.

"She takes too many risks, Captain," Needle said as he spun his compass on its chain. "Too many risks, I tell you."

The captain wore a proud smile. "It's the only way to learn."

Ismara's opponent was at least a head taller than she was and a good hundred pounds heavier. Surprisingly, she was holding her own. Her form was good. Her stance was perhaps a little long, but she seemed to be managing it. The main problem was in her defense. She was overcompensating. If he swung, she'd swing right back and with twice the power. It was like she had something to prove.

If she continued to use that much force with every block, she was going to wear out before her opponent did. I remembered doing the same when I had first started my training. I would want to keep my opponent's weapon as far from me as possible. I'd try knocking their sword from their hands with every parry. It had taken me a while to learn that you only needed to deflect a blade a few inches for it to miss its target.

Her opponent held his weapon well, but his movements were choppy—block, strike, parry, thrust. Every motion clear, concise. No finesse. No real flow. It was the kind of technique you saw from someone with military training.

They circled each other for a moment to catch their breath. Ismara looked like she needed it, judging from the sweat on her face and the way she was panting.

Ismara advanced. She swiped at his head, side, and shoulder in quick succession, leaving her opponent with little room for his own advances. She got close enough to elbow him in the stomach, and he stumbled backward. She lunged with a single thrust, but he recovered and deflected it, punching her in the shoulder with his free hand.

She spun and retreated.

Her opponent showered her with strikes to the side and head, intent on overwhelming her. She grunted as she worked to hold him back, sidestepping left to break his advance. Her fatigue was showing now in the amount of effort it took to maintain her balance, and her guard was slipping.

He came at her again, concentrating on her left side, where she was weakest. She parried, but her movements were sluggish. Instead of deflecting, she was chasing the blade, swinging wildly in a desperate attempt to force his guard down. It seemed to work, and she lunged for the opening.

I shook my head, seeing her mistake.

Her opponent had left it open on purpose. He used her momentum to deflect the strike and spin around behind her. His final swing stopped at the back of her neck, and the match was over.

She conceded the win to the cheers of those gathered around. Our crew wasn't quite as enthusiastic as Horis's men, but they clapped and offered smiles of encouragement.

Pops stood off to the side, chewing on his pipe, back far enough to not get hit by a wide swing. He also seemed to be keeping his distance from our guests. He wasn't the only one. Most of our crew had gathered to one side, giving Horis and his men plenty of room. I couldn't blame them. We might be fighting alongside this new crew, but I didn't know them well enough to trust them. Most appeared a little too eager for a fight.

Horis put his arm around Ismara. "Quite the spirited fighter you have here, Treygan. A few more years of training and a little more meat on these pretty bones, and even I'd be afraid to stand against her."

Ismara's lips tightened.

"And what does our resident Upaka have to say?" Horis asked, turning his attention up to the quarterdeck and to me. There was a hint of a challenge behind his words. "Any wisdom to impart for our captain's daughter?"

She glanced at me briefly, then lowered her eyes. Her fists were clenched. I swallowed. I didn't like being put on the spot. Worse yet, he was forcing me to judge someone who was just starting to warm up to me.

"I think she would make an exceptional Upaka."

On my left, I heard the captain release a slow breath.

"High praise indeed," Horis said with a nod. "Would you care to give us a demonstration? Upakan training is legendary. It's not every day we have the pleasure of enjoying one's company." He smiled mischievously. "They say if you ever lay eyes on an Upaka, it's the last thing you'll ever see."

I smiled politely. "Another time, perhaps."

"Come, come," he said, waving me down. "I'm sure there's much we can learn from such instruction." Horis sounded friendly, but it was obvious he was trying to goad me into participating.

The rest of the crew now turned eagerly in my direction.

I glanced at the captain and he shrugged. "You won't hear the end of it unless you do," he said with a wry smile.

He was right. They probably wouldn't stop pressuring me until

I did. Besides, a small demonstration might go a long way to winning me their respect, and it might give some of the new ones pause if they had any intention of testing me further. I raised my hands in defeat and made my way down the stairs to the main deck.

"Aye, there's a good lad," Horis said with a slight tug on his beard. The men on deck moved to make room. Ever since our first run-in with Horis and his men, I'd taken to wearing my sword at all times. I felt comfortable enough leaving my bow with the rest of my gear, but I didn't want to get caught without my blade.

"Who'll put their sword to the test?" Horis asked as he looked around the ring. "Who'll be willing to match their steel with our young Upakan friend here?"

No one stepped forward.

"Come, now. Surely we have a brave-enough soul here willing to put this young man to the test."

"I will."

I turned. Worg, who looked just as ready to fight as he had the night before, stepped forward and drew his blade. It was almost as big as I was. I guessed if I had to face one of them, it might as well be the biggest and meanest of the lot.

Even his own crew didn't seem to care much for him. In the time he'd been on board, I'd never seen the man smile. But that could have been because of the long scar that pulled one side of his mouth down in a permanent frown.

Pops walked over to me and placed an arm around my shoulder. "Be careful with this one," he murmured. "I've heard he's not lost a fight. I've also heard he's put more than one opponent in the ground."

I couldn't tell if he was trying to warn me, frighten me, or both.

"I'll be careful. I'm sure the captain won't let it go that far."

Pops looked at me as if to say more but then finally nodded and lowered his arm.

"Let's have a clean fight," Horis said as he limped with his gout-ridden leg to the center of the deck. "First to force the other to concede wins." Horis raised both hands, inviting us to the center of the deck. "Back up and give them some room," he said, "or suffer the consequences."

The two crews quickly backed away, not wanting to lose an arm or head from a foul blade.

I drew my sword and walked to the middle of the deck. My sword balanced well in my hand. I could feel the ship's sway deepen as we hit rougher wakes. I bent my legs slightly for balance.

Worg raised his sword. He looked eager. A little too eager. Like many of the boatmen, he carried a cutlass, but his was at least a foot longer than usual and broader at the hilt, with a more defined curve toward the point. A sword that size would have made fighting aboard ship more difficult, but Worg didn't seem to care. He carried his blade like a club, his entire hand wrapped around the hilt, ready to swing it like a chunk of wood, which told me a lot about his tactics. Someone as big as Worg didn't rely on skill or speed. He used his size and strength to intimidate his opponent.

When facing a smaller, less-trained fighter, Worg would have had a clear advantage because of his reach, but when facing an Upaka, size and strength didn't count for much. And when facing an Upaka who also happened to wield magic . . .

"Are you ready?" Horis asked, his arm raised, anxious to get the fight underway.

"Ready," I said, not looking away from Worg. I kept my blade pointed toward the deck instead of bringing it up into a customary guard.

Worg didn't say anything. He simply growled.

"May the best man win."

I released my magic, letting the heat of it come alive inside me. I wanted to test Worg the same way I did with every new opponent I faced. I needed to see what they were capable of, how far they were willing to go.

Horis swung his arm to begin the fight, but before he got a chance to step out of the way, Worg raised his sword with both hands and swung. His blade missed Horis's chest by a hairsbreadth as it drove for my head. His swing was powerful. Too powerful. Instead of simply retreating out of the way, I let his blade come. I felt the burn as it sliced through my neck. Worg hadn't even attempted to slow. The man was out for blood, and he'd just found it.

I heard Ismara scream somewhere behind me. Then everything shifted, and we were back at the line once again with Horis's hand in the air.

". . . best man win." Horis flung his arm to signal the start of the match.

As disturbing as it had been to let myself get killed, I'd wanted to test my opponent's resolve. Thanks to my magic, I now knew how far he was willing to go.

My plan hadn't been to embarrass Worg during our duel. I had intended to give those watching a good fight and then disarm him. But when someone up and kills you for no other reason than to prove he's capable, something inside you snaps.

Now I was going to make an example of him.

Worg shouted and his blade swung around.

I retreated, and he hit nothing.

"What do you think you're doing!" Horis shouted as he staggered back to get out of the big swordsman's way. "You nearly hit me!"

Worg ignored him. He was focused on me, clearly upset at not having finished the job with his first swing. He advanced with one monstrous cut after another. I almost laughed. The way he swung his arms around, telegraphing every move, I had no need of magic. His shoulders let me know exactly what he intended before he did it. Clearly, he'd never faced an opponent he couldn't muscle his way through.

I never once raised my guard, never once used my sword. I dodged left, ducked and feinted right, then sidestepped just far enough to feel the wind from his steel as it passed. With each failed attempt, Worg grew angrier, his attacks fiercer. Before long, I had no choice but to use my sword, but only enough to simply swat the strike away like I might an annoying fly. I yawned. I wiped my eyes. I scratched my head, all while deflecting, parrying, and blocking every attempt at my life.

The men were shouting at Worg, at first in encouragement and then to berate him. Pretty soon they were all but laughing at him. One man, Jenner, I thought his name was, shouted something about Worg not being able hit to the side of the boat had he been standing there trying to urinate on it.

Worg immediately took a swing at his shipmate. Jenner screamed and dove to the right, knocking three others down in the process.

Taking advantage of the distraction, I backed to the edge of the ship. I ended up against the break in the railing for the gangplank. The safety rope tied across the gap tapped the back of my knees as I waited, giving me an idea.

I tested the rope's strength with my foot. I hoped it would hold.

"That's enough!" Treygan shouted from the quarterdeck, but Worg didn't listen.

Worg spun. "No one makes a fool of me," he hissed, his head jerking back and forth in search of me.

Our eyes met.

From the corner of my eye, I could see the captain coming down the stairs on the left. "Horis! Get your man under control!" I sighed, knowing there wasn't much the captain, or Horis, was going to be able to do to stop him.

Another vision hit, and I dove forward, rolling under a swing bent on cutting me in two. I was back on my feet in time to deflect the next three, each more determined than the last.

With each parry, I retreated farther toward the opposite side of the ship, giving me enough room to make a mad dash back to the opening in the railing on the other side. For this to work, I needed

Worg to chase me.

"What's wrong?" I said mockingly. "A thirteen-year-old too much for you to handle?"

Worg brought his cutlass up and over. I never even lifted my sword. I waited till the last moment and then dodged to the side, letting it sink into the top of the rail behind me. I tried getting around him, but one of the pallets of crates caught my leg, and I went down, just about the time Worg yanked his sword free.

He turned and brought his blade down like an axe. I rolled, and it struck the deck where I'd just been, sending wood chips flying. I jumped to my feet and ran for the other side of the ship as if my life depended on it. It didn't take much acting on my part.

I could feel him right behind me. I didn't dare look. The edge of the boat was only steps away and I ran straight for it. My foot hit the rope, and I prayed it would hold. It took my weight as I kicked off it in the opposite direction and hit Worg just below the shins. His feet flew out from under him, and he sailed straight over the side of the ship. I heard the splash and then the shouting when he finally broke the surface.

"Man overboard!" Horis shouted, as if we hadn't all just watched it happen. "Drop the anchor. Throw a line."

"Belay that order," Treygan said as he joined me and the others at the rail. He leaned over and watched as Worg desperately swam for the ship. The current, however, was too strong, and we slowly pulled away.

Horis pushed through his men and found a spot at the edge to see for himself. "Well, aren't you going after him? We need all the men we can get."

The captain turned and walked back across the deck. "Not men like that."

"Good riddance," Bones said with a scoff. He turned and followed Treygan up the stairs.

Horis looked down at me and tugged on his beard. I couldn't tell if he was angry. What I could see was a hint of fear in his eyes, and the others', after what they'd just seen me do.

## Chapter 31

WE REACHED OUR DESTINATION by the afternoon of the next day.

The storm from the south had come and gone, and in spite of it, the captain had managed to find the branch in the river leading west toward the Black Hills. I could see where the mountains had gotten their name. The granite was even darker than that of the Northern Heights. Its black reflection in the water gave it an impenetrable sort of feel.

The channel through the mountains was beautiful. The dull echo of our passage off the rock reminded me in a small way of home. It was a comforting presence.

After yesterday's unsettling duel and the decision by the captain to leave Worg behind, no one had felt it necessary to discuss the situation further, at least not in front of Treygan. Worg's ousting from the ship had come as a relief to many. Apparently, I wasn't the only one Worg had threatened while on board. I had a feeling that if it hadn't been for me, the captain would have ordered him off either way, which would have led to Worg challenging Treygan. In the end, it had worked out for the best.

I studied the mountain face as we passed, encouraged by the amount of deformation visible on the surface. It would make for much easier climbing. The captain wanted me to wait until dark to start my trek up, so they could row me in as close as possible and then wait for my signal before trying to take the dock.

"You're not seriously considering climbing that, are you?" Ismara asked as she joined me at the bow. Treygan had anchored the *Wind Binder* far enough back from the mouth of the lagoon to avoid being spotted. "Don't get me wrong. After seeing what you did to Worg, I doubt there's much you can't do, but it's one thing to stand against a single man. It's quite another to face a mountain." She tilted her head and looked up at the crest hundreds of feet above us. "Doesn't that frighten you? I'm getting dizzy just looking at it."

"It won't be the first time I've scaled the face of a cliff." I cocked my head to the side. "You sound worried."

"Hardly," she said, and took a step back. "I just . . . I'd just hate for you to fall and alert them to our presence, is all." She stared at me for a moment. "Fine," she said, folding her arms. "It wouldn't be completely wrong to say that some of us have grown used to having you around."

I stood there staring, not sure if she was expecting me to say something.

She huffed. "I'm trying to tell you to be careful, Eelface."

"Oh." I offered her my most charming smile.

"Ugh! You're so annoying," she said, walking off.

Not quite the send-off I'd hoped for, but with Ismara, it was probably the best I would get.

I left my perch at the bow and went below to check my gear. Heavy snores were coming from the men who'd stood watch the previous night. I tried not to disturb them as I walked across the hull to where Pops was sitting beside his chest. It was already open and waiting for me.

"You got what you need to make it to the top?"

"I believe so," I said as I pulled my travel pack out and laid it on the floor. I was grateful Father had packed my picks. I probably would have left them behind. Who would have thought I'd find myself climbing another mountainside?

Pops leaned forward on his seat. "In all my years," he said, pointing the tip of his pipe at me, "I've never seen anything like what I saw up on that deck." He fixed me with his eye. "Worg could've swung a hundred times, and I doubt he'd even have come close. It was like you knew what he was going do before he did." He shook his head. "Nope. Never seen anything like it before."

"Lucky, I guess."

"Lucky?" Pops laughed. He had to catch his pipe before he dropped it. "You need to pass a little of that luck on to me, lad."

"I don't think you'll want any of my luck. Don't forget, I'm the one who got volunteered to climb up there and dispose of the sentries."

Pops nodded solemnly. "Aye. Suppose you're right."

"Which reminds me. Do we have any spare rope?" I asked, looking around the barely filled hull for an extra few coils not being used to tie down the cargo. "And not the thick stuff. Something I can use to tie off some hands and feet."

"I reckon I can find some," Pops said, standing. "How much you think you'll be needing?"

I thought about it a moment. "Fifteen feet. Five coils' worth should do it."

Pops smiled. "This is a cargo ship; I'm sure we have some spare cord around here somewhere. I'll see what I can scrounge up and meet you topside." He left me there as I continued packing my bag. This time, I was going to have to take more than just my axes. It wouldn't be as easy of a climb, but I needed to make sure I had enough to get the job done.

I put all the gear I wasn't taking back in Pops' chest and locked the lid before going topside to return the key. As luck would have it, he'd found the cord I needed. The only thing left was to wait.

There was a nervous energy among the crew as they went about their duties. Normal conversations had been reduced to cautious whispers. All eyes watched the rising cliffs on either side of the ship as if worried they'd somehow close in on them if not kept under constant surveillance. Those not on deck were in the hull, catching up on some much-needed sleep.

"It's time," Treygan said as he brushed past me on his way to the port side of the ship. "Lower the longboat and prepare the men."

Bones nodded and motioned for Whitey to give him a hand. A couple of others from Horis's crew joined them as they lowered the boat over the side and into the water. Bones had applied some sort of white paint to his face. There were stripes down his chin, under his eyes, and across his cheeks. I wasn't sure why, other than to make him look even more intimidating.

The captain left the men to their work and headed across the deck to his cabin.

I felt a tap on my shoulder and turned around.

"Just wanted to wish you well before you left," Needle said, which was uncharacteristic for him. His gold compass swung from its chain in his left hand. "We'll look for your safe return."

"Thank you." I didn't know what else to say. It was the most he'd said to me since the first day I'd come on board. He turned and headed back up to the navigator's station on the quarterdeck.

"Got everything, lad?" Pops asked as he strolled across the deck.

I checked my supplies for the hundredth time. "Looks like it," I said, then hefted the satchel and headed for the longboat, where the crew were already climbing over the side to take their places at the oars.

"Hold your sails," someone said behind me.

I stopped and turned.

Kettle stepped out of the crew cabin and walked over, carrying a small, wrapped package. He had his sword strapped to his waist and his butcher knife sheathed in a small leather case on his belt. "Thought you might want this," he said, handing the package to me. It was warm to the touch, and something inside smelled good. "It be a long climb up. Figured you could use a bite to eat once you reach the top." He smiled, as much as his grumpy face would let him. "Put some of that bacon you like so much in there as well."

"Thank you," I said, surprised by Kettle's sudden show of concern. I added the bundle to my pack.

"Well, don't just stand there burning light, boy. Get a move on." With that, Kettle walked past and climbed over the side of the ship, down into the boat.

Pops pulled his pipe from his mouth and pointed it in the direction Kettle had just taken. "That be the first time I've seen that man do anything like that before. Guess you've made an impression." He popped his pipe back in and started chewing. "He be right, though. Best you get a move on. Sun disappears mighty quickly in these mountains. By the time you make it into the lagoon, it'll be good and dark."

I walked with Pops to the side of the railing and looked down at the longboat as it floated against the *Wind Binder*. I could see Whitey, Bones, and Kettle were already in and waiting, along with Horis and five others.

"Wait for the signal," Treygan said from somewhere behind me.

Pops and I turned around.

The captain closed the door to his cabin and walked toward us with Ismara in tow. "When you see it, I want you and the rest of the men to sail the *Wind Binder* into the lagoon and meet us at the dock on the other side."

"Aye, aye," she said, coming to attention. For a moment there, I thought she was going to salute.

"You ready?" Treygan asked when he reached us.

"As ready as I'll ever be, I guess."

He looked me over. "Good. Everything rides on you. If you don't get those sentries, then all of this will have been for nothing."

"So, no pressure, then?"

The captain smiled and laid a hand on my shoulder. "After what I witnessed between you and Worg, I'm not too worried. Just be careful. I want to get those people out of there, but I don't want to risk you in the process."

The captain turned to Ismara. "The old girl's in your hands now. Keep her safe." He spared a quick glance around the *Wind Binder*'s deck and then climbed over the side.

I nodded at Pops, then grabbed my pack and started over myself.

"Wait," Ismara said. She walked over and kissed me on the cheek. "For luck."

I was thankful it was getting dark, so she couldn't see how red my face was. I left her there and shimmied down the rope ladder into the bow of the boat. I waved at Pops and Ismara as the longboat began to pull away from the ship.

The river was slow this evening, the oars sending ripples across its surface with each new stroke. The opening to the lagoon was just ahead.

The sun had lowered far enough to keep the open basin smothered in darkness. The colors that had saturated the sky earlier had now turned to slate gray. We rowed through a narrow spot between the rock faces. It was barely large enough for a single ship to pass. I hoped Needle was up to the challenge. He was going to have to do some fancy threading to make it through undamaged.

I could see the dock on the far side of the cove. It was the only spot not bordered by cliffs. The mountains lowered there, forming a depression between the peaks large enough to build a small port. I wondered if the water was deep enough to allow the *Wind Binder* to unload the men straight onto the dock.

We kept to the left side of the lagoon. The cliff face wasn't quite as sheer, and more importantly, it was the side where the sentries had always been the other times Treygan had made his supply runs.

By the time we'd reached a spot on the wall where I felt there were enough grips for me to start working my way up, the stars had begun to wink into view. The sky was clear and the wind was down, good conditions if you found yourself needing to climb a granite wall in the middle of the night to subdue lookouts.

The captain guided the boat as close to the rock as he dared.

I slipped my pack around my shoulders and looked up at the cliff. I couldn't see the top. My hands shook a little as I thought about what was ahead of me. Unlike my climb up Howling Gorge, there was a whole lot more at stake than simply passing a test. The crew's safety depended on me.

The questions weighed heavy as I patted the two picks at my waist, reassuring myself they were still there.

"Good luck to you, lad," the captain said.

"Aye," Horis agreed. "Once you dispatch the watchers, use the signal and we'll hit the dock."

I nodded, took a deep breath, and stepped off the boat.

Chapter 32

$\mathcal{O}$ HE CLIMB WAS MUCH EASIER than I had expected, even with the added weight of my pack. Far easier than the one I had faced at Howling Gorge. The rock under my feet was a nice change to the constant sway of the ship. The climb, however, wasn't the challenge. The real challenge was what awaited me at the top—subduing three guards without anyone knowing I was there.

After a couple of hours of climbing, I dug my feet into a small alcove and took a moment to rest my arms. According to the map, I should have been just east of the first guard's position. I looked down to see if I could spot the longboat, but there was no sign of it. Obviously, the captain had wanted to get as close to the dock as he could without risking being seen, so they could storm the dock as soon as I took care of the sentries.

Moonlight illuminated the cliffs on the other side of the lagoon, still too low in the sky to reach the water. I found my next set of holds and pushed on. The weathered face of the rock was proving to be much more stable than what I had been forced to use during my run at the Tri'Nephrin.

The crest was within sight. A few more stable handholds and I'd be there. Kettle's bacon was whispering in my ear to hurry, a sentiment my growling stomach agreed with wholeheartedly. I looked for the next outcropping and swung. My arms ached from the extra weight I carried, and my fingers were beginning to go numb. I needed to hurry.

I reached for the last hold and pulled.

I didn't know who was more surprised: me or the Cylmaran lookout. He shot to his feet from where he had been sitting in front of a small fire, whittling a piece of wood. "What in the name of—"

"Give me a hand. It's a long way down."

The man stood there for a moment in silence, his mouth hanging open. Finally, he dropped the stick of wood and walked to the edge. "What are you doing?" he asked in a rather annoyingly high-pitched voice. I understood his words, but they came with a strong accent I wasn't used to hearing. "Who are you?" He looked over the side. I didn't know if he was trying to see where I had come from or if there were more with me, but either way, he eventually grabbed my hand and helped me up.

"Thanks, mister," I said as I took a moment to unsaddle my pack from my aching shoulders.

"I'll have an answer," the guard demanded, reaching for his sword. "Who are you?"

"I'm Ayrion," I said as if nothing was amiss. "Didn't they tell you I was coming?"

"Who?" The guard's hand was on the hilt, but he hadn't drawn.

I leaned over and picked up a large rock with one hand, using my pack to hide it. "Mind holding this?" I said as I shoved my gear at him. If you don't give people time to think, you'll be surprised what they'll be willing to do.

As soon as he reached to take it, I clubbed him in the back of the head.

He fell forward, dropping my pack as he hit the ground. He started to squirm, so I wrapped my arm around his neck, shutting off his air until he was unconscious. I tied off his hands and then his feet before gagging his mouth to keep him from warning the others. I was half-tempted to roll him off the side of the cliff, but the splash would have alerted everyone that something was wrong. Besides, I didn't want to openly kill someone who was doing nothing more than enjoying an evening fire.

My goal wasn't to kill all the guards, only subdue them. I didn't have the taste for killing that many of the other Upakans had. I was more like my father. I preferred not to, if given the choice. Sure, the men we were after were slavers and deserved whatever punishment they got, but other than the word of some very determined shipmates, I hadn't seen anything yet that warranted killing. For all I knew, we had the wrong location. Last thing I wanted was to carry the deaths of a bunch of innocents on my conscience.

With the first guard down and no one in sight, I decided to take a break. I walked over, sat by the fire he had so graciously started for me, and warmed my hands. Opening my pack, I pulled out Kettle's wrapped bundle. Inside, I found three thick slices of bacon he had saved for me, along with a biscuit, a couple of slices of cheese, and an apple.

After devouring the last piece of bacon, I retied the top of my pack and tucked my dagger into my belt. I left my sword tied to the top of my bundle instead of strapping it on. The bouncing would have given me away before I'd gotten within a hundred feet of the next lookout. I was starting to wonder why I had brought so many weapons, but like my father used to say, better to have them and not need them than to not have them when I did need them. Hefting my pack, I left the trussed guard to his dozing.

One down, two more to go. At least according to the map.

A narrow footpath led off in the general direction of where I was guessing the next lookout station was positioned. The top of the ridge was filled with boulders of varying sizes, scrub brush, and a few sporadic trees. I was careful to keep from kicking up any loose rock in case someone was close enough to hear. I was feeling very thankful for my Upakan eyes. On a night such as this, it would be easy to take a wrong step and tumble right over the edge of the bluff without knowing it.

To my right, moonlight worked its way down the side of the cliff on the opposite side of the lagoon. It would soon be high enough to illuminate the waters below. Of course, that also meant my time was running short. I needed to take care of the last two sentries before the light gave away the captain and crew's position.

The trail twisted back and forth along the edge of the cliffs. At times, the lagoon was visible, but at others, the trail cut inland, hiding the water below. I hoped the guards stayed at their posts and didn't wander the trail between them.

A shift in the wind sent the aroma of fresh-cooked meat in my direction. I stopped, sniffing to locate where it was coming from. The next watch station must have been just ahead. I stepped into the shadows of a large rock and quickly lowered my pack. I couldn't see the guard, but I knew he had to be just on the other side.

Slowly, I edged around the massive piece of granite until I caught my first glimpse of his campsite. Like the other guard, he was seated about fifteen feet from the edge. A small fire crackled and popped in front of him. He was surrounded on all sides by rock, making sneaking up behind him all but impossible. So, if I couldn't get to him, I needed him to come to me. I smiled as an idea began to form.

I made my way back around the rock to where I was out of sight of the lookout and then ran back down the footpath to where I had left the first guard. Grabbing his cloak and his hat, along with a stick of firewood, I made my way back to the second lookout, sliding along the rough wall to where I'd left my pack. With the sentry's cloak around my shoulders and hat angled low, I moved halfway out of the shadows, enough for him to see part of me and hopefully recognize the outfit, but not enough for him to see me. I bent at an angle toward the rock to help hide my shorter size.

Mimicking the first guard's high-pitched voice wasn't too difficult, considering my voice hadn't lowered yet. "Hey, come take a look at this." I kept my back turned to make it look like I was staring at something on the ground up near the rock.

"Why aren't you at your post?" the guard asked. I could hear his boots thumping across the rock as they approached. "What are you looking at?"

He was nearly on top of me when I spun around and clubbed him across the side of his face. My swing was a little too hard, and he hit the ground with a thud. He didn't move.

I checked to make sure I hadn't killed him before grabbing a few more pieces of rope to bind him with. His face was already purpling from where the wood had hit him.

"Two down. One to go."

I retrieved my pack and walked to the edge of the cliff. The water in the lagoon below sparkled as the pale light of the moon washed halfway across its surface, giving it the appearance of freshly polished gems. I idly wished I had time to sit and drink in the sight, but I still had one more sentry, and time was running out.

On my left, I could see the dock running out from the natural inlet between the sides of the mountains. So far, no other ships had entered from the Cylmaran side. The longboat, with Captain Treygan, Horis, and the others, was hidden even from my eyes. They must have been up against the face of the cliff, hiding in the darker shadows of the mountainside.

Once again, I hefted my travel pack. The path ahead descended gradually as I got closer to the other side of the cove. I kept my ears open for anything ahead, but nothing more than the occasional call of an owl or the howl of a lone coyote broke the stillness.

How much farther was the final sentry? As the slope down steepened, I figured I had to be getting close to the inlet and the dock. Had I somehow missed the third guard? Maybe there weren't three lookouts. Maybe there were only two. Or maybe I had started my climb too far to the west and the third guard was still behind me. The farther I walked, the more worried I became.

The wind whipped across the mountainside, blowing my hair across my face. I readjusted my new hat to keep it at bay, but it had been made for a much larger head. A single gust ripped it off and sent it on ahead. I chased after it. It came to a stop at the foot of an old tree just off the path. I walked over and snatched it up about the same time the third guard stepped out from the other side.

One look at me, or more importantly at the light reflecting off my eyes, and he turned and ran.

There was no way I was going to catch him, so I threw off my pack and grabbed my bow. I strung it as fast as my trained hands would go and grabbed an arrow, forcing myself to use calm, precise movements. The guard was at least a couple dozen yards and gaining. He raced along the widening path as it sloped down to the dock.

I took a deep breath and drew the string. I sighted down the shaft, watching as his head bobbed up and down over the rock. There was an opening just ahead of him. It would be my only chance.

*Three. Two. One.*

I let go. The arrow spun through the air, cutting a path straight for the guard. He hit the straightaway, took three steps, and dropped. He screamed as he rolled to a stop.

I snatched up my pack, bow still in hand, and chased after him. The damage was already done. There was no need for a signal. If anyone had been watching the dock, they would have certainly heard the man's screams. I didn't doubt those still on the *Wind Binder* could have as well.

The guard was still writhing on the ground when I reached him. I yanked the arrow out of his backside and kicked him in the head. He was still moving, so I kicked him again. That seemed to work.

I tied his arms and legs but didn't bother with the gag. There didn't seem to be much point, and I needed to get to the dock.

By the time I reached the bottom and started down the dirt road leading toward the water, I could hear the sound of battle ahead. I rounded the corner and was saved by one of my visions as an escaping guard attempted to run me over with his horse. I dove to the side. The rest of the horses were tied not ten feet away, so I jumped on the first one and took off after him.

The captain shouted something behind me. I didn't need to hear him to understand. If this guard managed to get to the camp and warn the others, not only would we not be able to rescue the workers, but our odds of surviving a full-on conflict would be extremely slim. The Cylmarans outnumbered us three to one.

I dug my heels in and gave my horse its head, which was not

something a rider would ever consider doing in the dark on unknown terrain, but my eyes could see hazards that the man I was chasing couldn't. I could push my horse faster without having to worry about breaking its legs.

The trail led straight back into the mountains, a wider version of the Squeeze back home. I quickly gained on the Cylmaran. We cut back and forth around the bends, pushing the animals faster with every turn. My horse was panting hard, sweat caking its flanks. The clay turned to rock as the route cut deeper into the Black Hills. The echo of the horses' hooves off the stone was deafening as we surged through the passageway.

I hadn't realized until now that my hand was still gripping my bow. I snatched an arrow and tried nocking it, but it slipped from my fingers when the horse jumped to miss a rock. I gripped the horse with my knees and grabbed another, managing to nock it. I raised it and tried to aim. The arrow flew by the man's head and ricocheted off the wall. This was useless. I wouldn't hit anything like this. Instead of pulling another arrow, I swatted the horse with my bow, giving me a small burst of speed.

I didn't like hitting the animal, but there wasn't much else I could do. One more hit and the horse pulled alongside the fleeing guard. We were running neck and neck. One wrong move and we'd both go down.

I had to do something. For all I knew, the mining compound was around the next corner. I pulled my legs up under me and groaned, knowing this was going to be one of the stupidest things I'd ever done.

I balanced on the back of my horse, my knees bent and moving to its rhythm. The man saw what I was about to do and reached for his sword, but I jumped before he could draw. I landed on top of him, grabbed his cloak, and yanked him off his horse.

We hit the ground and rolled, bouncing across the stone like skipping rocks across the surface of a lake. I managed to protect my head with my arms until finally coming to a stop against the rock wall. I had been spared the worst thanks to my pack, but I could tell I was going to be nursing some very deep, very nasty bruises for the next few weeks. I prayed nothing was broken.

I couldn't say the same for the Cylmaran. The man was barely moving.

I made it to my knees, checking myself for damage. I didn't think anything was broken, but the pain was enough to make my head spin. I crawled over to the Cylmaran. He was on his back, bloody face pointing skyward. Thankfully, he was still conscious, because I needed to get information about this compound we were heading for and who all was in it.

I pulled my knife and placed it against his throat. After being nearly trampled by the man's horse, I wasn't feeling very merciful. One way or another, I was going to get what I needed.

Chapter 33

"LARINGER . . . my name's Laringer," the Cylmaran said, coughing up blood as he lay there with my knife at his throat.

"Where are the mines?"

"Are you going to kill me?"

"Guess that depends on what you tell me. Now, where are the mines?"

His eyes shifted to the left. "Over there," he said, raising his arm. "Way I was headed."

"How far?"

"Not far. Few more bends."

"How many guards?"

He didn't answer, so I pressed the blade a little harder.

"About three dozen," he said, trying to swallow. Blood trickled down the side of his mouth.

"How many standing watch tonight?"

"You promise not to kill me? I don't wanna die."

"You tell me what I want to know, and I'll spare your life."

He studied my face for a moment, then nodded. "There's four, maybe five standing watch." He started coughing uncontrollably, spitting blood as he did, so I helped him to a sitting position against the rock wall. The guard was in bad shape. His arm was clearly broken, the bone jutting partway out. He didn't appear to be that old, probably younger than most of the crew of the *Wind Binder*, other than Ismara and me.

I kept up the questions, and he, between bouts of coughing, gave answers. By the time I heard horses coming up the canyon from the direction of the dock, the guard had told me everything I needed to know about the compound: the layout of the mines and buildings surrounding them; where the workers were being held; where the guards were likely to be standing watch; and most importantly, where the best place to enter without being seen was.

"I see you caught our runaway," Treygan said as he dismounted.

Horis slid off his horse, wincing when his bad foot hit the ground. "Good. Since it was your flaming fault he did. What was all that ruckus and shouting up in the hills?" He limped his way over. "I thought you Upakans were supposed to be silent killers."

I bit back my retort. "It couldn't be helped."

Treygan shot Horis a hard look. "I'm glad you were able to stop him. If he'd made it to the camp, this would have all been for nothing." He looked down at me. "Are you hurt?"

I winced when he touched the side of my forehead. "I'll be fine."

"No broken bones, I hope—"

"What's he told you?" Horis asked impatiently, staring hard at the man against the wall. "Has he told you how many of those faerie-lovin' mongrels are holed up in there?" He had a dangerous fire in his eyes. "Well, you got a tongue, boy. What did he say?"

"He said they're expecting new recruits any day now, but for the time being, they have around three dozen guards on post."

"Three dozen, you say?" Horis glanced at the wounded man.

"That's more than we had figured, Horis," Treygan said.

"Aye, but nothing we can't handle."

The captain raised a brow. "Heroics aside, we need to know more about the compound before we go any further."

Horis waved the captain off. "Yes, yes, but let's be quick about it. We don't have all night, and I know a few slavers who have an appointment with the tip of my blade."

"We wait for the rest of our crew," Treygan said, turning back to me. "What else has he told you?"

I relayed everything I'd learned from the guard, then Treygan questioned him further. The Cylmaran was too scared to do anything other than answer.

"We got everything we need?" Horis asked Treygan, towering over the guard.

"As much as we're going to get."

"You believe him?"

The captain looked over at the man and nodded. "I don't reckon he has cause to lie."

"Too scared to do otherwise, if you ask me," Bones said, moving up alongside the captain. I still couldn't get used to the paint on his face, which I was sure was the point. I wondered if something like that would work for me.

Horis looked down at the injured man and pulled his belt knife. "Good." Before any of us could stop him, he slit the man's throat.

"What do you think you're doing?" I ran for the guard and clamped my hands on his neck. His blood was warm as it squeezed through my fingers. The guard sat there with an expression of confusion and horror as his eyes went lifeless and his head drooped forward.

Treygan grabbed Horis by the arm and yanked him around. "The man was unarmed."

Horis sneered as he wiped his blade. "The man was a slaver and deserved much worse."

I spun around. "I promised him his life if he talked."

"Shouldn't go making promises like that," Horis said, and limped back to his horse.

I wiped the man's blood from my hands as best I could on his pant legs and turned to Treygan. "I'm going in first. That way, I can find where they have the workers and mobilize them before you storm the place." I glanced over at Horis. "Last thing we want is for the innocent to get mistaken for the guilty."

"Aye," Treygan said. "Better get a move on. Once the rest of our crew shows up, we'll follow."

I nodded and lifted my pack from where I had dropped it against the wall. Thankfully, there was no permanent damage. I was afraid I'd snapped my bow when I'd first hit the ground, but it appeared intact, if a bit scuffed. I took one last look at the bloody guard and then hefted my supplies onto my back.

Treygan put a hand on my shoulder. "Keep yourself safe."

I glanced past him at Horis. "You do the same."

"Don't worry about Horis. I'll rein him in. He's not a bad man, just eaten with hate." Treygan shrugged. "Can't say as I blame him."

Bones walked over, holding my stolen horse's reins. "Here you go."

I waved it off. "I'm going on foot. From what the guard told me, we're close. I'd rather them not hear me coming."

Bones nodded, and I turned and started walking. I lost sight of the men once I made it around the next curve. I stopped at each new turn and peeked around the corner, hoping to catch a glimpse of the mining compound. On the fifth, I finally did.

Here, the passage opened into a wide canyon. Not nearly as wide as the lagoon we'd boated in on, but enough to fit four or five buildings, a corral, a loading area with a number of wagons, and stacks of barrels filled with tools. I looked around for the tunnels leading into the mountainside, but I didn't see any. Instead, they had three large holes dug straight into the ground near the far side of the canyon, with a large pulley system built over each one. I wondered how deep they went.

I scanned the outer perimeter of the compound. I didn't see much activity. It wasn't like the prisoners had anywhere to escape to. If they managed to flee the compound and make it to the dock, they were still left with nowhere to go.

Three of the five buildings were bunkhouses for the workers. From what the Cylmaran had said, they were the three closest to the holes on the far side. The building closest to me was the guards' bunkhouse, and the final one was supposedly for storage and meals.

I hid my pack behind some large rocks at the edge of the passage and unstrapped my bow, slinging it and the quiver over my shoulder. My sword hung belted on one side and my dagger on the other. I felt ready for anything.

The moon was nearing its peak, bathing the clearing ahead in pale light and making it that much more difficult for me to move about unseen. I would need to keep to the edge of the mountain, where the shadows were thickest, if I planned on making it around to the workers' bunkhouses unnoticed.

From where I was standing, I could see three members of the patrol. The first was on my right, not twenty feet away, probably there to guard the entrance. It wouldn't have taken much to subdue him, but if I did and one of the guards found him before our people arrived, then the element of surprise would be gone. So, I waited until the guard's back was turned and headed for the opposite side of the passage, careful not to kick up any loose rocks.

Once I reached the other side, I hugged the wall, and not a moment too soon. The guard on my right turned unexpectedly and looked right at me. I didn't move. I didn't even breathe. This would be my luck, I thought. I hadn't even made it into the camp, and I'd already managed to alert the first guard I'd seen.

After a long, nerve-wracking moment, the guard finally turned back around.

I released the breath I'd been holding, counted to ten, and pushed on.

The trip around the left side of the encampment took longer than I had expected. Twice, I ran into obstacles that needed skirting—forcing me to leave the protective cover of the shadows—and once, a guard I hadn't seen stepped out from behind one of the wagons.

I ducked behind the wheels as he passed. Another man met him on the far side of the wagon. I didn't move, too afraid they'd spot me.

"It's my turn, Sim," the man on the left said. "Fagan was last night. I'm tonight."

"Fine. But don't let me catch you roughing this one up like you did the last. We need them to be able to work."

"I give you my word. She'll be at her post tomorrow."

"Then be quick about it," the man on the right said, and walked off.

The other man headed straight for the smaller of the three worker bunkhouses. I watched him go inside. A few minutes later, I heard some shouts, and then he came back out, dragging someone behind him. I couldn't see much from under the wagon, but I could tell it was a woman.

She clawed at him as he dragged her over behind some crates

near the wall.

I scanned the compound. The only movement I saw was from the other side of the mining holes. If I were smart, I'd have used the man's appetite as a distraction to get inside the bunkhouse, but I couldn't just listen to the woman's cries and do nothing.

Sticking to the shadows of the wagons, I made my way back to the mountainside. The large stack of supplies between me and the guard kept me from seeing what was happening, but it wasn't hard to figure out.

"Shut your mouth," the man said. His words were followed by a loud slap. The woman fought back her sobs. "Turn around, or you'll get worse."

Now I could see why Horis had been so outraged by these Cylmarans. I slipped my dagger from its sheath and moved slowly around the crates, watching for any sign of the other guards. No one was coming.

"No," she pleaded. "Please. Don't."

The Cylmaran's back was to me. I couldn't see much else, thankfully, as it appeared the man was busy trying to unfasten his trousers. By the time I made it completely around, the guard had the woman bent over a large barrel. The thought of what he intended had me gripping my knife even harder. For the first time, I wanted to kill someone. Flon I'd killed by accident. The bandits I'd killed out of necessity. But this was different.

I waited until both his hands were busy yanking his pants down before I attacked. I used one of the crates to leap onto the man's back and grab his mouth. I planted my dagger to the hilt in his chest. The feeling was eerily similar to the stuffed sacks of meat and grain we used to train on in the Lost City. I remembered wondering how it would feel to really do it.

Now I knew.

I twisted the blade, and he dropped to his knees. I twisted again, and he went still, falling sideways into the dirt.

The woman turned, and I grabbed her mouth as well, just before she screamed.

"I'm not going to hurt you. I'm here to help." I wasn't sure how much she believed me, with my blood-soaked hands covering her mouth, but she eventually nodded.

The woman turned out to be a girl no older than my sister. Her hands were trembling as she reached up to grab my arm.

"If I release you, are you going to scream?"

She shook her head, and I let go slowly.

"We need to hide the body. Are there any guards in the bunkhouses?"

She shook her head again, on the verge of tears.

"Good. We'll hide him inside. Here," I said, grabbing one of the guard's hands, "help me drag him."

She hesitated at first but then grabbed the other hand, and we both pulled. It was slow moving, considering the guard's size, but we eventually made it, and without being seen. I hoped the others didn't come looking for him anytime soon. The girl opened the door, and we dragged his body inside.

"What's going on?" someone asked as the other prisoners peered from their beds.

I closed the door and turned around. Moonlight poured in from a couple of the windows, lighting the inside enough for me to see. The bunkhouse was filled to overflowing. Two rows of beds lined the walls on either side with a single-file walkway down the middle. The smell of unwashed bodies hit me in a suffocating wave.

I pointed at two men on my left. "You, help me get him out of sight."

One of the two men walked over and looked down at the guard. "Is he dead?"

I pulled the knife from his chest and wiped it on his shirt.

"Never mind," he said, then kicked the guard in the side before spitting on him.

I didn't say anything. From what I'd seen so far, the man had deserved much worse. The men helped me pull the guard's body behind a couple of the cots and throw a blanket over him.

I turned to face the workers.

"Listen up," I said as loudly as I dared with the guards roaming around outside. "I'm here to rescue you."

I didn't exactly hear any giggles, but there wasn't much in the way of cheer or excitement either.

"I hope you brought more than yourself, son," an older man near the front said, looking a bit worried at the prospect of a single child coming to rescue them.

"I did. But they aren't here yet. I was sent in to make sure you were ready." I glanced out the front window. "How many workers are in the other buildings?"

The girl I'd saved earlier was the first to speak. "That building," she said, pointing out the window to the one on the left, "is as full as ours, and the one beside it is about half as much. Used to be more, but we lost a number this winter to the cold."

I nodded. "I'm going to let them know to be ready as well. I'm not sure when my friends will be here, but you'll know it when they are. Make sure to stay inside until I come and get you. If you go running out in the open during the battle, you're likely to be mistaken for one of the Cylmarans. Best to stay here until the fighting's over." I pulled back on the door's latch and started to open it. "I'll be back as soon as I can." I stuck my head out to see if anyone was nearby. I was about to slip through when a voice behind me stopped me in my tracks.

"Ayrion, is that you?"

I turned as someone pushed their way to the front of the crowd. My breath caught in my throat. "Magistrate Sirias?"

Chapter 34

"**W**HAT ARE YOU doing here?" I asked.

Magistrate Sirias met me at the door, out of earshot of the others. "We were attacked on the road and brought here about two months ago. Have you seen Merilyn or Rosella?" he asked desperately, almost in tears. "I haven't seen them in days."

"No," I said, shaking my head. "Sorry. I just arrived tonight. You're the first captives I've come across so far."

"What are you doing here?" Sirias asked as he glanced out the window. "Is your father here as well?"

"No, it's just me. Well, me and the group of rivermen I'm with."

"Rivermen?"

"It's a long story, and I don't have time to tell it, but I'll make sure to look for your wife and children in the other buildings—"

Sirias grabbed my arm before I could make it all the way out the door. "You're not going anywhere without me." From the look on his face, I knew arguing was out of the question.

After telling the others to remain where they were, we slipped outside and closed the door behind us, waiting patiently in the shadow of the porch for any sign of movement. We needed to hurry. I didn't know how long it would take Ismara to bring the *Wind Binder* in and unload the rest of the men, and as anxious as Horis was, I wasn't even sure he could be persuaded to wait that long.

"This way," I said, motioning for the magistrate to follow me to the side of the bunkhouse. We stopped at the corner long enough to spot three guards chatting on the other side of the mining pits. Torches marked each hole, giving us a clear view of the men. Each carried a sword at the waist and nothing more. They didn't seem to be all that worried with keeping watch. Escape attempts were probably few and far between, what with there being nowhere to run. This really was the ideal location for a prison camp.

I motioned for the magistrate to stay low as we started across the open area between buildings.

Partway across, Sirias tripped and grabbed me to keep from falling. But instead of stopping his fall, we both went down. We hit the ground and didn't move as we waited to see if the guards had heard us. Two of the men turned and looked in our direction. From this distance, I hoped we blended in with the rest of the rocks. The ground was cold against my face, the feeling all too familiar. It hadn't been too long ago since we'd been doing the same thing outside the magistrate's home.

*Turn back around. Please, turn back around.*

I was sure the guards had seen us. My hand slid slowly toward my blade, and I was about to tell Sirias to run for the bunkhouse when they finally turned back to their conversation.

I exhaled, sending a small puff of dust off the ground. With a single touch, I signaled the magistrate, and we crawled the rest of the way. Bringing the magistrate might not have been the best idea after all. His arms and legs were so weak, they trembled with every push. There was no telling how little these people had been fed, or how little rest they'd been permitted.

We reached the other building and moved onto the porch and out of sight of the three guards. Sirias was the first inside, not even bothering to knock.

"Merilyn? Rosella?"

I shut the door quickly and grabbed his arm. "Not so loud. They might hear us."

Sirias wasn't deterred as he headed down the center aisle. "Merilyn? Rosella?"

"Sirias?" Merilyn hopped out of a bed near the back with her infant in her arms and Rosella beside her. They raced across the room and embraced. Rosella and her baby brother were squished somewhere in the middle. "What are you doing?" Merilyn asked, fear in her voice. "If the guards see you . . ." Then she saw me. Her head tilted with a blank stare. Suddenly, her eyes widened.

"Ayrion?"

Rosella released her father's leg and rushed over to wrap her arms around me. "Have you come to take us away from this bad place?"

It was the most affection I'd received since my farewell parting with Hobb. I smiled. "Yes. I've come to take you away. Take you all away."

"Did you hear that, Mama? Ayrion's come to take us away . . . again." She hopped with excitement.

By now, the others had left their beds to see what was happening, so I took the time to address them as I had with the first bunch. I let them know what we were planning to do and that for their own safety, they should stay right where they were.

"What about the others?" Sirias asked, pointing out the window at the final bunkhouse. "We need to warn them as well."

I started to say something when a loud eruption sounded from the other side of the gorge. Shouts broke out from the general direction of the pass, followed by the familiar clash of steel.

We were out of time.

"Stay here," I said as I headed for the door. "I've got to warn the prisoners." I opened the door but quickly ducked back inside when two guards ran past. They were too preoccupied with the sounds of battle to notice me.

I slid back out and ran across the front of the bunkhouse. I made it two steps off the porch when something hit me from the side and sent me tumbling. I yelped as I landed on the bruised areas from my fall off the horse. I glanced behind me. The third guard was picking himself up from where he'd tripped over me in his rush to catch up with the others.

I barely made it to my feet before a vision sent me diving once more as the guard took a swing for my head with his already-drawn sword. I was back on my feet before he could try again.

I drew my blade and deflected the next swing as he lunged for my chest. I knocked his sword away and circled. The door to the third bunkhouse opened, and prisoners started pouring out.

"Get back inside!" someone shouted behind me. I didn't need to look. I recognized Sirias's voice.

I ducked again and blocked the next attack while trying to see where Sirias was. About the time I turned, the magistrate ran past, on his way to the other building.

The Cylmaran guard was too focused on me to worry about the magistrate. However, having one of the prisoners run past did offer a little distraction, and I used it to kick him between the legs. It's amazing what you forget to protect in the heat of battle. The man dropped to his knees, and I finished him with a quick thrust to center chest.

Leaving him there, I ran after Sirias. He was busy trying to get the people back inside, but those who had escaped before he got there were already heading in the direction of the pass, directly into the thick of it.

"Here, take this," I said, tossing him the extra sword. "Stay inside. I'll try to stop the others."

I ran after the fleeing prisoners, but they didn't run like a bunch of half-starved workers. They ran as though the Defiler himself was after them.

"Wait!" I shouted, willing my legs to go faster. "Come back! You're going to get yourselves killed." Why were they running? They didn't have anywhere to go. Or were they so desperate that reason didn't matter anymore?

Up ahead, I could see the battle taking place near the mouth of the pass. The Cylmaran guards had somehow managed to assemble in time to repel our fighters. I couldn't tell for sure, but we looked to be missing about half of the force we should have had. I had the sinking feeling that Horis hadn't waited and had decided to attack before the rest of our crew had arrived. Idiot.

I was nearly there. "Stop running!" They wouldn't listen. In fact, the more I shouted, the faster they seemed to go. I had to do something. Reaching the back of their ranks, I grabbed one woman and pulled her off her feet, sending her skidding across the rocks screaming. I elbowed a man in the side and sent him careening into a third. Both went down shouting. It was the only way to save their lives. "Stop, you fools!" The rest of the workers were coming up behind the battle, not slowing in the slightest. What was wrong with these people?

I managed to kick the legs out from under a fourth and fifth, but I wasn't able to reach the rest before they ran headlong into the back of the Cylmarans. The fools didn't stand a chance. The guards didn't look to see who it was they were fighting; they simply reacted to what looked like an assault from the rear. The defenseless workers were cut to pieces before they could reach our men.

I turned and shouted at the few I'd managed to stop. "Get back to your bunkhouses!" My efforts had at least brought them out of their delirious flight long enough to realize the danger they were in, not to mention the rage in my Upakan eyes was enough to send them running back to their quarters.

Two of the Cylmarans, having heard me, rushed my position. I cut the sword from the first guard's hand, then removed his hand for good measure. With a little help from my magic, I swept past the second's attack and opened the back of his leg, cutting straight through the tendons and leaving him incapable of standing. Knowing neither would be rejoining the fight, I left them wallowing in the dirt and went to help the rest of our men.

Instead of running straight up the Cylmarans' backside like those poor dead workers had done, I skirted the fight altogether and headed left for the mountain wall. From there, I worked my way around the battle in the direction of the pass. Our men were being overpowered. The Cylmarans had them outnumbered nearly two to one. Out in front, Captain Treygan moved like a master swordsman. He cut and parried, deflected and lunged, throwing his attackers back with every advance. By the way he fought, I would have thought he was Upakan.

Our men were being forced to retreat farther into the pass. At least they had enough sense to keep themselves from getting pressed against the side of the mountain, not that it was going to matter, as outnumbered as they were.

Horis was struggling on Treygan's right. His sword was bathed in blood, along with his clothes. Some of it was his, but most was from the Cylmarans who lay at his feet.

Bones fought on Treygan's left, his painted face clearly working to his advantage as the Cylmarans seemed scared to face him. His dark, skinny arms flew with deadly accuracy as his kamas cut and sliced away at those brave enough to stand up to him.

I reached the pass about the time I heard Kettle release a string of curses. The cook's sword flew from his hand, and he grabbed his arm. Blood was gushing from a deep wound. He stumbled backward, trying to get away from his attacker's blade.

I broke from my place near the edge of the pass and ran to help him, cutting down one of the closer slavers on the way—a quick upward block to lift his guard, followed by a swift opening of his abdomen. I kept running, but I could see I wasn't going to reach Kettle in time. He was too far away.

The Cylmaran lunged for him, but Bones managed to kick the hefty cook in the side and send him flying just in time to save his life. The guard didn't stop. He raised his sword with both hands and swung it at Kettle like an axe ready to split firewood, but my blade was there to block him.

Our swords sparked as they hit. The Cylmaran hadn't seen me coming, and I used it to my advantage as I spun the man's blade far enough to stab him in the side with my dagger. The slaver dropped his sword and grabbed the open wound, staggering out of the fight. His place was quickly filled by another.

"Get back!" I shouted at Kettle, who was still on the ground, trying to reach his weapon. I blocked the next guard's attack and opened the top of his thigh with my dagger. He'd been too focused on my eyes and my sword to pay attention to my other hand. Stupid mistake. I glanced over my shoulder. "You're not doing us any good if you can't hold your sword."

Kettle grabbed his weapon with the other hand and pushed his way back to his feet. "Watch me!" He jumped in beside me and nearly took off my arm with a wild swing.

"Flaming fish scales! You nearly killed me!" I blocked the next guard's lunge, sweeping his sword to the right and kicking him in the side of his knee. There was a brittle *crack* followed by the guard dropping to the dirt. I finished him off with a cut to his neck and then moved on.

Horis went down on Treygan's right.

"I've half a mind to let them kill you!" Treygan shouted at him as he fought to reach the big man and pull him back to his feet. "If you'd have waited for the rest of our crew like you was supposed to, we wouldn't be in this mess!"

Horis didn't say anything. He just continued to fight. At least three of his men had already fallen. We were being overrun, and with no chance of retreat, we had little choice but to keep swinging.

I was fighting two guards at once when Kettle went down again, this time with a stab to the top of his leg.

"Get out of there!" I shouted at him over my shoulder. I couldn't do anything for him this time. If I turned to help, one of the two men I was holding back would kill me. I could see Kettle from the corner of my eye, crawling backward, desperately trying to get away from the man coming for him. I turned my head. At least I didn't have to watch.

I waited for the inevitable wail—or, knowing Kettle, the angry curse—as the guard plunged his sword in, but it never came. Instead, I heard a high-pitched battle cry and another clash of steel. I couldn't turn to see what was happening.

I ducked to the side and blocked high, swinging wildly at the guard on my left, forcing him to retreat a step. Using the break, I glanced over my shoulder. Ismara was standing over Kettle, fighting back the taller guard trying to kill him. There was a ferocity in her eyes that surpassed even that of her sparring match with one of Horis's men. She threw back the slaver's advances and cut his sword from his hand. Kicking him in the leg to drop him to her level, she took his head with a single swing.

Behind her, the rest of our crew charged into the fray.

I released a heavy sigh of relief. Now it was the Cylmarans who were in retreat. And with the onset of fresh fighters, the battle didn't last much longer.

Horis and his lot gave the Cylmarans no chance to surrender. They continued fighting till the last Cylmaran was dead on the ground. Afterward, they sifted through the wounded and made sure those who remained joined their comrades in the afterlife.

I didn't stop them, but I didn't help them, either. After seeing what the slavers had been doing to these poor people, I felt no pity for them. Besides, if we had left any alive, they would have eventually gone right back to the pillaging they'd been doing all along. This was an evil that needed to be destroyed.

Chapter 35

"WHERE'S THE WORKERS?" Captain Treygan asked as he wiped the blood from his blade.

I pointed to the buildings on the other side of the encampment. "The last three are where they keep them. I told them to wait inside until I came back for them, but a few didn't listen." I looked at the bleeding bodies of the fallen workers and shook my head. "I wasn't able to save them all."

"If you hadn't been here, we'd have lost a great deal more."

The captain grabbed a torch and followed me back to the bunkhouses. The sky was beginning to gray, and the last of the stars had already faded from view. Morning was almost here.

"Where's the prisoners?" Horis asked as he limped his way over, meeting us about halfway.

"Ayrion's taking us there now," Treygan said.

Horis and some of the other men followed.

I directed them back toward the second bunkhouse, where I'd told Sirias and his family to wait. To his credit, the doors were still shut, waiting for me to return.

"Magi . . ." I caught myself before giving away his former title. No one was supposed to know he and his family were still alive. "Sirias." I knocked on the door. "You can come out. It's over."

The latch flipped, and the door opened partway, then was jerked open completely as little Rosella came charging out, wrapping her arms around me. "You came back, Ayrion! You came back!" Sirias, Merilyn, and the others were right behind her.

"You're safe," I said, hugging the little girl.

"Do you know these people, Ayrion?" Treygan asked with a quizzical expression.

"I do. This is Sirias, and his wife Merilyn, and their daughter—"

"I'm Rosella," she blurted out.

Treygan smiled. "It's nice to meet you, Rosella."

"I met them in Oswell this past fall," I said, careful not to say how.

Horis shook his head. "If that don't beat all. Quite the coincidence."

"*Providence* is more like it," Sirias said.

"I'm surprised to find children here at all," Horis said, gawking at the babe in Merilyn's arms. "Can't see that they'd be considered anything but extra mouths to feed. Surely, they didn't have them digging as well."

Sirias put his arm around Rosella. "The children clean the guardhouses and the tools."

Treygan took a step back to let the rest of the workers out of the bunkhouse. "We need to get these people back to the ship."

People were filing out of the other buildings, tears streaming down their faces as they came to thank us. Even Horis had to wipe an eye after seeing what was left of the poor wretches we'd come to save.

Treygan moved to the edge of the bunkhouse. "Whitey, Bones, hitch up some teams to those wagons," he said, pointing. "We can use them to carry these people out of here."

"How can we help?" Sirias asked, still holding the blade I had given him.

"Get these people into groups. Once the wagons are hitched, make sure they all get on board. The sooner we are loaded, the sooner we get out of here."

I followed the captain back to the passage.

"Ayrion, can you give me a hand?" Ismara called when she saw me coming. She was kneeling beside Kettle, trying to bandage his leg.

"Ow!" Kettle shouted. "You trying to finish the job?"

I knelt and held the bandage as she tied it off. Together, we helped Kettle over to a nearby boulder. He groaned and whined the entire way. Once down, he straightened himself. "Yes, well, I suspect the two of you will be wanting a double ration for your assistance, huh?"

Ismara smiled. "Just see to it that our cuts of bacon are on the thicker side next meal, and we'll call it even."

He nodded reluctantly. "Go on. Get out of here. I don't need the two of you standing there, gawking at me."

It was about as close to a thank you as either of us was going to get.

"Over here!" one of Horis's men shouted, standing outside the building we'd been told was used for storage and meals.

"You'll never believe what we found." There was an eager look on his face.

Ismara and I headed for the building just behind her father and Horis. Horis pushed his way past Treygan to be the first inside, but since Treygan held the torch, there wasn't much Horis could do except wait for the light. Once inside, we found a number of tables lined up across the main room with a small kitchen area on the right.

"In there," one of Horis's men said, pointing to a door at the back. Ismara and I followed the captain and Horis as they went inside. Along with their food stores, the room was filled to the top with spoils the Cylmarans had pillaged during their raids. From the amount of expensive furnishings, it appeared their looting had been going on for some time.

"There's enough here to buy a whole fleet of ships," Horis said excitedly as he patted Treygan on the back.

"Aye, but what would that make us if we were to just take it for ourselves?"

Horis lowered his head, looking a bit embarrassed by his earlier excitement. "Well, we have no way of returning it. Just look at it," he said with a sweep of his arm. "We don't have the first idea where it even came from."

Ismara took a step forward and cleared her throat. "I say before we do anything, we make sure those poor souls outside are provided for. Some of this stuff could be theirs, anyway."

Horis tugged on his beard. "You've got a good daughter there, Treygan. Must take after her mother." He took a moment to make one last sweep of the room before turning and limping out the door. "Let's get it loaded. We can sort out the details later."

I helped the men load everything from the room onto one of the wagons, one not already filled with passengers. With the number of refugees we had liberated, it was going to take more than one trip, even with the wagons.

I gathered my gear and shared a mount with Ismara back to the *Wind Binder*. Pops was there with a warm smile to welcome us on board.

"That be quite the haul, my lad," he said as he counted the new passengers. "I'm glad to see the two of you safe and unharmed."

Ismara kissed the older man on the cheek and then headed for the top deck to talk with Needle. His compass was certainly spinning at the sight of so many people walking up the gangway. He kept shaking his head and mumbling. I couldn't hear what he was saying, but I could certainly guess.

"Reckon we're going to have a hard time making room for them all," Pops said, pulling his pipe from his mouth. He scratched the back of his head with the stem. "Hope they brought blankets."

The sun was high overhead by the time we got everyone on

board. We stowed the valuables in the captain's cabin, the one place we could manage to keep them from prying eyes and hands. Across the deck, the passengers crowded the railing to watch the Cylmaran dock shrink behind us as the *Wind Binder* sailed back across the lagoon toward the river pass leading out of the Black Hills.

The refugees had to be split into groups. There wasn't enough room for everyone to be on deck at the same time, so they went in rotation. Those not sprawled across all three decks were below decks, trying to rest.

In the mess, Kettle was busy trying to stock all the extra supplies the captain had brought back from the compound. If there was ever a time he needed my help, it was now. With his wounds, he could barely tend to himself, let alone a crew of hungry passengers.

Sirias and his family stayed close to me, helping wherever they could. I introduced them to Kettle as we worked to get supper underway. A couple of the ladies from the camp offered their assistance, and as much as Kettle fussed and bickered about how to properly run a riverboat kitchen, I could tell he was enjoying their company.

With the additional hands, it was soon apparent that my services were no longer required, so I left the mess and went topside. I found Pops and Ismara up on the bow and introduced them to Sirias and his family. We spent the better part of the afternoon talking about the circumstances that had reunited us, mainly my banishment from the Lost City.

"It appears we're all in the same boat," Merilyn said. Having said it, she seemed to realize how silly that sounded, and started laughing. "I guess we really are in the same boat," she said, looking down at the deck. The rest of us laughed as well.

I leaned over the railing and let the wind rustle my hair. "You're welcome to sail with us south to Aramoor."

"I should say not," Merilyn said with a huff.

Sirias sighed. "We had intended to ride south to Terhi or Laneer, someplace near the coast where I could find a position in shipping, but after what we've been through, I've no intention of taking my family anywhere near the Cylmaran borders. I'll get a wagon as soon as we reach the next town and ride east around the Sandrethin Mountains. I'm sure I can find work in Vinten or Fayburn. No chance of running across slavers there."

I wasn't exactly sure where those cities were located. It had been a while since I'd studied my map, but I thought they were somewhere on the coast between Aramoor and the Riverlands. After what the magistrate's family had endured, I'd be looking for an alternate location to settle down as well.

By the time supper was over and everyone had made it through the very long line to get their bowl of fish chowder, we found ourselves sailing out of the Black Hills, leaving the last remnants of the dark mountains behind us.

"It will be good to get back underway," Pops said. "If we can catch the wind, we might even make it in time to deliver Elis's crops."

I'd forgotten all about our shipment. I would have thought we'd already missed that deadline a while back. It seemed like we'd been sailing the river for months.

The fork leading back into the main branch of the Shemoa was just ahead. We crossed out of the last of the trees on the west side only to be greeted by two ships anchored just offshore. They were still too far away to see on board, but I recognized the larger of the two.

"Hang me!" Kettle said as he pushed his way to the railing and spat over the side. "It's Captain Owen. How in the flaming Pits of Aran'gal did he know we was here?"

"DROP ANCHOR!" the captain shouted behind us. "Get everyone below deck."

I heard the splash and felt the deck shift as the *Wind Binder* slowed.

I joined Treygan and the rest of the crew on the main deck as the last of the refugees shuffled through the mess door and down into the hold.

"How'd they know we was here?" Needle asked, spinning his compass in his hand.

"Doesn't rightly matter at this point," Horis said. "The question is, what are we gonna do about it?"

For an uncomfortable moment, there was complete silence as uneasy glances passed among the crew. To have come as far as we had only to be met by something like this was enough to break anyone's spirit. The festive grins and earlier merriment had been replaced with fear and trepidation as the thought of what awaited us sank in.

"We set a trap," I said finally, not able to take the silence any longer.

All eyes shifted in my direction.

"We lure Owen on board."

"And how, pray tell, do we do that?" Kettle asked, rubbing his hands on his apron. "Offer to cook him a meal?"

"We surrender the ship."

Another awkward silence.

"The blazes we will!" Horis said, slapping the sword at his waist. "I'll be hung before I give in without a fight."

Treygan laid a hand on the big man's arm. "Let's hear him out." He nodded at me. "Go on."

I cleared my throat. I hadn't exactly had time to think the plan through, so I did my best to come up with it as I went. "Well, we know there's nothing Owen wants more than to get his hands on the *Wind Binder*, so we tell him that we'll turn the ship over without a fight if he'll promise us safe passage to the nearest town—"

Needle spun his compass. "And what's to stop him from simply coming on board, slittin' our throats, and taking the ship for himself?"

"He won't want to risk us setting her ablaze just to keep her out of his hands."

Whitey scratched his head. "I'm confused. Sounds like we're just giving Owen everything he wants. How's this good for us?"

"Aye," Needle said, his eye twitching nervously. "Where's the trap? What sense does it make to offer surrender?"

"Because of what he can't see."

And apparently neither could the crew, because *everyone* was now scratching their head. Or maybe this whole idea was about as terrible as my luck. "Even with Horis and his men," I pointed out, "Owen has the advantage. But what he doesn't know is that we have nearly a hundred refugees below deck who would likely do just about anything to keep their newly found freedom. You let Owen and his crew on board and then release a hundred half-starved miners on them . . ."

I looked at the captain to see what he thought of my ridiculous idea and was surprised to find a smile creeping across his face.

Horis tugged his beard. "It could work. Half those people below deck look like shades themselves."

My head shot up. "Paint!"

Ismara gave me a funny look. "What?"

"Paint," I repeated, pointing at Bones's face, where the markings he'd applied for battle were still visible. "Horis just said some of the refugees looked like shades. Let's make them all look like that."

Bones crossed his arms. "I don't have enough for all those people."

"There. We can use that." I pointed at Kettle's midriff.

Everyone turned to look at Kettle.

"What?" Kettle asked, looking down at his outfit. "You want to use my apron?"

"No. I want to use what's on it. Flour. And not just for a few stripes. Let's cover everything—"

Treygan smiled. "Well, you heard the man. Get to work. We need to have them ready before Owen gets tired of waiting and shows up with a boarding party."

The men scattered. Even with the added help of Horis's crew, it took a while to get the refugees prepared. As luck would have it, Owen kept his distance, no doubt waiting to see what we would do.

Below deck, Kettle pulled out a large washtub he'd been using as a storage bin for some of Elis's grain and filled it with water. He then added a couple of sacks of flour until he had a runny paste. Too much flour and it would have formed a batter too thick to apply.

The refugees took turns dunking themselves in the basin—clothes and all—while Kettle kept a steady supply of the stuff on hand. The leftovers were then painted over anything that didn't get coated the first time.

Watching them all get in the tub, roll, and get out had me wanting to do the same. It looked like fun. The goo hardened to the outside of their skin and hair and clothing, making them look less than human.

"By thunder!" Horis said when he and the captain came down to inspect the work. "My skin's crawling just looking at 'em."

A few of the refugees made scary faces just to simulate the desired effect.

Magistrate Sirias walked over to greet the two men, and Horis took a step back. Sirias's shoulder-length hair had dried into points, much like the stars on a mace. If I hadn't been worried about whether this insane plan would work or not, I would have laughed.

Horis rubbed a finger along one of the points of Sirias's caked hair.

Treygan simply smiled. "If this doesn't loosen Owen's bowels, nothing will."

"Aye," Horis said, looking at the others who were starting to gather around the two men. "Let's get out of here before I do the same." He shivered slightly, and the two men left us to our work.

"You do look scary," I said to Sirias.

He smiled, his teeth matching the paste.

I grinned right back, another idea forming. "Kettle, do we have any more jars of berry preserve?"

He rubbed his long mustache and gave me a hard look. "What's swimming around in that head of yours now?"

It wasn't until the sun had begun to set behind us that Captain Owen finally had a boat sent to deliver his demands. The single occupant carried a white flag. He stopped rowing well before reaching the *Wind Binder* and shouted:

"I have a message for Captain Treygan, if he be aboard."

"Where else would I be?" Treygan shouted back. "Does your captain wish to offer his surrender?"

The man in the boat laughed. "Captain Owen says to set your affairs in order. There will be no quarter given."

"Tell your captain that I'll sink this ship and all hands before I let him have her."

The man in the boat looked confused. Clearly, he hadn't expected such a brash statement from the captain in front of his own men.

"That be your final answer?"

The captain raised his hand. "Give me a moment to confer with my crew."

The man in the boat sat back down.

Treygan waited an appropriate amount of time before responding. "Tell Owen that if he'll agree to safe passage for me and my crew to the next available town, then we'll relinquish the *Wind Binder*."

The man nodded, then swung his oars around and headed back the way he came.

"How long do you give us, Captain?" Whitey asked as he lifted his wide-brimmed hat and wiped his forehead.

Treygan looked at the two ships in the distance. "I reckon we have till dark before they come."

Barely an hour had passed when the first few longboats were spotted. We heard their oars striking the water before we saw them float out of the fog like wraiths moving up the river in our direction. There were three boats altogether, each with at least a dozen men, outnumbering us two to one. Owen was in the first.

Those sitting at the front and sides of each boat bore wooden shields, no doubt to protect against arrows had we not been entirely truthful about our desire to peacefully turn over the ship.

"Now I see how they knew we was here," Horis said, pointing to the back of the first boat. Sitting beside Owen, with his sword in his lap, was Worg. His smile was dark and vengeful. "I figured he'd make it to shore, but I wonder how he managed to flag Owen down."

The longboats made their way slowly around the port side of the ship. Worg was the first one up and over the side, pulling himself up by the rope he'd previously sailed over during his tussle with me. A single lamp hung from the front of the captain's cabin, giving little light to the main deck. The rest of the rivermen followed Worg on board. Owen clearly had no intention of setting foot on our vessel until every one of his men was aboard.

I stood between Horis and Ismara at the edge of the foredeck railing. Treygan, who stood at the center of our group, wanted to keep Owen and his men as far from the door leading down to the hold as he could. He figured the best way to do that was to force Owen to come to us, while at the same time making it look like we were cowering at the front of the ship. Everything was relying on my silly plan. If it failed, it would mean not only the lives of our crew but also of all the newly freed slaves down below.

"I told you I'd have the *Wind Binder* one day," Owen said as stepped onto the deck. His smile was that of a man who had found winning to be a way of life.

Treygan cleared his throat. "Our agreement was that I would turn over the *Wind Binder* in exchange for safe passage."

"Aye," Owen replied, still smiling.

"Then why do your men carry their swords?" Treygan asked.

Owen looked at his men. "Because they don't trust you. And frankly, neither do I." He craned his neck to get a look at us. "Now throw down your weapons, or we'll come up and take them."

"If we give up our weapons, what's to keep you from killing us?"

Owen glanced at his men and shrugged. "My word?"

The rivermen below laughed and then followed Owen across the deck in our direction.

Owen stopped in front of the mast and looked up. "Now, where's those weapons?"

Captain Treygan sighed and nodded. "Do as he says."

I joined the others in tossing my sword over the railing to the deck in front of Owen and his men. Of course, my sword wasn't the only weapon I carried.

"How many do you have up there with you?" Owen asked, pointing his sword at us.

"Fifteen, including myself," Treygan said.

Owen looked at Worg. "Is that all of them?"

Worg took a moment to scan the faces. "No. We seem to be missing a few. Where's Sim and Jakes? And I don't see Craye anywhere."

Horis leaned against the railing. "They ain't missing, Toadface. They's dead, fighting the Cylmarans."

Owen pointed toward the door leading below to the captain's cabin. "Check it out."

Worg shoved one of Owen's men forward. The man turned, but one look from Worg and he decided not to push the issue.

"What's wrong, Owen?" Treygan asked. "You don't trust me?"

"I don't trust anyone. It's why I'm still alive."

After a while, the cabin door opened, and the sailor returned. "No one's there, Captain."

"Then check below deck. I don't want any surprises."

Worg pointed at two men on the end. "Go help him."

My hands tightened on the rails. If they went down into the hold, it would give everything away. I kept my eye on my sword down on the deck. A single leap and I could be over the railing and on top of it before Owen and his men could get to me, but then I'd have to hold them off long enough for our crew to reach me.

The three men opened the mess door.

Owen pointed his cutlass at me. "I told you I wouldn't forget you. I have something—"

Screams pierced the night from somewhere below deck. They only lasted a moment, and then everything went silent. The men on deck turned to face the open door. Those who didn't already have their weapons drawn certainly did now.

"What was that?" Owen demanded. "You got men below—"

A faint wailing rose from the empty doorway, soft enough that it took a moment to even notice. And then it grew. Ten voices, twenty, a hundred. All blending together like something otherworldly, something that made my skin crawl. It wasn't like anything I'd ever heard before. I was beginning to wonder if the underworld had opened up.

"What nonsense is this?" Owen shouted, his eyes on the open door leading into the bowels of the ship.

Many of the men below drew an *X* on their chests and spat on the deck.

"This ship's cursed, Captain," one of his men said. "We shouldn't be here."

"Why do you think this ship's never been taken?" Treygan said, leaning over the railing as he looked at the men below. "Why do you think she's never been caught?"

The men didn't move as they waited for the answer.

"Because," Pops said, interrupting Treygan with his rough, scratchy voice, "we made a pact with the Defiler, and now no one's gonna lay a hand on this ship."

"I told you the *Wind Binder* was haunted, Captain," another of Owen's men said. "I've seen it steal the wind from other ships' sails."

Owen backhanded the sailor across the face. "Shut your hole! The only ghosts on this ship are going to be those of Treygan and his crew."

"We had a deal, Owen!" Treygan shouted. "Safe passage in return for my ship!"

"You didn't actually expect me to honor that, did you?" Owen turned to his men. "Kill them!"

This entire plan was collapsing. Owen was supposed to agree to terms, not demand we throw down our weapons and then order us killed.

"What are you waiting for?" Owen shouted, turning to see why his men weren't obeying. That was when he noticed everyone staring at the open doorway leading to the hold.

The wailing had stopped.

My knuckles were white as they clutched the rail in front of me.

Owen's men screamed as white bodies poured out of the doorway, their mouths covered in blood. The slaves didn't even need the flour and jam to look terrifying. After enduring years of rape, torture, hard labor, and starvation, they were nothing but skeletal. One look at the creatures flooding the deck, and the rivermen began to fight each other to reach the edge and jump. Owen was knocked down in the stampede. He crawled as fast as he could toward the captain's cabin.

I leaped over the railing to the deck and grabbed my sword. I ducked as a vision kept me from losing my head to Worg's blade, then spun back to my feet in time to deflect the big man's next attempt.

All around us, sailors rushed to escape, many discarding their weapons in the process. Those who tried making it to the top deck were met by Treygan and the crew.

Our swords clanged and sparked in the surrounding darkness as I fought to hold Worg back. It was clear the man wasn't leaving until one of us was dead, and since I'd left what little mercy I possessed back at the mines, I was more than happy to accommodate him.

I threw back his advances, dancing around him as he hurled one heavy swing after another. He hit the cabin door, tearing a hinge partway out of the wall. He swung again and almost decapitated one of his fellow sailors. He hit just about everything except me, but then he did something I hadn't expected. He grabbed one of the slaves, an older man, and lifted his blade to his neck.

Worg threw me a vicious smile.

I raised my free hand. "Don't. You don't want him; you want me."

Before I could say anything more, Worg slit the old man's throat and let him drop at his feet.

This time, I attacked. I slashed for his arm, then his leg, then neck, spinning from one side to the other. Worg couldn't keep up. I opened his calf, then his forearm, but he kept going. He roared and swung for my chest. I ducked and stabbed him through the thigh. He dropped to one knee and I cut off his sword hand. The blade clanged against the floor.

He snarled as I walked over to him. "Go ahead! Finish it!"

I didn't get the chance. Before I could raise my sword, a horde of screaming former slaves swarmed, attacking him with their bare hands and teeth.

Worg's screams were long and unpleasant. I was actually thankful when they finally ended.

Behind me, Captain Owen had managed to get the cabin door opened, but before he could get inside, a group of slaves latched on to his legs and yanked him backward.

"Please! Please don't kill me! Please . . ." He curled into a ball and whimpered like a newborn as he waited for the wraiths to devour him.

I wanted to laugh at the sight of the fearless Captain Owen curled up at the feet of half-starved slaves with berry juice dripping from their mouths. The light had been perfect.

The rivermen who didn't make it off the ship were huddled in groups near the door that led below deck, surrounded by ghostly slaves. They threw down their weapons, hoping it would appease the white faces in front of them.

I couldn't believe this crazy idea had worked.

Someone slapped me on the back, and I turned to find myself staring into a flour-caked face. He smiled, and I flinched.

"Pretty frightening, isn't it," Sirias said with a chuckle. "I can't even get Rosella to look at me."

"That was the point," I said, trying not to stare too hard.

Sirias turned and scanned the deck. "Looks like we won."

"Aye," Whitey said as he walked over and retrieved his sword. "That we did."

"It worked a little too well," Ismara said as she joined us. "I didn't get to lock swords with a single riverman." She looked upset by the situation as she studied Sirias's hardened hair. "What does it feel like?" she asked, reaching out to touch a small clump that had bent downward.

"Uncomfortable," he said with a wry smile. "I'll be glad when I can finally wash it off."

Pops sauntered over, pulling his pipe from an inner pocket and placing it between his teeth. "Well, that was quite the excitement," he said. "A story worthy of a ballad, I reckon. At least four stanzas."

"Get on your feet, you coward," Treygan shouted behind us.

We turned to watch as Owen struggled to stand. His legs were shaking. Once the slaves had backed off far enough, he finally managed it. He limped over to the mast, surrounded by at least twenty white faces, all looking like they were ready to tear into his flesh. I half-believed that if given the chance, a few of them would.

"Line the rest of them up," Treygan said, pointing at the two groups of rivermen cowering over at the side.

Whitey and Bones herded Owen's men to the center of the deck to stand alongside their *brave* captain. Needle remained up top, too afraid to come down and join the others. He stood there shaking his head and mumbling.

Treygan leaned against his sword. "The question now is what to do with you."

Owen sneered. "Give me my sword, and I'll show you what you can do."

Captain Treygan smiled. "I've got a better idea."

Chapter 37

"YOU CAN'T JUST LEAVE us here!" Owen shouted, his face beet-red as he half-demanded, half-pleaded to remain onboard.

"It's no worse than you deserve," Horis said, spitting over the side.

Treygan stood at the railing. "I'd say this is a fitting end for a group of river pirates. At least you'll be in good company. Maybe you can swap stories with your new brothers. I hear the Cylmarans are a friendly sort." He laughed as he pointed his blade out toward the lonely dock and the road that led back to the Cylmaran mining camps. "Now jump. It's not that far of a swim."

With the threat of a sword hanging over them, Owen and the rest of his men jumped overboard and swam for shore. Those who had escaped over the side the previous night had disappeared. I doubted we'd ever see any of them again.

Treygan waited for the last of Owen's men to make it ashore before setting sail. The captain was right. It was the perfect punishment. They had spent their lives taking advantage of others, and now they would end theirs having the same done to them. Once another boat of Cylmarans arrived, they'd find a new batch of miners waiting on them.

I couldn't help but smile as I watched the dock fade into the distance. I glanced up at the top of the ridge and wondered what had happened to the lookouts. I was sure they had found a way to free themselves by now. They would have quite the surprise when Owen and his men came walking into camp.

I spent the rest of the day helping Kettle in the mess as we prepared the evening meal for the crew and refugees. Afterward, I spent time with Sirias, Merilyn, and Rosella. They were eager to be on their way toward a new life.

Ismara stuck her head out of the cabin door and spotted me over at the railing with Sirias. "Captain wants to see you," she said.

I left the magistrate and followed her inside. Not much had changed since the last time I'd been there. The table was a bit more cluttered, and the curtains on the windows had been drawn.

"Ah, Ayrion, please." Captain Treygan motioned to a seat by the writing desk, and I sat down. Ismara did the same on a nearby stool. "This has been quite the journey, my young friend." He walked around the table to our side and leaned against it. "It appears that we won't be able to make for Aramoor quite as soon as we would have liked. In fact, it might be some time."

"I had a feeling," I said. "It wouldn't be right to travel all the way to Aramoor for one passenger when you have a hundred others who haven't seen their loved ones in years."

"I'm glad you agree," Treygan said, "because I have a proposition for you."

Ismara leaned forward in her seat with an excited smile. "We'd like you to stay on with us, at least until we can finish returning the rest of the refugees."

"Aye," her father said. "You're a good man to have around. I can use rivermen like you—men that can hold their own, that are not afraid to do what's right. It might be some time before we can make it as far as Aramoor, but you'd be welcome to stay with us as one of the crew until we do. Or if you have a hankering for the river life, there'll always be a place for you here."

I sat tall in my seat. It was the first time someone had referred to me as a man. Thirteen or not, I felt much older just listening to him.

"What do you say?" Treygan asked. Ismara rubbed her hands, eagerly awaiting my answer.

I took a deep breath and slowly released it. "I almost wish I could say yes."

"Then why don't ya?" Ismara said, a slight frown forming at the corners of her mouth.

"Because it's partly my fault that Sirias and his family were taken by slavers, and I owe it to them to make sure they reach their destination safely."

"How is it your fault?" she asked.

I wrung my hands. "I can't say."

She crossed her arms. "You can't, or you won't?"

"His business is his own, daughter," Treygan said. "He's old enough to make up his own mind."

Ismara huffed. "That's debatable."

"As much as I've enjoyed my time on the *Wind Binder*, I believe it's time for me to move on. My father had wished me to go to Aramoor, so I want to at least try."

Treygan sighed but nodded. "No need to say more." He leaned forward and held out his hand. "You'll be missed."

I stood and took it. "Thank you."

He smiled. "How soon will you be leaving us?"

"The next town we make port that's large enough to purchase a wagon and some supplies."

Treygan nodded. "I'll make sure you get your share of the takings."

"What do you plan to do with the other two ships?" I asked.

"Start building my company once more," he said with a smile. "I'll turn one over to Bones, and Horis has already agreed to take the other, at least until we manage to return the refugees. But with no family to speak of, I have a feeling he'll be with us for a long time to come." The captain lifted his hat and rubbed his forehead. "Of course, I'm not sure if that's a good thing or not." He smiled and walked around to the far side of the table. "Well, I'll bid you good night, then. Lots of work still to do."

I said good night, and Ismara walked me out. She was still wearing a frown as we climbed the stairs to the top of the foredeck and walked over to the railing. There was a soft breeze blowing in from the north, filling my nostrils with the scent of jasmine from her hair. We stood there for a moment without saying anything as we stared at the two new additions to the fleet.

"I'm going to miss having you around," she finally said, keeping her attention out on the water. "It was nice having someone younger around to talk to."

"I'll miss being here," I said, sparing a glance her way. I remembered the first time we'd met, how brusque she had been. I almost didn't recognize that girl now.

"The river's a great place to live," she said.

"For those of us not born there, it's an adjustment."

"One you could make."

I sighed. "It's not that I don't want to be here. It's just . . ." I looked out at the water again. "It doesn't feel like home."

Ismara turned and looked at me. "I understand." Before I could say anything more, she turned and headed back down to the cabin.

Captain Treygan took us as far as Trillen. Not only was this the stop for Elis's goods, but it was also the closest city to the main road that led east around the Sandrethin Mountains.

The *Wind Binder* actually made it to market a full two days before our deadline.

"Not forgetting anything, are ya, lad?" Pops asked as the *Wind*

*Binder* crew stood on deck to see me off.

I shook my head and hefted my travel pack. "Nope. I have what I came with. Well, mostly." I reached up and gave the old man a hug. He nearly lost his pipe trying to hug me back.

"Wipe your eyes, you old woman," Kettle said as he smacked Pops on the arm. Kettle handed me a wrapped bundle. The aroma had my mouth watering.

"Bacon?" I asked hungrily.

He just smiled.

To Kettle's right, Whitey stuck out his hand. "It was good knowing you, Master Ayrion." His hand was big enough to completely wrap around mine. "You're a good man to have in a fight," he said with a nod.

I leaned in and whispered, "Every time I eat a fig tart, I'll think of you."

Whitey smiled and raised his wide-brimmed hat.

I moved down the line to Needle. He pulled out his compass, and for a moment, I thought he was going to hand it to me. Instead, he popped the top and looked inside as if judging our heading. "Make sure you chart a straight course, young man," he said, sounding very fatherly and not at all like the nervous Needle we generally saw. "Maybe one day it will bring you back our way." He flipped the lid closed and spun it in his hand with a smile.

Bones was next. His skinny arms were crossed as I approached. He had finally washed off the paint, all but a single line that ran down the center of his chin. "I keep this for you," he said, pointing at the line. "It will remind me of the time I shared passage with an

Upaka and was the better for it." He made an *X* on his chest but refrained from spitting. He then undid one of his earrings and handed it to me. "Something to remember me by."

"Thank you," I said, looking at the gold loop. I hoped he didn't expect me to wear it. I tucked it into the outside pocket of my jerkin. "You're a hard man to forget."

Bones smiled and gave me a nod, and I moved on to the next person in line.

"We might not have seen eye to eye," Horis said with a tug on that thick red beard of his, "but there's no questioning the respect I have for your abilities. We wouldn't have managed this rescue without you, and I'll be forever in your debt."

I reached out and offered the old veteran my hand. It was the kindest thing he'd said to me since our first meeting. "I'm glad it all worked out the way it did."

Horis smiled and then took a step back to let Ismara get her turn.

She surprised me with a hug. I closed my eyes and took a deep breath, drinking in her fragrance, wanting to remember it as long as I could.

"You sure you won't stay?" she asked.

"You keep hugging me like this and I might consider it."

She chuckled and let go.

Captain Treygan was last in line. "We've come a long way since our meeting at Cretollo."

I nodded. "If I'd known half of what I was signing on for,

I'd . . . I'd . . ." I looked down the row at the faces of the crew staring back at me. "I wouldn't have changed a thing."

Treygan smiled and laid a hand on my shoulder. "You're a good lad, Master Ayrion. The Upakans are fools to have gotten rid of the likes of you. But their loss has been our gain. Just remember, if you ever find yourself in need, you'll always have a place here on the *Wind Binder*. You're one of the crew now, which makes you family."

I smiled, tears forming at the corners of my eyes. I tried holding them back, but they fell regardless. I hadn't been away from the Lost City six months, and already I had found two new homes. One with Hobb, and one on the decks of the *Wind Binder*.

I didn't like good-byes. But as good-byes went, this wasn't a bad one.

I waved at my new family, wondering if I'd ever see them again. With my pack under my arms, I walked down the gangway to the dock and up to the wagon Sirias had purchased the day before. It was loaded with the supplies we'd need to make the rest of the journey.

So much had happened since the Tri'Nephrin. It almost didn't feel real, like I was living someone else's life, walking in someone else's shoes. With a full heart, I climbed onto the back of the wagon alongside Rosella and turned to get one last look at the *Wind Binder* and her crew before she sailed away. Ismara stood at the bow, waving.

Tears burned my eyes as I took my seat, and Sirias snapped the reins. I hoped I would see them again one day. Until then, it felt like I was missing another part of myself.

If there was one thing I could take away from my time in exile, it was this: no matter where you go, you can always find a place to belong, if you look hard enough.

Thank You

## Dear Reader,

I HOPE YOU enjoyed this first book in the Street Rats of Aramoor series. If you found the story entertaining and would like to see more, then please consider helping me reach that goal by leaving a quick review on Amazon.

Reviews are very important. They help encourage other readers to try the book while at the same time showing Amazon that the book is worth promoting.

Thank you in advance!

Love fantasy merchandise? Stop by the **Aramoor Market** and take a look at the new Aldoran store. New arrivals every month.

<<www.store.michaelwisehart.com>>

**\*\*Keep reading for a FREE offer.**

# Free Offer

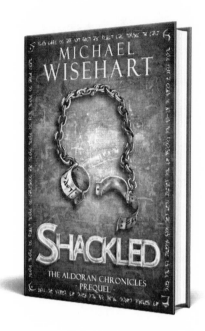

I F YOU WOULD LIKE to get a FREE copy of the prequel to the Aldoran Chronicles series, type in the address below:

« www.michaelwisehart.com/shackled-wt »

The Aldoran Chronicles begin twenty years after the Street Rats of Aramoor series.

*Born in a world where magic is not only feared, but outlawed, Ferrin's choice to use his abilities brings the Black Watch to his doorstep. Caged alongside a helpless band of half-starved wielders, he formulates a strategy to escape. Armed with nothing more than his sarcastic wit and a determination to never give in, Ferrin attempts the impossible.*

# Author Note

YOU CAN LEARN more about the World of Aldor on my website. Don't forget to read the *History of Aldor* while you're there. It will give you a better understanding behind the internal struggles and conflicts taking place between those with magic and those without.

**My website:** www.michaelwisehart.com

## For the Latest News

« facebook.com/MichaelWisehart.author »

# Acknowledgements

I THANK GOD for the doors and windows He's allowed to open in order for me to reach this point.

I want to thank my parents *Mickey and Julie Wisehart* for their unending loyalty, encouragement, and support over the years. None of this would be possible without you—love you both.

I want to thank my Author Team, whose endless talent, time, and dedication have made this project possible:

## AUTHOR TEAM

To my illustrator and sister, whose creativity and talent continues to impress—*Janelle Wisehart*

To my cover artists, who have given us our first look at the Lost City—*Whendell Souza, Rodrigo Ramos*

To my conceptual artist, who brought the Wind Binder and its crew to life in ways I couldn't have imagined—Dongjun Lu

To my content editor, who has spent countless hours advising me on the proper structure of my thoughts—*Nathan Hall*

To my line editor, who managed to take a floundering script and turn it into something readable—*Danae Smith*

To my copy editors, whose patience has managed to surpass my continual lack of commas—*Tammy Salyer, Mia Darien of LKJ Bookmakers, Richard Shealy*

# About the Author

**M**ICHAEL WISEHART graduated with a bachelor's degree in business before going back to school for film and starting his own production company. As much as he enjoyed film work, the call of writing a novel got the better of him, and on April 14, 2014, he started typing the first words of what would be two new epic fantasy series: The Aldoran Chronicles and Street Rats of Aramoor.

He currently lives and writes in South Georgia.

Visit « michaelwisehart.com »

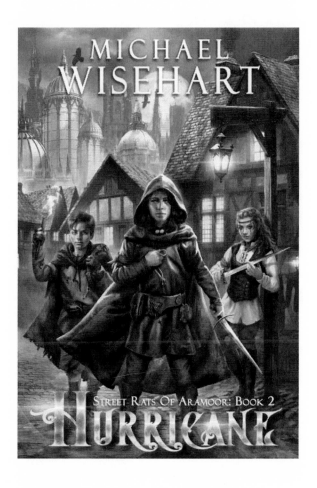

$\mathcal{M}$ Y JOURNEY was nearing its end.

After leaving the *Wind Binder* and her captain and crew behind on the Shemoa River, I traveled east around the Sandrethin Mountains with Magistrate Sirias and his family. The trip had taken nearly two months, but we were in no rush, and with having the magistrate's resources returned after freeing the slaves at the Cylmaran mining camp, plus the share I'd received from Captain

Treygan for my part in the rescue, we decided to take our time and enjoy the trip. After our harrowing experiences over the last few months, it was a welcomed gift, a time to heal both physically and mentally.

Once we had rounded the southern tip of the Sandrethins, we parted ways. Magistrate Sirias, Merilyn, Rosella, and their infant son continued south toward the coastal cities of Vinten and Fayburn, while I took the west road to Aramoor.

Not wanting to waste my coin purchasing a horse, I spent the next couple of weeks enjoying the open road on foot. A day outside of Aramoor, I was lucky enough to be picked up by a farmer and his family, where I found myself bouncing along in the back of a wagon filled with half a dozen large melons and a barrel of cucumbers that smelled of last week's pickings despite the FRESH CUT label on the front.

They told me no thirteen-year-old should be out on these roads by themselves. There could be highwaymen just waiting to snatch me up. I almost laughed.

Their son, who was seated across from me on a small crate of lettuce, was several years younger and definitely not shy about speaking his mind.

"What's wrong with your eyes?" he asked, his head cocked slightly to the side. "They look funny."

"Hush, Enon. That's rude." His mother was trying her best not to stare herself.

Enon reminded me of my younger brother, Jorn. He was about the same age and just as feisty.

The little boy folded his arms. "Well, they do."

I smiled. Having passed through as many cities, towns, and villages as I had on my way to Aramoor, I'd grown accustomed to the stares. It would seem colorless eyes were something of a rarity. Growing up in the Lost City of Keldor, I'd never known anything different. I was just as amazed at the variety of color I'd seen.

"All of my people have the same eyes," I said.

The farmer's wife twisted in her seat. "Your people?"

"The Upaka."

The woman's expression darkened, and her husband threw me a sharp look over his shoulder. "Upaka?" There was a hint of concern in his voice. "That's a name I haven't heard in quite some time. What are you doing this far south?"

"It's a long story," I said, not feeling in the mood to share the tale of my banishment with strangers, even strangers kind enough to give me a ride.

They got the hint and didn't pry further. I doubted their silence had anything to do with common courtesy. After all, my people were well known as mercenaries for hire.

A gust of wind caught my hair and sent it whipping behind me. It had grown long enough to tickle my shoulders, nearly half as long as my sister Rianna's, which would have earned me some time with Mother's shears were I at home.

We crested a small rise, and I could see Aramoor looming in the distance. It was larger than anything I had imagined. The capital city of Elondria was the home of the High King. It was also the largest city in the known world. Nothing in the five kingdoms came close to its magnitude. The thought of calling it *home* both excited and terrified me.

"So, this is your first time to Aramoor, is it?" the farmer asked.

He'd turned his attention back to his team as the horses plodded down the main road leading toward the city.

"Yes, sir."

He smiled. "Bet you've never laid eyes on the likes of it before."

"I haven't."

"That wall is one of Aldor's great wonders, if you ask me."

I stared off into the distance at the protective barrier surrounding the city. Its white stone could be seen for miles in all directions.

"I can see why."

"They say it was built by wizards after the defeat of the Kuhl hordes. It was probably one of the last great feats of magic before the Purge." The farmer shook his head. "It's hard to believe something as evil as magic could create such beauty."

I bit my tongue. Having magic was no more likely to make someone evil than having too much gold. I could speak from personal experience.

The road grew more congested, the closer we got to the city's eastern gate. It was as though the townsfolk from the surrounding communities had decided to make a sacred pilgrimage to the capital, all at the same time.

We passed a number of other wagons toting wares to sell to those living within the protection of the great wall.

Our pace slowed as we reached the first of two gatehouses leading in. This close, I could see that the blocks used to build the fortification were as wide as the farmer's wagon. I wondered at the amount of magic it must have required. The wizards from that age must have been truly powerful.

A sentry waved the cart in front of us on, through and we pulled forward to the first checkpoint. "State your name and purpose," the guard said. He bore the insignia of the Elondrian Lancers—a high sun overshadowing a golden crown.

I'd seen pictures of that emblem in my studies back home. I'd been required to learn of the various militaries within the five kingdoms. Their crests and colors had been just as important to memorize as their styles of combat.

"The name's Neelan," the farmer said to the guard. "We're from Cadwyn. This is my wife and my two boys. We have fresh produce to sell at the lower market on South Avis."

The guard stepped over to my side of the wagon and looked in. Thankfully, my back was to him, so I didn't have to worry about hiding my eyes. One quick glance and he was walking back around to the front. He waved us forward. "Move on through."

We passed a second guard station once we were through the gate, but no one bothered stopping us. The lancers at that station were concerned with traffic leaving the city.

"Where would you like us to drop you off?" Neelan asked as we started down the main thoroughfare leading into the heart of Aramoor.

In the distance, I could see great domes and spires rising above the dwellings we were passing between. They reminded me of the snowcapped peaks of the Northern Heights back home.

With this being my first time inside the city, I needed to get my bearings before attempting to explore any deeper.

"I'll get off here, thanks."

"Here?" The farmer's wife turned in her seat. "Do you have family nearby?" She looked at the closest buildings as if expecting to see some nice couple standing there waiting on me.

"Uh, yes," I lied. "Uncle Fen . . . der . . . stad." Of course, I didn't have an uncle, and if I did, his name certainly wouldn't have been Fenderstad. I wished I'd given it a little more thought.

The farmer directed the horses over to the edge of the road and stopped the wagon. "Are you sure? It's easy to get lost in here if you don't know where you're going."

"I'll be fine. He doesn't live far from here." I grabbed my travel bag and slung it over my shoulder before hopping down from the back. "My parents gave me directions. Thank you for the ride. It was most kind." I waved, not giving them a chance to argue. I was too embarrassed to tell them I was homeless with nowhere to go.

"Well, good luck to you, lad," Neelan said with a concerned look and a polite wave. "If you change your mind, we'll be on South Avis. It's off of King's Way East." He pointed at the wide cobbled road in front of us leading into the heart of the city. "Just follow this to the main square and then turn left. You'll find us somewhere near Marrow Lane in Cheapside. You can't miss it. We usually sell out before dusk, so if you can't find us by then, just wait for us at the east gate."

"Thank you. I will." I waved once more and casually walked down the first street on the right. I hoped it looked like I knew where I was going. Behind me, I could hear the farmer snap the reins and the wagon wheels thump over the cobblestones.

I stopped at the corner of the next building and listened as the wagon blended into the cacophony coming from those on their way to market. Taking a deep breath, I scanned the street, mesmerized by the flow of the crowd. I was surrounded by more people than I'd ever seen in my life, and yet I had never felt so alone.

I knelt and adjusted my boots. The coin pouches were starting to chafe. With the money my father had given me, along with what

I had salvaged from the two dead highwaymen, and the proceeds I'd received from Captain Treygan, I hoped it would be enough to keep me sheltered and fed until I was able to find some type of work or purchase an apprenticeship with a local merchant.

At the thought of my father, I lifted the thin chain from where it was safely hidden under my tunic and stared at the ring hanging from its end. The black onyx band had a single white rune at its center, the crest of my clan. Tears welled near the corners of my eyes, brought on by the thought of once again being alone. Being this far from home, now, more than ever, it was the small things like this ring that helped remind me of who I was.

I tucked the chain back into my shirt and pulled the hood up to hide my eyes as I made my way north up the street. I let the natural flow of the people move me along. The farther I walked, the more the crowds began to dwindle. I kept an eye out for a place to stay, somewhere not too far from the eastern gate, in case I needed to take Master Neelan up on his offer.

I was looking for somewhere reputable, but not too reputable or the cost would be too high. I would have been fine with four walls and a mattress, as long as it came with clean sheets and an owner who wouldn't try mugging me in the middle of the night.

The farther I traveled from King's Way East, the more dilapidated the buildings became, not to mention the people mingling around them. I generally judged a location by the hairs on the back of my neck. So far, they hadn't risen, which meant it was a reasonably safe place to find a room. But I couldn't quite shake the feeling that someone was watching me.

Across the street, a sign swung back and forth with a rusty moan. The faded gold letters under the painting of a large buck proclaimed it THE WHITE STAG. It seemed a typical name for an Elondrian inn. Many carried the names of wild animals: The White Stag, The Wild Boar, The Dancing Bear. Although I found it hard to imagine a bear dancing.

The building looked reliable enough. A couple of windows on the upper floors were lit, letting me know it was in use, so I headed across the street. I reached for the front door, but a sharp cry kept me from entering.

"Help! Someone please help!"

A young boy, several years younger than myself, was being dragged by two older boys into a narrow alley a few buildings away. The bigger of the two slapped the kid across the face.

"Shut your mouth or I'll slit your throat."

I looked to see if anyone was going to help, but the few people I saw didn't seem to care enough to stop what they were doing. For most, that meant sitting around, smoking pipes and nursing drinks while pretending nothing was amiss.

I knew I shouldn't get involved. I looked away. The last time I got involved, it had me attacking a Cylmaran compound. I tried to act like the rest of those sitting around and ignore the problem, but the boy's desperate pleas stopped me, and I turned back.

What kind of citizen would I be if I just let this kid be taken without trying to help? My father's voice answered from somewhere in the back of my mind: *A smart one.*

I sighed, dropping my hand to caress the hilt of my dagger. With a quick adjustment to my pack, I took off for the alley. *It's just a way to test my training*, I told the voice in my head. *Don't want my skills to get rusty.*

I didn't believe that for a minute.

# Character Glossary

**Ayrion** [air-ee-un] Thirteen-year-old Upakan. Born with two magical gifts.

**Bones** [bones] Captain Treygan's first mate. Tall and lanky with dark skin.

**Bray** [bray] Navigator on Treygan's ship, whom everyone calls Needle. Nervous man who carries a compass.

**Brim** [brim] Head of Ayrion's clan in the Lost City.

**Craye** [crae] A mercenary paid by Horis to fight Cylmaran slavers.

**Dorin** [dor-in] One of the Upakan trainers who prefers using a whip to get his students to obey.

**Elis** [el-iss] Farmer who contracts Treygan instead of Owen to transport his crops to market, sparking an armed conflict between the captains.

**Fanon** [fuh-non] One of the Upakan men in charge of dispersing contracts.

**Flon** [flon] Seventeen-year-old son of Brim. Ayrion's rival.

**Haran** [huh-ron] Friend of Orvil in Norshag.

**Heflin** [hef-lin] An Upakan warrior.

**Hobb** [hob] Shemoa River ferryman. Lives west of Oswell, just south of the Slags.

**Horis** [hor-iss] Old friend of captain Treygan's who raises a group of mercenaries to attack a Cylmaran mining camp.

**Ismara** [iz-mar-uh] Captain Treygan's daughter. Beautiful. Arrogant. Good with a sword.

**Jakes** [jakes] A mercenary paid by Horis to fight Cylmaran slavers.

**Jorn** [jorn] Ayrion's younger brother. Age ten.

**Kettle** [ket-el] Short but stout cook on board Treygan's ship. Long mustache that hangs to his chest.

**Lea** [lay-uh] Ayrion's mother.

**Lorna** [lor-nuh] Heflin's wife.

**Magistrate Egleman** [eg-el-mun] Former ruler of Oswell. Ousted by a rebellion. Has a contract placed on Sirias's head.

**Magistrate Sirias** [sir-eye-us] New leader of Oswell. Husband to Merilyn

**Merilyn** [mare-uh-lin] Magistrate Sirias's wife.

**Milly** [mil-ee] Innkeeper in Oswell whom Hobb has feelings for.

**Narris** [nar-iss] Ayrion's father.

**Ness** [ness] The third member of the Peltok, the ruling council of Ayrion's tribe.

**Nykl** [nih-coal] An Upakan warrior.

**Orvil** [or-vil] Grizzly of a man who owns the stables in Norshag.

**Owen** [o-en] Ship's captain and river pirate who threatens Treygan and demands he hand over his contract.

**Rianna** [ree-on-uh] Ayrion's older sister. Age sixteen.

**Ronan** [roe-nun] One of the Golden Tassel's kitchen staff.

**Rosella** [roe-zel-uh] Magistrate Sirias's daughter. Five years old.

**Selfer** [sel-fir] Older Upakan man who raises mountain wolves.

**Sim** [sim] A mercenary paid by Horis to fight Cylmaran slavers.

**Talarin** [tuh-lar-in] The second member of the Peltok. Cousin to Brim.

**Tillman** [till-men] Mousy-looking ship's captain whom Hobb tries to get to take Ayrion downriver.

**Treppin** [trep-in] Hobb's late wife's younger brother.

**Tressle** [tress-el] Old sailor everyone calls Pops. Takes a shine to Ayrion. Loves to smoke his pipe.

**Treygan** [tray-gen] Rough ship captain who agrees to take Ayrion when no one else will. Owns a cursed ship called the *Wind Binder*.

**Whitey** [why-tee] Large, pale man who wears a wide-brimmed hat to shade from the sun.

**Worg** [worg] A mercenary paid by Horis to fight the Cylmaran slavers. He duels against Ayrion and loses.

### Stop by and visit:
www.michaelwisehart.com

Made in United States
North Haven, CT
19 May 2022

19265569R00226